RIPPED UP THE MIDDLE IN TWO

Viggy Parr Hampton

First edition, July 2026
ISBN Paperback: 979-8-9935980-3-1
ISBN Hardcover: 979-8-9935980-4-8
ISBN Ebook: 979-8-9935980-2-4
Illustrations by Joey Powell
Book Design by Nuno Moreira, NMDESIGN
Excerpt from *Rumpelstiltskin* reprinted with permission from D.L. Ashliman

RIPPED UP THE MIDDLE IN TWO

Viggy Parr Hampton

To all the moms out there. In case someone hasn't told you lately—
you're incredible.

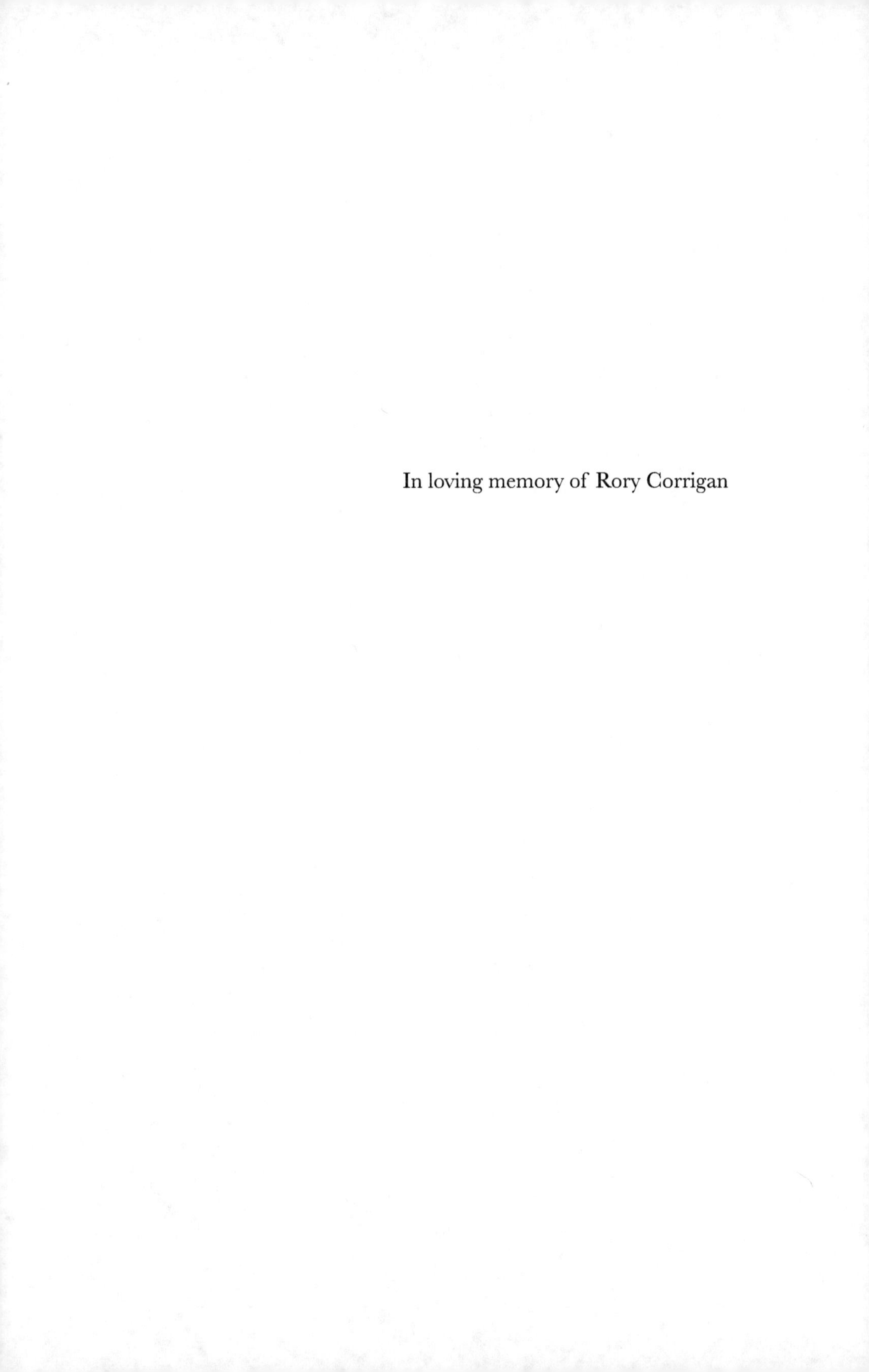

In loving memory of Rory Corrigan

ALSO BY VIGGY PARR HAMPTON

A Cold Night for Alligators

A determined CDC epidemiologist goes rogue to tackle a mysterious outbreak in Savannah, only to find himself entangled with a pair of urban explorers and a dangerous, tortured soul in an abandoned theme park where dark forces stir.

Much Too Vulgar

Disturbed pre-med student Keely Rexroth is unable to take 'no' for an answer when she is denied entry into a prestigious research program. As her ambition curdles into dark mania, she embarks on her own curriculum of twisted experimentation, fighting to keep her secrets from a campus priest who is too perceptive for his own good. If she can't get what she deserves on her own merit, she'll eliminate her competition.

The Rotting Room

When a young nun with a troubled past joins a new religious order, she quickly comes to realize that this abbey has its own share of sinister secrets, along with a disturbing burial ritual. She must race to uncover if the abbey is full of divine miracles—or unspeakable evil.

A Veritable Household Pet

Darla Gregory received a lobotomy at the age of 11... and she was never the same.

Soon afterward the little man came in and asked, "Now, Madame Queen, what is my name?"

She first asked, "Is your name Kunz?"

"No."

"Is your name Heinz?"

"No."

"Is your name perhaps Rumpelstiltskin?"

"The devil told you that! The devil told you that!" shouted the little man, and with anger he stomped his right foot so hard into the ground that he fell in up to his waist. Then with both hands he took hold of his left foot and ripped himself up the middle in two.

—*Rumpelstiltskin*, by Jacob and Wilhelm Grimm,
translated by D.L. Ashliman

CHAPTER ONE

Is This Really the Best Use of Your Time?

"Is this really the best use of your time?" Cash asks as he walks into the dining room, startling me. I'm painting a fairy door I ordered on Amazon, the wood thin and brittle, more likely to break than to bend. There are milk and spit-up stains on my shirt, and my head is fuzzy from lack of sleep.

He sidles up next to where I'm seated at the dining table and gestures at the bottles of outdoor acrylic paint, cheap paintbrushes, and flimsy miniature wooden doors.

"I thought you were on the golf course."

"I was supposed to be, but something happened to the first tee box. It got destroyed. Somebody put nails all over the grass, if you can believe it," he says. "Course is closed until they fix it. Probably some stupid kids, ruining it for everybody."

I accidentally flick a spot of cotton candy pink onto a stripe of sky blue. "Dammit," I say, scowling.

"Sadie," Cash says, leaning over me. "Holly won't even know the doors are there. Hell, she won't even be able to grasp the concept of a 'fairy' for years, at least."

I keep my eyes on the door, trying to scrape away the pink blemish with my fingernail, but only succeed in smearing it around into a purplish blob. "I don't care."

Cash sits next to me, getting his face way too close to mine. "Go take a nap, huh? You'll feel much better after you get some sleep."

Clearly, he won't let me ignore him. I lay the door on the plastic-covered table and look at him. Whereas I look like a survivor of a zombie apocalypse, Cash looks like he just stepped out of the pages of *GQ*. How does he do that? He's a new parent, too. Why is he allowed to take care of his appearance and I can't take care of mine?

"Cash," I say, trying to muster every ounce of the limited patience I have. "I need this creative outlet, okay? Let me have this. I'm a milk-making cow with constantly leaking tits and a saggy stomach and I can't sleep for more than two hours in one night without screams waking me up and Jesus Christ I need something I can control!" Well, so much for patience. My breath is coming in animalistic heaves.

"Whoa, whoa. Calm down," Cash says, hands up, trying to placate me. "It's okay."

Tears threaten to obscure my vision. I try to blink them away, but they overflow and run down my cheeks. "It's not okay, Cash! It's not. Your life has barely changed at all, and mine couldn't be more different!" We're not talking about fairy doors anymore, but I don't think we ever really were.

Cash's eyebrows shoot up to his hairline. "What are you talking about? That's not true! Holly isn't just your baby. She's our baby."

I sneer, thinking about how I insisted Cash sleep in the spare room instead of getting up at night with me, because there was—is—no sense in him being tired, too, especially since he can't breastfeed. Sure, I could figure out the whole pumping thing, or try to go for formula, but pumping seems too overwhelming and confusing when I can barely hold things together as it is. Honestly, if I'm capable of breastfeeding on demand, that seems like the easiest option. I thought if he were fully rested, he could help me more during the day, but what he actually does with all that energy is channel it into playtime on the golf course with his friends. Swallowing back angry bile, I snarl, "Really? She's our baby? Then how come I'm the one changing ninety-nine percent of the diapers? How come I'm the one up in the night four, sometimes five times? How come I'm the one who looks like a wreck and can barely get away long enough to take a shower?" To emphasize my point, I plunk my paintbrush into a plastic cup of water. Immediately, the resistance and clink of the ice tells me I've made a mistake. I stare at my fingers, still clutching the paintbrush, as my iced coconut water slowly turns a bruised purple. "Motherfucker!" I hiss.

"It's okay," Cash says, putting a hand on my shoulder. It's far too heavy, and I shake it off. "Let me get you another. What was that? Coconut water?"

"That was the last one!" I wail. I know I'm being immature, but I can't help it. Lack of sleep has turned me into a different person, someone I can't understand or control, someone who acts on impulse and instinct. "You should have gotten more at the store like I told you!" This isn't fair, but I don't care. I want him to hurt like I do, even if it's only a little.

He closes his eyes and sighs heavily. "Sadie," he says, in an infuriatingly gentle tone, as though he's talking to a wild animal who may pounce on him at any moment. "I know you've been through a lot. I get it."

I want to scream, but I settle for a harsh whisper. Holly's still sleeping, and hell no am I going to wake her up. "No, you don't, Cash! You can never 'get it!' You didn't just push a whole flesh-and-blood human out of your body!"

"Sadie, come on. It's going to be okay," Cash says, and his patronizing voice irritates me even as it's meant to soothe. "You seriously need a nap." Before I can protest, he adds, "And if you say you barely have time to shower, why aren't you showering now? Why are you wasting time with this stuff?" He sweeps his hand to encompass all the paints, brushes, and fairy doors again. "Why are you doing this when you could be taking care of yourself?"

I can't control the rage any longer. "This *is* taking care of myself!" I bellow. The tears are coming faster now, pouring down my face, pooling at the corners of my lips, my breath turning into noisy, body-wracking sobs.

The baby monitor crackles to life, and Holly's piercing wails mirror my own.

"Great," I sputter. "You've woken up the baby."

Cash glares at me. "I didn't—"

I don't want to hear what lame excuse he has to offer. As I stand up to leave, my hand catches the cup of dirty coconut water, overturning it. Cloudy liquid floods the table, spilling over onto the upholstered dining chairs, the floor, Cash's lap. The last one I don't mind so much, but the others are simply more messes I'll have to clean up.

I leave Cash mumbling "Jesus," and attempting to sop up the water with a roll of paper towels as I stalk off to get the baby, because really—who else is going to do it?

* * *

I clip the nursing pillow around my waist and settle into the couch to feed Holly. My nipples are cracked and sore, prone to bleeding. Cash sits across the room in an armchair, watching me.

"Sadie," he says, once Holly's latched and suckling. "About earlier…"

"I'm sorry," I blurt. I don't want a lecture from him, but I do feel bad about how everything went down.

"I know you are," he says. Why does he have to be so damned forgiving all the time? I mean, I'm grateful that he can sweep some things under the rug and move on, but every now and then, there's a part of me that wishes he would fight back, show a little bit of ferocity. I need to know

I'm not alone, that I'm not the only one who is feeling things I wish I weren't, who is being something I wish I wasn't.

"I..." Pain shoots through me as Holly tugs at my breast. When the discomfort subsides, I say, "It's just... lack of sleep is a real trigger for me. You know sleep deprivation is a literal torture technique?"

"Yeah, I've heard that," he says.

"It's brutal," I say. "My life is so... out of control lately. I can't control when I sleep, when I eat, what I do, anything. I wanted to paint those fairy doors because I need something I can control, something creative, something... calm, I guess. I wanted—no, I *needed* to do something that made me feel like myself. You've got your job, so you still get to be... you. I don't know if or when I'll start looking for clients again. Everything feels so alien right now."

Cash clears his throat. "Well, I can understand that," he says, and even though he's being nice, I can't help but think he actually can't understand, because he still manages to work, go to the gym, groom himself to perfection, and play all that golf. Meanwhile, I'm stuck at home, changing diapers, doing load after load of laundry, and trying to keep this infant alive.

"Yeah," I mumble, trying to sound like I believe him.

"Listen, Sadie," he says. "I want to be there for you. I want you to know I'm here. I can help. If you want to start doing client work again, you can do it—but you don't have to. I can take care of us, if that's what you want. You know all I want is for you to be happy, and for Holly to be happy."

"Yeah," I say again, wishing I could muster some genuine emotion—of love, of gratitude, of anything positive. Instead, I'm mostly numb. When I first started my health care content writing business two years ago, it was all I thought about, all I wanted to do, all I'd dreamed about. Now, with an indeterminate hiatus for maternity leave, I'm not sure if I'll ever go back. I miss feeling important, intellectual, professional... but I also can't imagine ever having the energy again to care about a holistic doctor's blog post performance or a press release for a small health care analytics company. Absentmindedly, I hook my finger into Holly's mouth to break her latch, then switch her to my other breast, wincing as she starts to suck.

"Still hurting?" Cash asks, nodding to my breasts.

"Yep," I say. "You have no idea."

"You want me to give it a try? I've been told I have very respectable B-cups." It's a lame joke, but he's trying.

"I wish," I say, summoning up a small smile.

"It really is going to be okay," he says. "This is normal."

I want to tell him he really doesn't know what he's talking about, because he's not the one who read countless parenting and pregnancy books, blogs, and articles, but I don't want to argue anymore. I'm too tired.

"Yeah," I say instead, looking down at Holly. A heaviness blossoms in my chest—a love so powerful it's agonizing. Oxytocin is flooding through my brain as Holly breastfeeds. My fingers brush against her soft head, and her little lips curve into the smallest smile while she continues to eat. She's perfect, and even though she's barely three months old, I can already tell she's the spitting image of her father—straight nose, bright green eyes, mop of curly brown hair, naturally tan skin. She's lucky.

"I love you," Cash says, and I jump slightly, making Holly cluck in annoyance. I'd forgotten Cash was still in the room. When I look up at him, his gaze is directed at Holly. I'm not sure if he was talking to me or her, but does it actually matter?

"You, too," I say, but the words taste bittersweet in my mouth.

He's treating me with kid gloves, as if he's afraid I'll explode at any moment.

Maybe I will.

CHAPTER TWO

It Was Probably One of the Yoga Moms

Another morning, another exhausted, semi-conscious walk through the undeveloped part of the neighborhood, pushing a stroller the size of a small shopping cart. My dog, a fluffy German Shepherd-poodle mix named Tater Tot, trots next to me, his curly white fur dappled with the sunshine filtering through the live oaks towering overhead. Chickadees and mockingbirds call to one another, and in the distance, there's the sharp rap of a woodpecker.

When I was pregnant, I would walk these empty streets all the time, enjoying the nature and listening to the bird calls, frog chirps, and the drone of insects that kept to themselves. This is our first summer in the Savannah-area gated community of Agua Roja, and now I understand why most of my neighbors flee Georgia and go north from May through September. Between the humidity, the heat, and the bugs, it's not a pleasant time to be outside.

Yet I still walk every single morning, mostly because Tater Tot needs the exercise—as do I—and walking is, usually, one of the few things that keeps Holly from constantly crying.

I should be happy, of course—Agua Roja is full of walking trails, small lakes, and beautiful meadows. There's even a citrus grove and a community garden, and no leash mandate for dogs. Cash and I could hardly believe our luck when we found this place, much less when we found we could afford it.

We'd barely settled into our first home together before I got pregnant with Holly. Part of me wishes I'd had more time to experience life in my new home on my own terms, without being on a baby's schedule. The other, more rational part of me is grateful that I get to have this wonderful baby girl when so many other couples struggle to conceive.

The still-healing wound between my legs throbs, my bladder contracts sharply, and my gratitude for this life I've built is totally inaccessible. What kind of horrible person—what kind of horrible mother—isn't grateful for their child twenty-four hours a day?

Holly is mercifully quiet in her stroller, staring up at me with Cash's big green eyes. The September humidity has curdled the air into a thick soup, making each step a struggle. I stop for a moment and pull the stroller fan from the bottom storage compartment. I turn it on maximum speed and aim it directly into my sweaty face. The relief is instant, the perspiration on my cheeks congealing into a sticky glaze. How anyone could survive in this climate without a handheld fan is beyond me…

"Shit," I say, and soak in a few more seconds of blessed coolness before I lower the fan and clip it in front of Holly's face. That's what a good mother would do.

Tater Tot lets out a single sharp "Woof!", and when I look up, there's another mom from the neighborhood approaching. So much for peace and quiet. Jessica is clutching a neon pink leash with a fully primped Shih Tzu prancing at the end. She's nice enough, but we didn't exactly click in the beginning when Cash and I first moved here. Plus, her daughter is a couple years older than Holly, so play dates aren't going to be a thing anytime soon, if ever.

Tater growls, so low I can barely hear it. My overlong fingernails find the dried spit-up stain on my nursing-accessible tank top and attempt to scratch it off. The top may be convenient, but it's unquestionably hideous. My baggy shorts, stretched to the limit from pregnancy, complete the look. I sigh and smooth down my poofy hair. Somehow, despite this Georgia heat, Jessica's hair always looks like a shining sheet of silk. She's wearing a hot pink athleisure set, and her toned abs belie the fact that she, somehow, has a child. My face stretches into something resembling a friendly smile, and I try not to feel self-conscious about my bloated stomach.

"Hi!" I call out to her, probably too brightly. Tater approaches Jessica's dog, Rosie, and gives her a sniff. Somehow, Rosie manages to look disgusted.

"Oh, hi," Jessica calls back, eyes wide in surprise, even though she must have seen me coming. It's hard to miss the bedraggled woman pushing the giant stroller with a white fluffy dog the size of a miniature horse.

I can't tell if she's going to stop to chat or continue with her walk, so I settle for a slow saunter as I get closer to her.

"How are you?" I ask when we're within a few feet of each other, because it's the polite thing to do.

"Great," she says. "How are you doing, mama?"

I try not to cringe. I've always hated it when women call themselves or other moms 'mama.'

"Good," I lie, because it's also the polite thing to not tell people like Jessica how you're actually feeling. It's one of the things Cash dislikes most about living in the South—the obligatory 'How are you doing?' and the equally obligatory 'I'm good.' He finds the greeting shallow and stupid. I disagreed at first, thinking it was charming, but now I'm starting to understand why he hates it so much, probably because nowadays, whenever I answer that question with the socially acceptable response, I'm almost always lying.

Jessica stops next to the stroller and peeks in at Holly. "She's getting so big!"

"Yep," I say, sucking my stomach in and trying to stand up straighter. "She's already fourteen pounds!"

Jessica smiles, the sunlight reflecting off of her porcelain veneers. "Wow. Hilda, right?"

A sour taste fills my mouth. "It's Holly, actually."

Jessica waves her hand. "Oh, right. I knew it started with an H!"

Before I can stop myself, I ask, "And how's Chelsey doing?"

Jessica clears her throat. "Chesley, you mean. Chesley's great. Definitely great."

We stare at each other for a beat, during which I contemplate the stupidity of the name 'Chesley,' and then I blurt, "Holly's only waking me up a few times a night now." This is only partially true. Last night, I was up with her seven different times. I barely slept at all.

Jessica frowns. "You don't have a night nurse?"

I frown back. "A night nurse?"

She tilts her head at me and blinks, then speaks slower, like she's talking to a silly child. "Sure. A nurse who stays with you at night for the first few months and takes care of the baby so you can get some rest? I don't know what I would have done without Irma."

I open my mouth, then close it again. I have no idea what to say. A night nurse? For real? Jessica doesn't even have a real job. But then again, if I had only a few more hours of sleep a night, I could get back into client work, I could exercise, I could take the time to cook a real meal that won't make me bloat, I could shower and maybe even put on some makeup…

"Sadie?" Jessica's nose is pinched, and as discreetly as possible, I lean my face to my shoulder and take a whiff. God, I stink.

"Yep?" I say, trying to compose my face back into the mask I have to wear in polite society. Why can't I think of something more interesting to talk about? Something to show her I'm someone worth hanging out with?

Jessica smiles again, blinding me with those Chiclets she calls teeth, and I know I've missed my opportunity. "Well, it was great seeing you,

Sadie! We should get together some time." For a moment, I allow myself to believe she's sincere, that I really could be wedged into an Instagram photo between her and the rest of the Yoga Moms, arms around each other's shoulders at a concert or all of us laughing, leaning out of a golf cart.

She's already walking away by the time I manage to squeak out, "Yeah, totally!"

She doesn't look back, and my face crumples into its usual grimace of exhaustion. I take a few halfhearted steps, but pushing the stroller is now a Herculean task. Tater Tot nuzzles up next to me, pressing his wet nose into my hip.

What would it be like to be a part of Jessica's little group? The Yoga Moms get together all the time, if their Instagram profiles are to be believed. They have group yoga sessions, of course, movie nights, game marathons, and dinner parties, always with copious amounts of wine (although, for morning yoga, I think they switch to mimosas). I wonder if they can smell the wrongness coming off me like a rotten stench—I don't drink, and I find yoga insufferably boring. Despite all that, and seemingly against all rational logic, I wish, just once, for an invitation.

* * *

Tater nudges my hip again, and we pick up the pace despite the pain between my legs. Holly's birth wasn't difficult by most standards, but, from what I've been told, the first baby is always tricky—it's the one that breaks you in. For the first month after Holly, I felt like I'd been ripped in half. It's better now, but even moderate exercise like this slow walk makes my lady parts swell with discomfort.

Then again, none of that actually matters. If I'm ever going to be a part of Jessica's group, I need to get back in shape. Gentle walks be damned.

"Hey, neighbor!" Ronald Callahan stops beside me with a screech of golf cart tires, making me scream. "Sorry about that."

When I catch my breath, I say, "No problem, Ron." Tater Tot is practically dancing with happiness at the sight of Ron. When Ron slips a bone-shaped treat from his pocket, Tater nearly levitates with joy.

"It's a lovely morning, isn't it?" Ron tosses the treat in the air, and Tater snaps at it, crushing it between his teeth and swallowing it in one bite.

"Sure is," I say. "A bit hot."

"Weatherman says we'll get a little breeze this afternoon, maybe a shower to cool things down. Great reading weather, I always say." He produces a second treat and tosses that one into the air, as well. Tater makes quick work of it, then licks Ron's hand.

"I wish I had time to read more," I say.

"There's always time, Sadie. You youngsters are always rushing around. You need to take life more slowly, do the things that make you happy."

"You're not wrong, Ron."

"Well, you don't get to be seventy-five without learning how to appreciate the little things." He snaps his fingers, making Holly jump. "You know what? I read a great article in the Wall Street Journal this morning. I think it would resonate with you. I'll slip it into your mailbox, okay?"

"That would be great," I say.

Tater jumps up in the golf cart next to Ron, pawing at him for another treat. "Not today, buddy," he says, patting Tater's head. "I'll come get you another day. I've got a tee time to get to!"

"Tater, come," I say, and Tater dutifully jumps down to sit next to me. "Have a great round!"

"I always do!" Ron winks and then, golf clubs clanking on the back of his cart, he's off, Tater whining as he leaves.

"I know you love Ron," I say. "You'll see him again soon, I promise."

Placated for now, Tater follows me as I round the corner at the end of the block and head down Laurel Lane, a stretch of undeveloped road. No houses have been built in this area yet, and enormous live oaks, maples, and sweetgum trees tower over the asphalt. The shade doesn't offer much respite from the heat, but I'm relieved to be enveloped in the leafy green embrace.

A large horsefly lands on my arm, and I'm not quick enough to swat it away before it bites me. "Dammit!" I shout. The bite stings, stirring the tears that are always wobbling right under the surface.

Holly whimpers, and my breasts stiffen and ache in response. "Shh, shh, it's okay," I whisper, hoping to soothe her before the wails begin in earnest.

I'm not successful. Holly opens her little pink mouth and bawls as though I've slapped her instead of the fly that bit me. I rock the stroller back and forth, a push-pull, push-pull motion that has, at best, a fifty percent success rate in calming Holly down. It sort of works this time; her sobs turn into hiccup-y cries that, while still devastatingly annoying, are at least a bit quieter.

I keep walking, trying to ignore how most of my body parts are working together to gang up on me.

Holly starts screaming again, because this is my life now. My left eye twitches, my heart races, and sweat pours down my back and between my engorged breasts in salty rivulets. With trembling fingers, I yank Holly out of her stroller, hoist her over my head, and chuck her furious little body at the nearest tree…

"No!" I shout, and when I look down into the stroller, Holly stares back up at me, momentarily stunned. "Jesus Christ," I whisper.

Holly screams.

How do other moms do this? Did Jessica ever want to rip out her own eardrums with a sharp fork? Did Heather ever hallucinate harming her baby, a desperate attempt to make the crying stop? Did Mandy ever seriously contemplate jumping off the second-floor balcony of her house to escape the heavy weight of responsibility? Did Tiffany ever stare at herself in the mirror and cry because she didn't recognize the shell of a person staring back at her?

I'm about to start crying along with her when Holly stops mid-wail, as though someone has pressed a hand over her mouth. Instant relief floods me like a drug, and I manage to take a deep breath that doesn't become a sob.

Something's wrong, though. It's not only Holly who's quieted down. I come to a stop on the side of the road and listen... but there's nothing to hear. Everything has gone utterly and completely silent. All the frogs, all the birds, all the insects might as well have disappeared off the face of the earth.

That's when I notice it.

Between a maple and a fat live oak, there's a break in the curtain of grapevines and trumpet flowers. A narrow trail leads into the woods, and before I know what I'm doing, I'm walking the stroller off the road and across the narrow stretch of grass to the trees. Tater Tot must sense the irresistible pull, too, because he trots out ahead of me, sniffing the ground as though he's picked up a scent. I manhandle the stroller up onto the dirt of the trail, even though it's tricky and I shouldn't be lifting this much or pushing this hard when I haven't fully healed.

It's strange—I've walked along Laurel Lane hundreds of times, and I've never noticed this path. It looks like it might have been used by deer, but I can't be sure. There are no wood chips or gravel to indicate a friendly walking trail built by the neighborhood association, but it still feels... enticing. This is more adventure than I've had in months—and no, I do not consider giving birth life's greatest adventure.

There should be a gossamer touch of spiderwebs, a lick of sharp leaves against my skin, a branch pushing into my hair, but there's nothing, as though the path has been deliberately cleared just for me, and recently. Ahead of me, Tater Tot is sniffing furiously, chasing a scent deeper and deeper into the thicket.

Miraculously, everything remains silent. The only sound is the soft crunch of leaves under the wheels of the stroller. There's not even the rattle and drone of insects to break the tension. Holly is staring at me, a question in her big green eyes. This is more adventure than she's ever known, too. Like me, she does not consider birth an adventure.

There's a yelp as the stroller runs into Tater Tot, who has stopped abruptly. "Sorry, boy," I say, reaching around to pet him. He doesn't even take notice of my hand; he's too busy staring at what's in front of us.

When I look up, all I can think is, *There it is.*

It's an odd thought, but it's the first thing that comes to me when I see the tree. There it is. As though it's something I've been looking for my whole life without ever realizing I've been searching. It's sprouting from a small clearing, the ground carpeted with dead leaves. The tree has a thick trunk, nearly six feet in diameter. About five feet up, the thickness gives way to dozens of thinner, spindly branches, looking like the tree was cut long ago and has kept growing despite that setback.

The atmosphere remains eerily quiet, everything holding its breath, until the rustle of a squirrel breaks the preternatural silence. Tater Tot clocks it, too, but he doesn't move to chase it. The squirrel emerges from the curtain of foliage to the right of the tree and runs toward it.

When it gets within a few feet of the tree, it jumps into the air like it's been jolted by an electric fence. With a squeal, it turns and runs back into the cover of the woods.

In front of me, Tater Tot is trembling. Holly is looking at me with her little brows knitted.

I clear my throat, unsure. "Well," I say. "That was interesting."

I step around the stroller toward Tater Tot, wanting to get a closer look. What spooked the squirrel? Did it see Tater?

That would be the logical answer, but my gut tells me that's not it.

It's the tree.

Far off, from another world, comes the call of a predator, maybe a red-tailed hawk. On autopilot, I pull out my phone and open the bird sounds app, which can identify bird calls. Cash and I have been having fun with it ever since we moved here, slowly becoming amateur ornithologists. I press Record to let the app start listening, then set my phone down in the stroller's cupholder as I step closer to the tree.

The thickest part of the trunk is encased in an almost solid mat of poison ivy, the telltale three-pronged leaves and reddish, woody vines giving it away. The ivy is the only color in the small clearing, which is mostly muted grays and browns in stark contrast to the riot of summer color all around us. The trumpet flowers, beautyberry, and other wildflowers encircling the clearing make the tree stand out even more, a monotone blot against the surrounding rainbow. Is it pesticides? Couldn't be, not this far out into the woods, surely?

Tater Tot presses his nose to the ground and takes a few tentative steps forward, placing his paws carefully in the leaf litter, but he doesn't go closer to the tree than the squirrel did.

I'm still a few feet away when I look to the base of the tree and see it.

The door.

It's about eight inches tall, made of a thick, gnarled bark with a doorknob that looks like a small ball of bone. The door is adorned with drifts of graying Spanish moss. It looks way more authentic than my flimsy rainbow-colored knockoffs. Whoever made this must have gone on a massive Michael's shopping spree.

"How did…" I trail off, my eyes locked on the door. Whoever put that there must have needed a gallon of calamine lotion after wading through all that poison ivy.

Because all the parenting books say you should talk to your baby about what's around you to help with their development, even if you feel like an idiot, I describe it to Holly. "Somebody put a fairy door here already, Holly! Can you believe it? It's a little door that the fairies use to get inside the trees, where they live. This one looks super cool, it's got moss and rocks and little decorations. This fairy must love the forest!"

My vision starts to tunnel as I stare at it. "I wonder which fairy put this here?" I supposed it could be my friend Kendall, who's fairly crafty, but she would have mentioned it if she had.

But if it wasn't her, who could it be? A bubble of resentment swells in my chest, threatening to burst. Fairy doors were supposed to be my thing. Who could have beat me—or Kendall—to the punch? I have a hard time imagining Jessica, with her Instagram-perfect manicure and skintight Lululemons, traipsing deep into the woods to nail a fake door to a tree.

My watch buzzes, breaking me out of my trance. It's nearly nine-thirty, time for Holly's mid-morning feeding.

"Ugh," I mumble. Time got away from me, and now I'll have to hustle back home to get her on the boob before she goes nuclear.

The dead leaves crunch under my feet as I walk back to the stroller. Tater Tot hasn't moved; he's staring at the fairy door like it's some animal he needs to keep an eye on.

"Come on, Tater," I say, picking up my phone from the cupholder. The bird sounds app is still running, but it doesn't seem to have identified any birds. Weird—I can see from the sound waves that it's recorded something. I press Play to hear it myself, and a strange, low growl comes through the small speaker.

Sweat breaks out on my forehead, and I quickly shut my phone off. "The app must be glitching," I tell Holly. "Don't worry, Mommy will try to fix it. Now, let's get you home and get you some food, huh?"

I execute a laborious five-point turn in the narrow path and scramble back toward the road. "Tater, come on!" I say, and finally, he tears himself away from his vigil and pads next to me, every so often turning his head to look back behind us.

As I push the stroller back down Laurel Lane, I can't get the tree—or its bizarre little door—out of my mind. I want to tell myself it's delightful, adorable, sweet, but I can't quite make myself believe it. The idea that something is wrong about that place is persistent, but, like most of my troubling and intrusive thoughts, I smother it and attend to my baby.

CHAPTER THREE

You've Got Mail

Later that afternoon, the front yard reeks like a slaughterhouse, the meaty smell coagulating with the heavy air to create a damp blanket that's more of an assault than a comfort.

"Ugh." I shove my finger under my nose, trying to block out the stench, but my skin still carries that sickly-sweet odor of newborn poop, and I have to stifle a gag.

Tater Tot hustles down the porch steps past me, bustling into the yard, nose pressed to the ground. He whips around, almost dancing with excitement, before stopping in front of the mailbox and whining.

"Oh God." My stomach lurches, and I really don't want to open that mailbox.

But, like most things I don't want to do, I go ahead and do it anyway.

If I thought the yard stank, it's nothing compared to the blast that slaps me in the face as soon as the mailbox door is open. I stagger back, nearly tripping over Tater, my eyes streaming.

"Jesus," I say, spitting out a mouthful of sour saliva. "What the..."

There's something furry in the mailbox. I can barely make out a fluffy brown tail, a pair of tiny claws, a strip of white stomach.

Against my better judgment, I take a step forward, breathing through my mouth to keep the smell at bay. When my face is level with the mailbox, there's no more room for denial.

There's a squirrel lying on top of my mail.

Correction: there's a *dead* squirrel lying on top of my mail.

"Ugh!" I shout, leaping back again, and this time I do fall over Tater Tot, my ass slamming into the street. My sore lady parts scream with agony, and oh God, what if I've managed to rip apart all the healing bits…

A car engine starts somewhere down the street. I can't let anybody see me like this, hair frizzy from sleep, eyes wild, slumping in a heap in the middle of the road.

With a grunt, I clamber back up to my feet. Tater Tot sits directly in front of the open mailbox, tail wagging, completely unapologetic.

With trembling hands, I grab a stick from a patch of undergrowth around the side of our house. Holding Tater's collar tightly with one hand, I use the other to maneuver the stick under the squirrel. I scoop up the body, slowly slide it out of the mailbox, and, with another grunt, heave it into the bushes, the stick flying along with the carcass.

Before I lose my nerve, I run inside, grab a garbage bag and a roll of paper towels, Tater Tot at my heels. When I return to the mailbox, the stench has dissipated enough that I can breathe out of my nose. There doesn't seem to be any blood on my topmost piece of mail—Ron's promised Wall Street Journal article, 'For Sadie' stamped at the top in his blocky handwriting—but I whisk it into the garbage bag with a paper towel-covered hand anyway. The rest of the mail is junk, so I slide the lot of it into the bag as well, followed by the paper towel. Who knows what germs that squirrel left behind?

The mailbox clangs as I shove it closed. It's not until the garbage bag is securely in the big bin around the back of the house that I let my shoulders relax.

It's not until much later that I finally ask myself, *Who put that there? And why?*

CHAPTER FOUR

Things Look Different from Another Direction

The blown-up rubber glove looks like an obese chicken. No matter how many times Kendall dips it in paint and rolls it across the canvas, it simply does not resemble a flower, even in the mid-morning sunlight illuminating the craft station we've set up in my dining room.

"I literally do not understand how this is supposed to work," Kendall says, setting her paint-covered glove down on a paper towel and picking up her La Croix.

"I feel like I say that all the time, about everything," I say, picking my nails, my eyes glued to the TikTok tutorial pulled up on Kendall's phone. In the video, a woman expertly rolls her paint-dipped glove across a canvas, creating the most beautiful peony-like flower.

Kendall takes a noisy slurp of La Croix and laughs. "This crafternoon is a bust, I think."

"But is it worse than that time we wrapped a bunch of wool thread around sticks?"

Kendall pauses, considering. "Well… no."

"My closet was covered in bugs for a week straight after that," I say. "Cash was so mad." It was funny at the time—Kendall and I hadn't realized we'd needed to let the sticks dry before wrapping them, and both of us had ended up with small but mighty infestations—but remembering Cash's anger wipes the smile off of my face. I look over at Holly, doing tummy time on her play mat. She's grunting, on the edge of a wail.

"Yeah, not our brightest moment," Kendall says, glancing at Holly. "Want me to get her?"

My shoulders lower about four inches. I hadn't even realized I'd been so tense. "That would be amazing, thank you."

Kendall drains her La Croix and goes to scoop up Holly. "Don't you worry, Hols, Aunt Kendall's coming to rescue you."

Holly smiles and coos in Kendall's arms.

"Want Mommy to tell you what we've been doing?" Kendall singsongs, bringing Holly to the table where our canvases, covered in unattractive blobs, sit in shame.

I dig too deep in one of my nail beds, and a bead of blood pops up. My finger is in my mouth before I know what I'm doing, the coppery taste of blood flooding my tongue.

"Sadie?" Kendall says. "You okay?"

"Yeah, yeah," I say, yanking my finger out of my mouth. "Fine."

Kendall gives me a lingering look, but then turns back to Holly. "I think that woman in the video is some sort of sorceress, Hols." She replays the TikTok tutorial. "Should we take some of the air out of the glove?"

"Worth a try," I say, pulling a fresh glove from the box. My finger leaves behind a smear of blood and I hastily wipe it away before blowing the glove up halfway. The glove slides into the paint, and I gently press it to the canvas, exactly as that woman in the TikTok video did.

Another unexciting blob—with a small streak of scarlet—spreads across the canvas.

"Dammit!" Kendall barks, then glances at Holly, still cradled comfortably in her arms. "Whoops. Sorry!"

"Don't worry about it, seriously," I say, fighting to keep my finger out of my mouth. “She won’t understand that for at least a year. You’re in the clear.”

“Good to know,” she says, chuckling. She sits down again, Holly cradled against her shoulder. Despite having no children of her own, she’s more of a natural with babies than Cash and me combined. “So.”

“So?” The image of the dead squirrel fills my brain, and my finger worms its way between my lips.

“Sadie, what’s up with you?”

I wrench my finger from my mouth and take another sip of my own La Croix washing away the salty taste of blood. “Actually,” I say, the word hanging in the air. Where do I begin?

“Besides, you know, having a baby and all,” Kendall says. “I know that’s a lot.”

“Right,” I say, sucking in a breath. My heart beats a bit faster. “Um… something weird happened the other day.”

“Weird how?”

“Someone put a… a dead squirrel in my mailbox.” I spit the words out like they taste bad.

“Oh,” Kendall says, more disappointed than shocked. “Oof.”

“It totally freaked me out,” I say. “And it reeked so bad.”

“Did you tell Cash?”

“Not yet… I don’t know, I didn’t want to worry him.”

Kendall sighs, shifting Holly to her other shoulder.

“You think it might have been Ron?”

“Ron? Ron Callahan?”

“Yeah. He left me an article in the mailbox, and the squirrel was right on top of it.”

“Why would he do that?” she says.

“I don’t know, some sort of weird neighborhood initiation ritual?”

Kendall barks out a humorless laugh. “No way. Ron wouldn’t do that. Besides… would it make you feel better if I told you you weren’t the first person here to get a dead animal in their mailbox?"

My throat tightens. "Um. Maybe?"

"Yeah, well. I know a few other people who've found rats, or opossums, even a fox once."

"Ew," I say, my skin breaking out in a chilly sweat. "That's… super gross."

"Yeah."

"Who did it?"

"Nobody ever figured it out," she said. "But it definitely wasn't Ron. Some kids, probably."

"That's… disturbing. Kids are weird, but I didn't think they were that weird."

"Who knows? But thank goodness you've brought another one into the world," Kendall says, giving Holly a pat.

"It could have been an adult, though. Adults are weird, too."

"No argument here. I once saw a dude in the parking lot of a Parker's gas station shove three whole taquitos into his mouth in one bite. Then he washed all that down with—get this—strawberry milk."

"Ugh," I say, grimacing. "That's a strangely disturbing combination."

"Like you said, adults are strange."

My leg starts to bounce. "Speaking of strange…"

"There's more?"

"Well, I was out walking with Holly and Tater Tot the other day, and I turned onto Laurel Lane—after running into Jessica, ugh—and there was this trail into the woods, one I'd never seen before. I turned onto it, because why not, and when I got to the end, there was this little clearing with this super odd tree in the middle. Oh, and all the bugs and birds were totally silent out there, and this tree was absolutely covered in poison ivy…"

"Okay…" Kendall says, one eyebrow raised. "There's poison ivy everywhere out there."

"Wait. There's even more." Kendall nods and tickles Holly under the chin. "Anyway, I looked down at the bottom of the tree, and there was a little, like… door there!"

"Seriously?" she says, cocking her head. "What do you mean, a door?"

"Like a little fairy door," I say. "Have you ever seen one of those?"

"I think so. People put them up in their yards and stuff? For kids?"

"Yeah, more or less," I say. "Supposedly 'fairies' live behind those doors and kids love to play with them, and there's all this miniature stuff you can buy for your fairies and put it all in a garden or somewhere."

"Huh," she says.

"Wait, that's not all. This one in the weird tree was kind of mossy, and it had this tiny white doorknob. Cool, yeah, but… I don't know… a little creepy?"

"What's so creepy about a fairy door?"

I shrug. "I guess not much, when you say it like that. Not compared to the dead animals in people's mailboxes."

"Not much can beat that."

"So I take it you didn't put that fairy door in the woods for me to find?"

"Not me," she says. "Who else? I'm guessing Miss Perfect Jessica wouldn't want to snag her leggings doing something like that. God, I'm glad I'm not part of their little group. They're all so fake, and I've heard their kids are absolute gremlins."

I laugh. "Really?"

"For sure," Kendall says. "One of their kids—Heather's, I think—is even in juvie."

"That's crazy!" I say. "What for?"

"I don't really know. As you can imagine, Heather doesn't like to talk about it. It must have been serious, though."

"Jesus."

"I know. Those women invited me to one of their parties once, but I was so bored I faked an emergency call from Jamie and got out of there."

"Yeah, they're so lame," I say, hoping Kendall can't see the longing on my face. "Right, so definitely not Jessica. Regardless, I was kind of mad someone beat me to the punch with that fairy door."

"Don't tell me," she says. "You want to make fairy doors for our next crafternoon?"

The fight with Cash comes flooding back to me, and my palms itch with anxious perspiration. "Well, yeah, I can't help thinking that a whole little village of fairy doors and fairy stuff hidden around the neighborhood would be really cool for the kids."

"Oooh, yes! I'm in, even though the kids in this neighborhood seem to lean more toward the macabre," she laughs. "But it's bound to turn out better than this." She sweeps a hand across the table at our blobby paintings.

"Right? I already have all the stuff for the doors, actually. I wanted to test it out before I brought you the idea."

Kendall studies the wreckage of our paintings again. "I suppose that's wise. Can I see what you've got?"

Tears prick the backs of my eyelids. After our fight, I'd thrown away all my painted doors while sobbing. Not my finest moment, but it seems most of my moments these days are far from fine. "Um," I say, and then it all comes spilling out like a tipped-over glass of coconut water. "I don't have anything to show you, and it's Cash's fault. I was painting the doors the other day, and Cash came in and was all, 'Don't you have something better to be doing?' And I don't know, I got so annoyed. It completely set me off, because who is he to tell me how to spend my time? He wanted me to go take a nap, or go shower or something. But you get it, right? Sometimes you need to be creative, to sort of reset."

"I totally get it," she says, rubbing Holly's back in circles, eliciting little snorts of contentment. "Why do you think I do so many home renovation projects? It's hard and messy, but it's… what's the right word?" She snaps the fingers not currently soothing my baby. "Fulfilling. That's what it is."

"Exactly! And Cash isn't an artsy person, so he couldn't understand why I needed something creative, something I could control. And then… okay, so we got over that, and the next day, I actually am trying to rest while Holly's playing and Cash says he'll watch her, and right as I'm falling asleep, I hear 'Honey. Sadie! Where are the wipes?' As though he's completely incapable of finding them himself."

"Oof," Kendall says.

"It gets better. I tell him where the damned wipes are, then I'm drifting off again when he comes over, pokes me, and whispers, 'Where are the clean diapers?' I literally wanted to kill him. This is why I don't try to rest during the day—it's so much more annoying to get up when I'm trying to rest than to just stay awake and deal with his questions. It's weaponized incompetence, that's what it is."

"Ugh, Jamie does that to me. All. The. Time. 'Kendall, where are the dog treats? Kendall, where are the leashes? Kendall, help me find the new bottle of detergent!' It's like, are you physically unable to look for things yourself? Or to think through the issue of where something might be and go find it?"

"Yes!" I say, and the tears that were threatening to burst the dams of my eyelids a few moments ago recede. Talking to someone who gets me is like therapy, I swear.

"But I like the idea of the fairy doors," she says, bringing the conversation back around. "You said you have all the stuff for it?"

"Yeah. The doors, brushes, paint… that's kind of all you need."

"But you said the one in the woods looks… well, woodsy. With moss and rocks."

"It did, but I wouldn't exactly call it cute."

"When have our crafts ever been cute?" Holly grunts, and Kendall hands her back to me. I'm probably being paranoid, but I swear Holly frowns with displeasure.

"I thought the homemade ornaments were cute."

"They were… not horrible," Kendall says. "But I won't be hanging them on my tree next year, I can tell you that."

"Mmm," I say. The thought of putting up decorations in a few months sounds overwhelming. And what if Holly decided to try to pull up to stand while holding onto the Christmas tree, and it toppled over on her, crushing her little body? Or what if she put a tiny light in her mouth and crushed it with her gums and broken glass lodged in her throat and—

Kendall slaps both hands on the table. "Well, let's go check it out!"

"Check what out?" My head feels like it's encased in fog.

"The door you found out on Laurel!"

"Right now?"

"Sure, why not?"

I shrug. Today's craft has gone to hell, and I've got nothing better to do. Plus, Tater Tot could use the exercise. "Okay, sure. Let me get Holly loaded up in the stroller and I'll show you."

"I could use some inspiration," she says.

As Kendall cleans up the kitchen table and I carry Holly with me to the garage to get the stroller, I think back to the bird sounds app and the weird, slightly threatening rumble my phone recorded.

It was probably nothing.

* * *

"It's the strangest thing," I say, as we round the corner onto Laurel Lane. "I've walked this street literally hundreds of times. I know every flower, every sapling, every vine, and I'd never noticed this trail until the other day."

"Are you sure it was a real trail?" Kendall asks. "You know, not just a break in the trees?"

"I mean, it didn't have gravel or wood chips or anything, but it was pretty clearly a trail."

"Weird."

"What's weirder was the fairy door I found on this tree at the end of the trail. Somebody else around here must be a crafter, too!" The false cheer is saccharine on my tongue. As we draw closer to where I'd found the trail leading to the tree, my legs stiffen, as though they don't want to carry me forward anymore.

"I bet it's Tiffany," Kendall says, laughing.

"Nah, she'd be too scared to break a fingernail. Have you seen those acrylics? They're like half an inch long!" I laugh, too, but there's a growing coldness spreading in my chest. Holly is staring up at me from the stroller, her green eyes oddly calm.

We're almost to the end of Laurel Lane when I realize we've somehow missed the trail. "Whoops," I say. "Let's double back—the trail was kind of obscured a bit by vines the other day, but it's there. I know it is."

"Okay," Kendall says.

We turn and walk back down Laurel Lane, toward my house. I'm searching the curtain of trees and vines for the entrance to the trail, squinting until my eyes hurt. Tater Tot sniffs the ground alongside us. When we reach the spot where the trail opening should be, there's nothing—just more saplings, more clumps of Spanish moss, a tessellation of grapevines obscuring everything. Tater crosses to the opposite side of the road and sits, whining. We keep walking, doubling back at least three more times. No matter how meticulously I look, there's no opening, not even the tiniest shred of evidence of snapped twigs, trampled grass, crushed leaves, withered flowers. The only sign that I'm not completely off the deep end is Tater Tot's continued whining whenever we pass this particular spot. He remembers, surely he does?

Is he as freaked out as I am by the patent fact that the trail is simply not there when it should be?

"Sadie?" Kendall says. "I don't see anything."

"It should be right here," I mutter.

"Are you sure?" Kendall says, and there's a note of concern in her voice that irritates me.

"I know what I saw."

"Well, regardless, we're not finding it, are we?" She's definitely not trying to sound snotty, but the irritation is now nipping at my back like an angry dog.

"I'm not crazy," I whisper.

Kendall stops and touches my arm. "Of course not. But stuff changes in this area all the time. Plants grow, plants die, animals move stuff, the weather shifts things around."

"It should be right here," I say again, but I'm not even convincing myself.

"We can try again another day," she says, but we both know it's a lie.

Before I can answer, Holly starts to cry. As the tears flow down her face and her lungs fill to power some truly epic wails, there's a loud thunderclap up above that drowns out both her anguish and mine.

"Yikes," Kendall says. "Come on, let's go."

She turns back toward my house and breaks into a jog. I shouldn't be running, but what else can I do? Rain starts to beat down on us as I turn the stroller around and follow Kendall, Tater Tot trotting dutifully next to me. With each step, my lady parts feel heavier and heavier. I wonder if my body will ever be normal again.

By the time I catch up with Kendall, she's already at her car, parked in front of my house. "I've got to head back! I'll see you next week!" she calls, waving.

"Yeah, okay!" I yell back, struggling to be heard over the rain, which is now pouring down in buckets.

Tater Tot runs under the cover of the front porch, leaving me to maneuver Holly's stroller into the garage all on my own. We're both sopping wet and crying by the time I finally get us out of the driving rain.

Holly's crying because she's cold and wet.

I'm crying because I can't stop asking myself—was the trail ever really there? And if it wasn't… what does that mean?

CHAPTER FIVE

I Asked for Two Sandwiches

Anxiety overwhelms me at Holly's three-month pediatrician check-up. The pen nearly slips from between my sweaty fingers as I circle 'Never' on the postpartum questionnaire, the clipboard cold and hard on my lap. It's a lie, but am I actually going to say 'Most of the time' to the statement 'I feel anxious for no good reason?' I look down at the rest of the statements, and my chest tightens. There are point values next to each answer. My head thuds, like it used to when I'd be in the middle of an exam and I couldn't recall what I'd studied. Cash is breathing too loud in the chair next to me, and he's scrolling on his phone when he should be at least attempting to engage with the sweet little baby nestled in the crook of his arm. Resentment bubbles up like swamp gas, but I shove it right back down, along with the anxiety. Maybe I'm not lying on this questionnaire, because, after all, don't I have a good reason to be anxious?

My lady parts ache against the too-hard seat, and I know I'm losing this fight with the anxiety. I mean, am I a good mom if I circle 'Never' for 'I have been able to find the joy in things like I always have?' For God's sake, I found a dead squirrel in my mailbox the other day. That doesn't exactly spark joy.

I scan the statements again. It's so obvious which one is the 'correct' answer for each question. Why would they do this if they weren't trying to send a message?

My throat clogs, the way it does before the tears come. Clearly, everybody wants moms to be 'back to normal.' The doctors, like the husbands, like the families, just want us to be okay. But it's more than simple want, isn't it? I see it in my own home, every day. My family *needs* me to be okay, because who else is the glue that holds all of us together? There's no room for me to fall apart, and now, with a new baby, there never will be again.

"Sadie?" Cash interrupts me as I'm circling 'Most of the time' (0) and 'Always' (0).

"What?" I ask.

He pauses, and I look at him, really look at him. The slight crinkling at the corners of his eyes is the only indication that he's feeling even the tiniest bit tense. And after all, why should he? The nurse has come and gone, and Holly's hitting all of her three-month milestones. Cash is sleeping through the night, not waking up over and over to shrill cries or dreams of grapevines and trumpet flowers, dirt and dead leaves, a forest-drowned door that may or may not be there.

"Are you okay?"

He's asked me that about a million times in the last three months, and I know it's more about him than it is about me. Fuck Cash, fuck his self-serving 'emotional check-in', as he calls it, and fuck this questionnaire and everything it implies, everything it demands. As long as I'm okay, nobody has to deal with my pain. Nobody has to deal with my aching shoulders, my sore breasts, my nipples that crack and bleed, or how I sometimes cry out in the night because I'm in too much pain, but there's nothing else to do and no one to help me.

But I'm complicit in all of it, aren't I? Because I'm a good mother. Because I love my baby. My lips curl into something that must pass muster for a smile. The deception of it all makes me hate myself. "Yep, I'm okay," I lie. "Of course."

I try not to scream when Cash visibly relaxes. What would he have done if I'd said no? What would he have said if I told him how I sometimes think about jumping off our second-floor balcony?

I finish the questionnaire and add up my score, a comfortable zero.

Holly starts to cry, no doubt because she's cold dressed only in her diaper, and it takes all my effort not to bawl right alongside her.

* * *

In the car on the way home from the pediatrician, Holly is still upset about the shots, crying in big hiccuping bursts. I'm in the backseat next to her, singing "Wagon Wheel." The song only has a 30% success rate at calming her down, but it's better than nothing.

Cash is saying something in the front seat, but it's nearly impossible to hear him over Holly's wails and my own out-of-tune singing. My apologies to Old Crow Medicine Show.

"What?" I say, when Cash repeats himself.

"I said, what's for lunch?"

My mouth twists into a grimace as I try to hold in the roar that wants to erupt from my lips. After that doctor's appointment, Holly's continued screaming, and my feeble attempts to soothe her, is Cash legitimately asking me such a trivial question? I don't know what's for goddamned lunch!

But, of course, I don't say this. Instead, I say, "I'm not sure."

"I'm hungry," he whines, competing with our daughter for Most Annoying Family Member.

"Tough titties," I murmur, but when he says "What? What was that?" I respond, "What do you want?"

I'm too exhausted to even think about eating lunch myself, much less cooking something for a grown man who knows exactly where the refrigerator is without any help from me.

"Hmmm," he says. "What are my options?" He's shouting to be heard over Holly, who, while a bit quieter, is still crying. How freeing it must feel to be an infant—you cry when you want to, you show all of your emotions, and people come to help you without you having to lift a finger. Honestly, that sounds a little bit like being a husband.

"Food," I snarl, flinching involuntarily at my own harshness. Like most things these days, my tone is often out of my conscious control.

"Jeez," he says. "Should I stop somewhere, pick something up?"

It's a nice gesture, but the thought of going out of our way and adding even more time to this car ride to grab some mediocre food when we have plenty of stuff at home is excruciating. I can't wait to get back to the house and finally lift Holly out of this car seat. She's hungry, too, and I'm currently the only person who can remedy that. I'm not going to make her wait any longer than necessary so Cash doesn't have to suffer through a tummy rumble. I didn't have time to eat breakfast before the doctor's appointment, and my own stomach is growling so insistently, I'm almost doubled over with hunger pangs, but it doesn't matter. I don't come first anymore.

"No," I say. "I need to feed Holly, so let's just get home."

"Fine," Cash says, all sulky now.

My hand hovers over the door handle. Would I die if I jumped out now, or merely be horribly maimed? Would those consequences be more uncomfortable than staying inside this car?

I lock eyes with Holly, and it takes all my strength to pull my hand away from the door. This precious little thing needs me, and she deserves everything I can possibly give her, including peace.

"You want a sandwich?" I say.

"Yes please! What would be on it?"

I sigh, but I keep it as quiet as possible. "Um… I think we have some salami. Cheese. Mustard. Pickles. That okay with you?"

"Yes!" he cheers. He says something after that, but Holly has increased her volume again, as though she knows we're talking about food and wants to weigh in with her own hunger. I say, "Mhmm," even though I don't really hear what he's saying—the tone is enough. There's so much joy in Cash's voice I'm almost appalled.

Is it actually that easy to make him happy?

* * *

When we finally make it home, I get the panini maker plugged in and heating while I bring Holly to the couch and strap on my nursing pillow. I never know exactly how long she's going to take; she hasn't settled into much of a rhythm yet. After ten minutes on the right breast, during which the pain dulls from pliers twisting my skin to the sensation of ripping off a particularly heavy duty bandage, I hook a finger into her mouth and unlatch her before switching her to the left breast, where the pain is more on the level of a nasty blister being rubbed repeatedly by a new shoe. Progress, I suppose. Two weeks ago, it felt as though someone was shoving a white-hot branding iron into both of my breasts.

After eight minutes, she unlatches on her own—miracle of miracles—and looks up at me. There's love there, it's unmistakable, and for a moment I don't even think about the pain. Her green eyes droop, and I wish I could go to sleep right alongside her, but I can't.

"Cash," I say, then, when there's no response from the dining room behind me, I say again, "Cash!"

"What?" he says, his fingers clacking away on a keyboard.

"Can you put Holly down for her nap?"

There's a brief silence, then he says, "Um, yeah, I guess. I mean, I was hoping to finish this real quick, but sure."

I tense my jaw, keeping the anger inside, always inside. "She's super tired," I say. "She had a big morning."

He clacks away some more. "Yeah, I heard you. Just finishing this email."

Holly looks up at me, her little mouth puckering into a frown. She's clearly overtired, and if she doesn't go down soon, it's going to be hellish around here.

"Cash?" I say again.

The incessant clacking doesn't even slow. "Almost done."

There's no use. 'Almost done' never actually means almost done, or maybe we have completely different understandings of the word 'almost.' To me, it means thirty seconds or less, to Cash, it means more like ten minutes, or even fifteen.

My stomach growls again, and I shift Holly to one side as I unclip my nursing pillow and stand, somewhat unsteadily.

Without a word, I head to our room, taking Holly to her bassinet. When I'm almost to the door, he calls out, "Oh, I was gonna take her!"

I don't even bother answering. It's not enough to offer to do something if you can't do it in time.

When Holly's settled, I go back to the kitchen and pull sandwich ingredients out of the fridge. The panini maker is searing hot, and I don't waste any time assembling—bread, mustard, cheese, pickles, and the last of the salami for him, and bread, cheese, pickles, and mustard for me. I need to go grocery shopping, but that's not going to happen today.

The sandwiches are almost finished in the panini maker when Cash finally stops clacking and comes into the kitchen. "Sorry about that," he says. "It was really important that I finish that email. We have this customer who's trying to level up to a higher subscription tier, which would mean a ton of money for the company, and it couldn't wait."

"It's fine," I say, because what else is there to say?

I grab two plates and lift the lid of the panini maker. With a knife, I slide his sandwich onto his plate, and my sandwich onto mine. I figure he's mature enough to grab any other lunch components he might want.

Even though I'm ravenous, I'm almost too tired to eat my food.

I close the panini maker and hand him his plate.

He takes it and looks at the innocuous sandwich, then back up at me. "Um," he says.

I try to keep my voice even. "Is there a problem?"

"You didn't make me two sandwiches?"

Something breaks inside of me. "Excuse me?"

"I asked you for two sandwiches, remember? In the car?"

"No," I say. My fists clench, my nails digging into the meat of my palms. "I don't remember."

"Well, I did. I'm super hungry… can you make me another one?"

I can't do this. I can't do this for one more second.

I shove my plate at him. "Here, take mine," I growl.

"What? No! It's yours."

"I'm not even hungry," I say, and at this point, it's the truth. My appetite has vanished, and rage has taken its place.

"Sadie, no. You need to eat. Maybe just make me another one?"

"We don't have any more bread. Or salami. Or pickles. Here. Take mine." I swear, if he doesn't take this sandwich out of my hands soon, I'm going to throw it at him.

"Jeez," he says. "Fine."

I turn to the sink to wash my hands, but he's not done with me yet. "I did ask you, you know. Did you not hear me?"

"I guess not," I say.

"Are you okay?" he asks through a mouthful of food.

This fucking question, again? No, I'm not okay. I'm extremely far from okay—but of course, as always, I don't say that. I say the ever-anodyne, "I'm fine."

"You don't need to be mad at me," he says, still chewing.

"I'm not mad at you," I say, my back still to him.

"You won't even look at me," he whines.

I whip around to face him. "There," I say. "How about now? I'm looking at you now. Is that okay?"

"Jeez," he says again. "Chill."

The broken thing in me rattles around, like I'm a box filled with shattered glass. Before I say something I'll regret, I turn to leave the kitchen. Instead of staying silent, as he should, Cash says, "Gosh, Sadie. I feel like I can't have fun around you anymore."

Where did that come from? And Jesus Christ, I'm sorry he can't have fun around me. Forget that I'm suffering from a slow-healing vagina, chewed-up breasts, and sleep deprivation on the level of torture. Not to mention how I'm constantly caring for a squalling infant who has completely taken over my life. Is it really such a surprise where all the fun went?

"That makes two of us," I hiss, then retreat upstairs into the guest bedroom that will become Holly's room in a few months when she's ready.

I lay on the bed, simmering, tears coursing down my greasy cheeks. I'm so angry, and I'm angry about being angry. I can't show my rage, so I have to keep suppressing it, and it's poisoning me. I deal with Cash's emotions all day, and if I'm anything but chipper, he can't handle it. He will never understand the weight of being a mother and all that entails. Even if I tried to tell him, I know how that would go—the same way as all of our 'discussions.' It would be me bringing something up, then Cash talking at me ceaselessly so I can barely get a word in edgewise as he tries to convince me why my feelings are wrong. He'd keep digging himself farther and farther into a hole and saying more and more hurtful things, and even though I'd want to scream at him to shut up and leave me alone, I couldn't.

What does Cash know about taking care of other people? Taking care of others means doing things you wouldn't normally do if you were only worried about keeping yourself going. Cash may think he 'takes care' of us, but how would his life be different if we weren't here? He would still have a job. He would still play golf. He would still go to the gym. Me, on the other hand? Without Holly and Cash, I wouldn't be up all night, crying out in pain and soaking through sheets with my postpartum sweats. I wouldn't be meal planning so fastidiously, I wouldn't be cooking so much, I wouldn't be doing load after load after load of body fluid-soaked laundry. I wouldn't be rage-crying over a missing sandwich. I wouldn't be organizing every waking—and sleeping—moment of my day around other people.

So, I ask myself again, what does Cash actually know about taking care of other people?

I don't know how long I'm in the guest room, lying on the bed, but eventually, the door creaks open. Tater Tot pads into the room and jumps up on the bed, wet nose prodding my leg. Cash is right behind him, holding a plate, which he sets down on the bed in front of me.

"I thought you might be hungry," he says. There's a few hunks of cheese, a sliced apple, and some crackers on the plate. My stomach growls, even though eating is the last thing I want to do right now.

"Thanks," I say without looking up at him.

"I'm sorry," he says limply.

If he would simply leave it at that, I could get over this. We could move on.

That big mouth of his opens again. "But, I mean, I did tell you I wanted two sandwiches."

I want to throw the plate against the wall, hear it explode into sharp shards. I want to howl and shove him to the ground. I want to run out into the street and see how long it will take until a car comes, either to hit me or give me a ride, it doesn't matter.

"Right," I say, and I reach for a cracker.

CHAPTER SIX

A Road Full of Squished Frogs

The bright orange plugs crackle as they expand in my ear canals. It's not the most pleasant sensation, but it's better than listening to Holly's disgruntled cries as she does tummy time.

"Shh, shh, it's okay," I say, barely able to hear my own voice. Holly clearly can't hear me either, so what's the point of talking?

What's the point of anything?

Even though I wanted to sleep in the guest room last night just to be alone, I ate the entire sorry plate of food Cash brought me, then I went downstairs and had a normal evening with my family. I played the role of the totally-okay wife and mother, even while I was still simmering with resentment.

Holly only woke me three times to breastfeed and change her diaper, which thrilled me so much I nearly cried. When the pounding of early morning rain woke me at five-thirty, I was actually happy, because the sound ripped me out of my troubling dreams—back to the tree, the door, the trail that was and wasn't there. The sweat that covered my body could have been a result of simple postpartum hormones, but I knew better.

Much like the trauma of childbirth, my body held my fear, and it wouldn't stop reminding me.

By the time I'd eaten my own breakfast and Holly had woken up an hour later, the rain had stopped. Tendrils of Spanish moss wept occasional tears onto the ground.

I press the earplugs further into my ears, watching steam rise from the warm pavement of our street. My own anger, much like the rain, has mostly evaporated into cloying mist. I haven't seen Cash yet this morning; he probably went to the gym. I could track him with Find My Friends, but I really don't care where he is as long as he's not here, bothering me, turning up the gas on my rage.

Tater Tot licks my leg. "I know, boy," I say. "I want to go outside, too. A bit more tummy time for your sister, then we're off."

When Holly grunts and complains more urgently with the effort of holding her torso up, I hook her under the armpits and lift her into my arms. She knows the routine by now, and she's happy to be nestled in her stroller. Even though it's unreasonably humid, we could all use the fresh air.

I manhandle the stroller out of the garage, through the lawn, and onto the road, which is completely deserted. I swap my earplugs for AirPods and put on a true crime podcast. After two deep breaths, I start walking, beyond grateful for the solitude.

I turn the corner onto Laurel Lane and immerse myself in the tunnel of flora, walking slowly to keep the lady pain at bay. Everything is still dripping from the rain, the leaves and bushes so green they're almost neon. All around me, frogs are chirping so loudly I can barely hear my podcast, which is fine because all I'm actually doing is replaying the fight with Cash in my head, thinking of all the things I wish I'd said instead, all the verbal maneuvers I could have performed to make him understand how I feel, just once.

Ahead of me, Tater Tot pauses in the road to sniff at something. When I get closer, I see it's a frog that has obviously been run over by a car. Its viscera have erupted out of its mouth, slimy pink entrails curling over the asphalt.

"Tater Tot, no," I yell.

To my great relief, he backs away and keeps walking down the road. I follow in his wake, spying four more squished frogs. Birds trill in the trees around me, reminding me plenty of living things escaped the frogs' fate. Holly coos happily in her stroller, staring up at me with her big green eyes.

I take another set of deep breaths, letting the petrichor invade my nostrils, my mouth, my lungs. I turn off my podcast and take out my AirPods, letting my ears fill with the birdsong and steady drip of rainwater.

Without warning, Tater Tot growls, a deep, low rumbling. He's on the side of the road, close to where I found—or thought I found?—the trail. He's facing the foliage, which, as I get closer, I see is far from immobile. From farther back in the woods, the sharp staccato of snapping twigs echoes. My fists clench around the stroller handles. Could it be a deer? An aggressive raccoon? At least Holly is unperturbed, staring up at the sky with a gentle smile on her chubby face.

In the underbrush, the snaps turn to crashes and then to crackling stomps. My bladder seizes. In front of me, leaves quake, sending raindrops waterfalling to the ground. The branches above shake like there's an earthquake, and now the leaves part to let something through—

I squeeze my eyes shut. When I open them again, there it is: the opening in the solid mass of grapevine and trumpet flower. The hole beckons me, taunts me, as if the trail has always been there… as if it had never hidden itself away from me.

The frogs have gone silent, and the birdsong is muted, as though someone has turned nature's volume to the lowest setting.

This is wrong—it's all wrong. The trail shouldn't be here, it can't be here, and it looks exactly like it did in my dreams, and my bladder is about to let go.

Tater Tot stops growling; he crouches five feet from the trail entrance, his hackles raised, his lips curled back in a snarl. I've never seen him look so vicious.

I've watched enough horror movies to know when a dog tries to tell you some bad stuff is about to go down, you better listen.

"Let's go!" I hiss, turning the cumbersome stroller around as quickly as I can. I jog back home, Tater Tot at my side. I'm aching and sore, but I don't stop until I'm back in my front yard, pushing the stroller up onto the grass. Holly is miraculously calm, even when I rip her from the stroller and run up the steps onto our porch.

When I get inside, the shock of the air conditioning turns the rivulets of tears on my face into ice. I'm actually relieved to find Cash sitting at our dining table, clacking away on his computer. He jumps up when he sees me and runs over, grabbing Holly from my arms.

"My God," he says, taking in my tearstained cheeks. "Are you okay?"

I still loathe this question, but that doesn't matter right now. I want to be comforted, to be held with the same ease with which he holds Holly. I want someone to take care of me, for once. So, I snuff out the flame of my lingering resentment.

"I'm so sorry," I say, letting the tears flow again. "I'm sorry for everything yesterday. I'm… I'm so sleep-deprived, I'm exhausted, I'm not myself. I want everything to be okay."

He sets Holly on her play mat and cautiously approaches me. "I know it's hard," he says, placing one arm around my heaving shoulders.

I ignore the voice in my head sniping that he doesn't know, he can't know, and even if he could know, he would choose not to. "I'm so sorry," I say again, even though I'm not sorry and I didn't do anything wrong. The truth is irrelevant when you're a mother.

"Let's forget about it and reset, okay?" he says, wrapping me in a hug. I let myself melt into him, pull strength from his warm solidity. I used to love his hugs, the way they totally engulfed me. Lately, the heat of his body and the weight of his arms repulse me.

He runs his fingers through my unwashed hair, gently massaging my scalp. “Shh, shh,” he whispers. “Everything’s going to be fine.”

I resist the urge to pull away when the touch becomes too heavy. I spend so much of my time being touched, being pulled, being sucked dry. He wouldn’t understand, and I don’t have the energy to explain right now, so I let him pet my head and squeeze my ribs. I let him whisper lies into my ears. I let him subsume me, finding a moment’s peace in being totally absorbed by another person.

CHAPTER SEVEN

Throwing Up Bones

A shaft of golden sunlight bounces off the bright pink of one of my finished fairy doors, making it glow. Two of them are dry and ready for installation. As Cash helpfully informed me, Holly won't even understand what these are until she's much older, but I don't care. The doors make me happy, and putting them up around the neighborhood might help erase my mental image of that weird little door in the poison ivy-choked tree down that silent trail that teases me with its disappearing act. Thinking about it makes my palms sweat, and my jaw clenches so hard it's painful to pry it apart. As with most unpleasant thoughts, I shove them away as roughly as I can.

Even if Holly doesn't care about the doors, this neighborhood is full of kids. Jessica's little daughter Chesley will clap and laugh when she sees the bubblegum-colored door, carefully nailed into the base of a towering maple. She might even knock on it, hoping to get a look at the sweet fairy who lives there. Tiffany's son—what's his name? Kaylor? Kyden? Something weird like that—will believe in magic for a tiny bit longer. He'll bring his friends around to visit the green-and-blue striped door. Maybe he'll even make up his own stories about it, and all the other kids can join in.

And even though the kids will believe it's magic, the adults will know better. They'll understand someone sweet and creative and interesting did this. Someone worth embracing. Someone nobody would cut out of the circle of chatting moms at the pool. Someone nobody would turn a corner to avoid. Someone whose text invitation to dinner would never go ignored.

My lip starts to hurt as my teeth dig in, but I welcome the pain. It's one I can control.

Maybe, if word gets around that I'm the one behind this whimsical and adorable art project, the Yoga Moms will invite me to join their private book club, the one where they drink bottle after bottle of wine and gossip instead of talking about the romance novels they were supposed to have read. It doesn't matter that I'm not drinking right now (and don't even like alcohol), or that I'd love to actually have in-depth discussions about books, about anything unrelated to children. What matters is that I'd be accepted, I'd be part of the group, instead of looking in from the outside, clicking the heart button underneath a photo of too many smiles with too many teeth holding too many wine glasses—'Best night ever'—or a veritable sea of matching yoga mats rolled out across a spotless wood floor—'Love these ladies to death!'

I desperately want to have a 'best night ever!'

I wish for someone besides my family to 'love me to death.'

On impulse, I snatch my phone from the table and open Instagram. Jessica has a new post, a ridiculously curated shot of her and Tiffany in cowboy boots and hats. She's captioned it 'Having the best time at the Taylor Swift concert!' I smash the heart button. In her Story, there's a looping video of her and Tiffany executing the most adorable line dance, bejeweled boots glinting in the low light.

I used to love going to concerts. I could get a cowboy hat, could pull on some shiny boots. I could learn a line dance, for God's sake! My hand cramps around my phone, and I let it drop back to the table.

Let it go, babe, Cash says in my head. *Why would you even want to be friends with them?*

"Because," I sputter aloud.

Stop scrolling. You should delete Instagram from your phone, Cash demands from somewhere deep in the back of my brain.

"But then I won't know what's going on," I say. From the corner of the living room, Tater Tot looks up at me, head cocked.

Why do you need to know? It only makes you mad.

"You're missing the point!" I yell, then cover my mouth because Holly's napping and under no circumstances can I risk waking her up early.

There is no point.

"They had that party last week, you know," I whisper.

I don't want to hear about it. Stop talking about it already.

"Why do they have to post about these get-togethers in the first place? Everybody who was there already knows what happened!"

Don't look at it!

I'm not listening to him even though he's in my head. "When you post those pictures, Jessica, you're doing it to show everybody who wasn't invited how exclusive your clique is. Do you actually think your husband's grandma's nephew's friend's daughter cares about what you're up to?" My chest is heaving when I finish, Tater still peering at me from across the room.

Clearly you care about it!

"I don't!" I hiss. "I don't!"

But of course, I do.

"Who are you talking to?"

I let out a breathy little scream as Cash rounds the corner and comes into the living room. He can be silent when he wants to, I guess. He's in his gym shorts and tank top, his damp skin glowing with post-workout endorphins.

"Shit!" I say.

"Sorry," he shrugs. "Didn't mean to scare you."

I close my eyes, take a deep breath.

"Who were you talking to, though?" he says, looking at me with the same head-cocked, puzzled expression as Tater Tot.

Blood rushes to my cheeks. "What? I wasn't talking to anybody."

Cash's brow furrows, but then he shrugs again, an Instagram-perfect smile lighting up his face. "Okay, then." He points at the table. "Still doing those doors, huh?"

I grit my teeth. "Yep."

"Cool, cool." He stands there a moment longer, and a knot grows in my stomach. I don't love that there's a version of Cash living in my head, but I'd rather talk to that one than this flesh-and-blood one in front of me. Incredibly, the Cash in my head is less irritating.

"What do you have going on today?" he asks.

"Gonna put these doors up around the neighborhood."

"Neat," he says.

"Yeah."

There's another pause, far too long, and then Cash cracks his knuckles. "Well, I've gotta get back to work."

"Great," I say.

"I hope you have a good day," he says, but there's a flatness to his voice that I don't care for. Does he really hope I have a good day, or is he just saying that?

"I will," I say, more to myself than to him.

When Cash leaves, I collect all the tools I'll need—a hammer, some nails—and get ready to go. I can hear the Yoga Moms now: *Isn't she amazing for doing this? Isn't she so creative? So fun! So sweet! And she had a baby not that long ago, too—can you believe it?*

Holly wakes up happy, thank God, and I load her into the stroller. I tuck the tools and the two doors into the stroller's storage compartment, which currently houses an extra diaper, dog poop bags, and a package of baby wipes. Everything clanks together as I wheel the stroller through the lawn and onto the road, Tater Tot trotting behind me.

Instead of taking a right onto Laurel Lane, I head straight, down Sweetgum Street. This road isn't as deserted as Laurel, but there are still only a handful of houses, making it one of the quieter areas of the neighborhood. People need to be able to find the doors, sure, but I don't want to make them too obvious. That would take away some of the magic.

I also have zero desire for people to see me, bent over and sweating, my slack stomach jiggling as I hammer plywood into the bark of a tree. It's not exactly dignified. It certainly doesn't scream Yoga Mom.

Judging by the slowly rotting pile of newspapers at the end of their driveway, the Masons are on vacation, so I stop at an empty lot full of sweetgum trees across from their house. I've scouted the area already on my daily walks, so I know exactly which tree will house my first door. It's an older maple with a knot near the bottom, about the same shape and size as my door. I park Holly in the grass off the road so she can watch. Tater Tot mills around in the grass, sniffing and stopping every so often to mark his territory.

I grab the hammer, the bubblegum-pink door, and a nail from the stroller and squat down next to the maple, ignoring the various aches in my body. Tater Tot comes up next to me and sniffs my arm.

"I'm hanging up a fairy door," I tell him and Holly, smiling. My shoulders relax, and I let out a whoosh of air. The sunlight is warm on my face, and my heart feels full to bursting. This is the kind of mother I want to be—the one who forgoes naps to spend hours painting and hanging tiny doors to bring even the smallest bit of joy to her daughter.

When I open my eyes, Holly is looking at me, her sweet little smile mirroring my own. "You'll love this when you're older," I tell her. "Fairies live behind these doors."

She coos and sneezes, sweet as a fluffy kitten, making me giggle.

I turn back to the tree, my legs trembling from the deep squat. I haven't been back in the gym since giving birth, and I can tell I have a lot of work to do.

"Okay, here goes nothing." I press the door into the crevice, where it wedges neatly, then line up the nail. The hammer, a silly little thing I got in college with a looping floral pattern, is heavy in my palm. I snort out a breath, tense my biceps, raise the hammer, and slam it against the nailhead.

The jolt radiates up my arm, niggling at my elbow, coming to rest somewhere between my ribs, throbbing in time with my heart.

The nail has pierced the thin plywood of the door, but that's it.

"Yikes," I say, shaking out my wrist. "Okay, let's try that again."

I rear back and bring the hammer down harder, this time driving the nail the tiniest bit into the tree. My abdominal muscles—what's left of them after pregnancy, anyway—burn in protest. "Progress," I say, then lean back for another blow, then another. The handle of the hammer grows slippery, forcing me to squeeze it with all the strength I've got. My wrist and fingers ache, and perspiration beads on my face, my back, in the creases of my knees and elbows. It's beyond difficult to penetrate the strong, old bark, but eventually, the nail makes enough headway to secure the door. My knees creak as I stand up, the sweat running freely down every inch of skin.

"Well. That was way harder than I thought it was going to be."

Next to me, Tater Tot lets out a long, low burp.

"That was handsome," I laugh, patting his fluffy head.

With the first door in place, I load my hammer back into the stroller and carry on down Sweetgum Street, taking a right onto Peach Grove Court. Like Sweetgum, Peach Grove has a handful of houses, most of them occupied only during the winter months by snowbirds with primary residences in New England. The undeveloped lots are heavily wooded, full of massive live oaks, loblolly pines, sweetgums, maples, and magnolia trees. Hanging curtains of grapevine, covered in serrated, heart-shaped leaves, stretch from the branches down to the leaf-littered ground. As I walk, I'm serenaded by the chirp of red-winged blackbirds, the trill of mockingbirds, and the occasional piercing cry of a red-tailed hawk. Woodpeckers drill against the trees high above me, but no matter how hard I squint, I can't find them amidst the leaves.

My next tree lies close to the intersection where Peach Grove connects with Laurel Lane. It's a young slash pine with a trunk barely wider than my hand. Hopefully, this tree will be a bit more cooperative than the maple. My arms are already sore from hammering, my wrists achy from the effort of squeezing the metal. A blister threatens to erupt on the meaty part of my thumb.

Like before, I park Holly on the grassy shoulder of the road and turn her so she can watch what I'm doing. I gingerly extract my second door, a blue-and-green striped mushroom shape, from the bottom of the stroller. This location is more off the beaten path than the other, but that will make it all the more delightful for the people who happen upon it. Tater Tot must agree, because he sniffs the grass around the slash pine perfunctorily, then lifts his leg and sprays the area with his scent.

"Hm," I say, frowning. "Thanks, boy."

Hammer, nail, and door in hand, I squat down next to the pine, trying to avoid stepping in Tater's fresh pee. I'm not sure I succeed, but who cares? I'm already gross, and I don't plan on seeing anybody but my family today.

The slash pine doesn't have a neatly-shaped crevice like the maple, so I place the door and nail against the flat bark of the tree and give it the first blow with the hammer. The nail easily pierces the door and even makes a bit of progress into the tree.

"Woohoo!" I cheer. Tater woofs.

I'm mid-hammer blow when Holly cries out, the sound so shrill and unexpected that I miss my mark and bring the shining head down on my own finger. Sharp pain shoots from my fingernail all the way up to my shoulder. It worms its way into my skull, where it curdles into a blinding rage.

"Holly!" I yell, surprised and somewhat frightened of my own anger, clearly still so close to the surface, even on a seemingly good day. Holly's green eyes sparkle with tears, and she lets out another wail.

"Shhh," I say, pushing away Tater's nose when he moves in to investigate my wound. I stand, inspecting the damage. Hot blood boils up around a jagged crack running through the middle of my nail. The warm slick of it coats my finger, dripping down into my palm. The coppery scent invades my nostrils, making my stomach roil.

Haven't I bled enough already?

This is what it means to be a mother—never having the chance to finish a single goddamn thing without interruption. Not a meal, a chore, a task, a conversation, a dream, a sentence, a single thought.

Frustrated tears cloud my vision, and I rummage through the stroller with my good hand until I grasp the ever-present pack of baby wipes. I pluck one out and wrap it around my finger, which now bleeds even more freely. I squeeze, trying to stanch the flow. Holly whimpers, her tiny forehead all wrinkled.

The humid air catches in my throat as I suck in a ragged breath. "It's fine," I say through gritted teeth. "Mommy's okay. I'm sorry I yelled."

The hammer's still on the ground next to the tree, the door installation half-finished. My enthusiasm has evaporated along with the morning mist. My arms, hands, and thighs burn with fatigue, refusing to do anything more.

I scoop up the hammer with my good hand, toss it into the bottom of the stroller, and push Holly back onto the road, pressing my injured finger against the handle of the stroller to keep the baby wipe in place.

"Time to go home," I bark. "Let's go, Tater."

Even though I'd rather avoid it, taking a right on Laurel Lane up ahead will be the fastest route home, and with blood now soaking the wipe and running down my wrist, I don't have a ton of time to waste. The last thing I need is for Jessica or Mandy or Tiffany to come along, looking like Lululemon models in their matching athleisure sets, wondering what the hell I'm doing out here and why I can't manage to get myself together.

"Oh, don't mind me, it's only a little cut," I whisper, trying out the phrasing, practicing the right inflection. "It's a funny story, actually, I was hanging up a fairy door—you know the kind, it's for the kids—"

The wheels of the stroller hit a patch of gravel, jolting me back to full awareness.

"You okay, Holly?" I ask, peering down at her. She stares back, stone-faced.

"Let's..." The thought dies in my throat as Tater growls, the only sound now permeating the silence that's crept up on us like a stealthy predator. No more woodpeckers, no more bird chirps, no more hum of cicadas or drone of lazy bumblebees. My body quivering, I force myself to turn.

There it is. Of course. The entrance to the trail, the grapevine and trumpet flower parted invitingly.

Am I dreaming? Unconscious from blood loss? Sleepwalking?

Or am I crazy?

I bite my lip hard, letting the pain center me. I'm here. I'm awake. I'm fine.

And I'm not going to let this break me.

I push Holly onto the side of the road. Without further hesitation, I walk us through the overhang of vines and onto the trail, Tater Tot stepping cautiously behind us.

"This is real," I say. "I'm going to prove it. I'm going to get a goddamned picture this time."

If I ever found any delight in this hidden trail before, it's gone now. As I reach the clearing, the atmosphere around me sours. A cloud passes over the sun, casting the tree up ahead into even deeper shadow.

I remind myself to breathe as I pick my way around the stroller, putting my body between Holly and the tree. Tater Tot sits at the clearing's edge, a low growl rumbling in his throat.

The door looks exactly the same as it did before.

Maybe I'm not crazy, after all.

My feet crush dead leaves and brittle twigs, crunching them like dry cereal as I creep closer. I clutch my phone in my uninjured hand, ready to snap as many pictures as it takes to prove I'm not losing it.

I'm three feet away from the door when I squat low, aim my phone, and snap a fusillade of pictures. Before I stand and walk out of here, I review a few to make sure I've captured what I need.

That's when I see it.

To the left of the tree, an enormous spider, possibly a wolf spider, crouches on the ground, legs curled, ready to spring.

I scream and jump back, dropping my phone and covering my face as though that will protect me from a spider attack. Tater Tot barks and takes a few tentative steps toward me. My body locks down, every muscle taut as a violin string, preparing for the sting of a bite… but nothing happens.

When I finally screw up the courage to lower my hands and open my eyes again, I see the spider hasn't moved. Its powerful brown legs are still curled, tense underneath its thick body. A retch rises in my throat, and I swallow it back down.

Tater Tot finally joins me, sniffing my knee. No doubt he can smell the anxiety pouring off of me in stinking waves. He takes a step toward the door, toward the spider—but it still doesn't move.

Now, morbid curiosity outweighs my fear, and I reach out with my uninjured hand, slowly, slowly, pluck a small twig from the ground, and stab at the leaf litter surrounding the spider.

Still nothing.

I go for a more direct approach, gently poking its body with the tip of the stick.

I scream again when it flips over, but it doesn't take long to realize something's not right. The spider has upended as though it weighs nothing, and, upon closer inspection, it has the same crumpled texture as the surrounding leaves. I poke it again, and there's a sickening crunch as it collapses in on itself.

There's no spider blood or guts—no goo of any kind, in fact. This thing has been sucked completely dry.

I gulp and try to make my muscles release without much success. Something doesn't feel right. My gaze travels from the shell of the spider to the door, then up the trunk of the tree. The tree itself is remarkable in its strangeness, in its quiet, understated malevolence. Forget its poison ivy shroud; the way its stunted, hardened body erupts into spindly, half-living branches not far from the ground makes it look uncomfortably similar to the wolf spider lying next to it, its legs reaching into the air.

I can't be the only one who sees this—the door, the tree, the desiccated spider. I toss the stick aside and squat down to retrieve my phone, my overtaxed thighs screaming.

This close to the ground, my horror grows teeth and jabs them into my flesh, because what I initially thought were scattered twigs surrounding the horrible tree are no twigs at all.

They're tiny bones.

My body freezes, still crouched low. There's no fight in me, not with this terror boiling in my veins, and flight is a no-go. All I can do is stare at the ground, air wheezing in fast little gasps through my teeth. Those bones… they're everywhere, they're crushed beneath my feet, they're poking at the soles of my shoes, they're… oh, God.

There's something wrong with these bones. They're gnawed, blackened, as though they've been cooked over an open fire. It's a veritable carpet of carnage: minuscule ribcages broken open like Easter eggs, spindly claws with split nails, toothpick-sized tibias with splintered ends.

Tater Tot is unperturbed; he's sniffing the ground with eagerness, even while he continues to growl. Before I can stop him, his jaws clamp around a jagged sliver of bone.

"No!" I yell, piercing the quiet of the clearing. I shove my phone into my pocket and lunge at Tater Tot, desperate to get that filth out of his mouth.

I clamp one hand around Tater's snout, trying unsuccessfully with the other to wrest the bone from between his teeth. I've forgotten about the baby wipe still squeezed around my finger; in the commotion, it falls away, blood spilling to the ground out of all proportion to the size of the injury.

"Son of a bitch!"

Tater Tot takes advantage of my distraction and lurches from my grasp before barreling around the stroller and back down the trail toward the road.

I dart to the stroller, turn it around, and run, Holly bouncing in the seat, panic sparking in her green eyes. Pinpricks of blood splatter my shirt as I chase Tater Tot back out onto Laurel Lane. The effort is exhausting, but I can't let him swallow that bone.

Tater Tot is almost back to our house by the time I finally catch up to him. When I do, he's licking his lips.

"Fuck," I gasp.

He swallowed that bone.

I park Holly's stroller and collapse onto my front steps, ignoring the blood still spilling from my wound, ruining my clothes, my shoes. Even my socks are speckled with red.

"Jesus Christ," I mutter. "Did you really have to do that?" I ask Tater Tot.

In response, he extends his neck and burps. The stink hits me like a slap.

"Gross," I whine.

Tater stretches out his neck and burps again, this one longer and more rattling. I can't help it—I laugh. I'm covered in blood and sweat, my muscles burning, my mind reeling. How ridiculous must I look? The laughter comes harder and faster, until I'm shaking.

I'm still laughing when Tater's third burp turns into a gargled, hacking sound.

He gags, and even though it's awful, I can't stop laughing. With a massive heave, Tater Tot disgorges the entirety of his stomach contents onto the sidewalk. The vomit is thin and watery, dotted with sharp shards of bone coated in bright yellow bile. I want to scream, but all I can do is keep laughing. Tater Tot retches again, and I can't catch my breath.

I'm in absolute hysterics by the time Cash emerges from the house and rushes down the steps, shouldering me aside, racing to save our choking dog.

CHAPTER EIGHT

You Were Freaked Out by a Tree?

An obese bulldog seated across from me in the waiting room at the veterinary hospital sneezes, his slobber landing on the toe of my sneaker. To my right, an elderly, piebald cat keeps pressing against my shoulder and purring. It would be cute if I weren't allergic to cats. My eyes sting like I've been chopping an overripe onion, and there's a persistent tickle in my nose that threatens to become a sneeze. I glare at the bulldog. If this tickle does become a full-blown a-choo, I know exactly who I'm aiming for.

Even though there's a snotty dog across from me and an allergen-shedding feline on my right, I almost prefer them both to what's on my left. After nearly a half hour of irritated silence, Cash finally speaks to me, almost yelling to be heard over the bulldog's sniffles, the cat's purrs, and the occasional screech of an anemic-looking parakeet. How Holly can sleep through all of this, nestled into her car seat at our feet, is beyond me.

"Sadie, what happened?"

Tears well in my eyes, completely unrelated to the cat dander, but I refuse to cry in this dirty waiting room while the vet saves our dog. "He threw up bones, Cash. Bones…" My stomach roils and I clench my teeth. Throwing up bones? What a horrible, disgusting image…

Cash snaps his fingers in front of my face. "Sadie, focus," he says. "It might be important if they have trouble helping Tater. Jeez, he's been back there a long time."

I take a deep breath, forcing my jaw to relax. "We were out on a walk. There's a trail off of Laurel Lane, and I've been down it before, and there's this weird tree and… well, we found all these bones on the ground, and Tater grabbed one. I tried to get it away from him, but he must've swallowed it and I guess it got stuck in his throat…"

I trail off again, and Cash sighs, drawing a hand over his face. For a tiny moment, he looks as tired as I am. "Sadie, you know not to take Tater off leash by the construction zones. Those builders are always leaving their trash everywhere, chicken bones and pork ribs and all that shit."

"It wasn't a construction zone!" I insist, trying to keep my voice level. "I told you, it was this trail off of Laurel Lane."

"I've never seen a trail off of Laurel," he says.

"Neither had I, until a few days ago. And I went down it, it goes into the woods, and there's this horrible tree, with this little door… wait! I'll show you!" I pull the zipper on my diaper bag so hard I lose my grip. The bag twists out of my hands, spilling fresh diapers, wipes, a pacifier, a small blanket, and, most embarrassingly, one of my massive postpartum pads onto the dirty floor.

"Christ," Cash hisses, but he doesn't lift a finger to help me. I fall to my knees, scooping everything back into the bag, trying to avoid jostling Holly's car seat. My cheeks burn, and this close to the floor, the mingled stenches of feces, urine, and vomit singe my nostrils.

Red-faced, I fall back into my seat next to Cash, lips pressed tightly together to keep a rising sob inside.

"Come on, Sadie," Cash says, sneering.

"I wanted to show you…" That's when I realize my phone is in my pocket, has been there all along.

Cash rolls his eyes. "Show me what?"

I blink, yank my shoulders back, and pull out my phone. "The trail," I say, looking through my photos to find the pictures I took only a few hours ago. I keep swiping, but after a series of Holly pictures and a screenshot of a dress I want to buy once I have my 'body back,' there's only darkness. Rectangle after rectangle of total blackness. Nausea rises in my throat, and my vision blurs. Did I eat anything today? I can't remember. "Where is it…"

Cash sighs far too loudly, and my entire body tenses as though I'm about to throw up. His sighs always say *That's right, I'm carrying the weight of the world on my shoulders, and everyone around me—especially you, Sadie—is supremely incompetent.* "Sadie," he says. "Come on."

I struggle to swallow a bubble of bile. "Okay, so, the pictures didn't turn out for some reason. But…" I suck in a sharp breath—what about the bird sounds recording from the first time I found the tree? Cash won't be able to ignore that menacing growl the app picked up. "Wait! I have something else!"

The cat on my right sweeps his furry head down my arm, leaving a trail of spit. The tickle in my nose becomes urgent, and I erupt, sending a shower of snot all over myself, Holly, and the floor. It's horrible, embarrassing, disgusting, but at least Holly doesn't so much as twitch. As a bonus, I also nailed the bulldog.

"Ugh," Cash snarls.

"Gesundheit," the bulldog's owner says. Despite me splattering his pet with mucus, the man is far nicer to me than my own husband.

Wiping my nose on the inside of my shirt, which smells of old spit-up and spoiled milk, I navigate to the bird sounds app and open my last recording.

Except… the last entry listed is from over a month ago, when I identified a particularly aggressive pileated woodpecker. "No," I breathe, refreshing the page again and again, hoping the recording from the clearing will magically appear.

Did I delete it? Goddammit, I can't remember!

"It's not here," I say. "But... Cash, I took a bird sounds recording near this freaky tree, and this weird growly noise got picked up, not like any bird I've ever heard, and the app couldn't identify it..."

Now Cash is staring at me, green eyes narrowed, mouth twisted into a frown. "So... help me understand, Sadie. You took Holly and Tater Tot into the woods, and you got freaked out by a tree?"

"It looks like a serial killer tree, Cash. And—"

"What does that even mean?" he says, snorting.

"It's not just the tree. There's this little door there, and I know you saw me painting fairy doors but I didn't put this one there, I swear, and I don't know who did, and there's something really wrong there! There were bones everywhere, all around it!" I'm shouting now, and all the people and animals in the waiting room are glaring at me. Cash puts a heavy hand on my wrist to quiet me, like I'm a naughty child caught telling a fib.

"Calm down, Sadie." He removes his hand, my snot glistening on his palm, and wipes it on the leg of his pants. His voice is barely above a whisper, his gaze roaming the room as his head nods, as if to say, 'Nothing to see here, I've got this under control, folks.'

"I am calm," I say, matching his volume. "I meant to tell you about the tree and everything in that little clearing earlier, but..." I trail off. He may be listening, but he's not hearing me.

"Right. Sadie, I think you need some sleep," he says, drawing his hand down his face again. I think it's the snot-covered one, and I have to grit my teeth to keep from barking with laughter. "It's fine. I'm sure it's nothing. Tater probably picked up a bone dropped by a bird or something. Forget about it."

And there it is—the invisible, persistent specter of everything he's not saying: 'Be okay, Sadie. Be normal, Sadie. Don't be hysterical, Sadie.

Stop making stuff up, Sadie. Stop overreacting, Sadie.'

I look down at my hands, chapped from so many washings after so many diaper changes, and grit my teeth.

Before Holly, I was Sadie. I was a wife, sure, but I was someone not defined by my reproductive success, by my place in a family. I was interested in birds. I liked learning about plants and naming flowers. I loved going to museums and musicals, and I even cried in the audience of a Jack White concert because the music was absolutely transcendent. I painted giant oil paintings of classic movie monsters on midcentury modern backgrounds. I was a three dimensional person.

Now, I am Holly's mother. I am Cash's wife. I am everybody to them—cook, maid, laundress, event planner, scheduler, administrative assistant—but I am nobody to everyone else.

I am a hysterical woman, and nothing I say can be believed.

As Cash picks up his phone to get lost in scrolling, my breasts begin to ache. It's past Holly's feeding time, but she's still sleeping. Her schedule is going to be way off from today's misadventures, which means my entire schedule will go off the rails, too. Should I wake her to feed now? Should I go somewhere else?

Holly makes my decision for me when she opens her little green eyes, so much like Cash's, and howls with hunger. I'm halfway to the door and the privacy of the car, arms aching from the weight of the car seat, when the veterinarian calls our name.

"Hansen?"

Cash leaps up, trotting over to the scruffy man in a white doctor's coat who's holding Tater's leash. I follow, lugging a crying Holly, my body throbbing in at least a dozen different places.

I set the car seat on the ground and try to listen to what the vet is saying. Tater leans over and licks Holly's tears, making her giggle.

"Tater Tot will be fine," the vet says. "There was a chunk of bone lodged in his throat."

"Jeez," Cash says.

"Don't worry, it's out now. He's very lucky—while we were examining him, he vomited, which dislodged the bone. From the looks of it, he ate some sort of animal. A rat, or a squirrel, maybe."

My entire body goes rigid. Tater saw me throw that squirrel from the mailbox into the bushes…

"If he hadn't gotten it out on his own, he'd have needed surgery. As it is, he'll need to rest and recover for a few weeks. His trachea is pretty bruised."

"Thank God," Cash says, visibly relaxing and leaning down to pet Tater's head.

"Only soft food and no long walks until he's fully healed," the vet says.

"Got it," Cash responds, now crouching down to envelop Tater Tot in a hug. Briefly, I let myself imagine I'm the one being hugged. It must be nice.

We thank the vet and then, after checking out at the desk, take our parade back to the car. I bet everybody in the waiting room is relieved to see us go—the crazy mother, the wailing infant, the giant horse-sized doodle.

When we get to the car, Tater Tot jumps in the front seat next to Cash while I breastfeed Holly in the backseat. I'm not going to make her wait the twenty minutes it will take to get back home, so I endure the twisted spine, the numb leg, the hunched shoulders. The pinched nipples would happen even with my ergonomic nursing pillow, but who really cares?

"No more eating squirrels, buddy!" Cash says, rubbing Tater's head. "You scared us!"

Thank God he did eat that squirrel, though! Otherwise, those gnawed bones from around the tree might have stayed wedged in his gullet. What would I have done if Tater had needed surgery? Or if he hadn't made it? Guilt lodges in my throat, sharper and more painful than any bone Tater might have swallowed.

"Cash?"

"What?" he says, still scratching Tater.

"I have to tell you something."

"Okay..."

"I think I know where Tater found that squirrel."

"Probably in the road or something. I told you, you can't take him off leash anymore."

"No, no," I say, shaking my head. "There was..." I struggle to find the right words, but, like vomit, the truth is better out than in. "There was a dead squirrel in our mailbox the other day."

"Huh?" Cash says. "What... seriously?"

"Yeah," I say. "I found it in the morning, and I got it out with a stick then threw it into some bushes. I think... I think Tater went and found it when I was cleaning out the mailbox."

Cash stops petting Tater and turns to face me. "That can't possibly be true. Are you messing with me?"

"No!" I shout, and Holly bites down on my nipple, making me wince.

"Honey, that's... no."

"Cash, it stank up our whole yard! And I saw it with my own eyes!"

Cash bites his lip. "Just like you saw that trail off of Laurel?"

I open my mouth to reply, but no words come out.

"Sadie," he says. "I think you need to get some sleep."

"You think I imagined everything?"

Cash sighs. "I think... sleeplessness is hard. It can make you see things, think things. I know when I get six hours instead of eight, I'm like a different person."

My mouth sags open again. I don't know where to begin—with his disbelief, or with the suggestion that six glorious hours of uninterrupted sleep is anything to complain about?

"Tater found a squirrel somewhere while you were out walking, I'm sure of it. Then he choked on it, then he threw it up. It's as simple as that, honey."

"Other people have found dead animals in their mailboxes, too! Kendall told me!"

Cash snorts. "I think she was trying to freak you out."

"She wouldn't do that!" What do I have to do to make him believe me?

"Whatever, Sadie. Believe what you want, but here's the truth: there's no pile of bones in the woods, there's no trail, there's no chance there was a dead squirrel in our mailbox. Once you start sleeping more, you'll understand all of that. I know you will." He smiles and gives a curt nod, as though he's wrapped the problem of me up and can now check that off his to-do list.

Rage replaces the guilt in my gullet, and it burns far hotter.

I definitely prefer the guilt.

CHAPTER NINE

Boring Is a Cardinal Sin

"I feel so bad for Tater," Kendall says. "Poor guy. I can't even imagine throwing up bones, of all things."

"I know," I say, huffing to keep up with her. "He was not happy about being left behind."

"I bet," Kendall says, leaning over to make a silly face at Holly, who rewards her with a sweet little smile.

"He's only been able to go on short walks, and even then it makes me nervous. It's so humid out, he starts panting as soon as we get outside. That can't be good for his throat." By the time I'm done talking, I'm panting myself. The wet air squeezes me like I'm a stress ball, but Kendall doesn't seem to notice, bouncing along as though it's a breezy spring afternoon instead of an oven-hot late summer morning.

"Remind me—how many fairy doors did you put up?" Kendall asks.

"Only two," I say. "Driving a nail through a tree is much harder than I thought it would be."

"Can't say I've ever tried it."

We go straight onto Sweetgum Street until we come to the first door. Kendall crouches next to it and dutifully oohs and aahs. With one fist, she gives a few delicate knocks, earning a grin from Holly.

It is cute, I have to admit. I did a decent job, for once.

"Holly is going to love this when she's older," Kendall says. When she rises to stand, there are no pops, creaks, or groans. She's as smooth as an elevator, and I try—unsuccessfully—to keep the jealousy at bay.

"I think so, too!" I shift to one hip, trying to take the weight off—also unsuccessfully—of my sore lady parts.

"I'm definitely going to make one," she says as we turn right onto Peach Grove Court. "I'm sure it won't be as pretty as yours, though."

"Psh," I say, struggling to turn the stroller onto Peach Grove. It's fine enough for light walking through, say, a mall, but not so much for asphalt roads. Miles of pebble and twig-strewn streets have taken their toll on the stroller's rickety wheels, making the thing a chore to push, but it's what I've got, so it's what I'll keep using until the wheels literally fall off.

Finally, I've got the stroller turned. Reflexively, I look behind me and call, "Tater!" When my brain catches up to my mouth, I frown. "Whoops," I say.

"Don't worry," Kendall says. "I'm sure he'll be out and about with us before you know it."

I nod, trying to peel the grimace off my face. It takes effort to remind myself Tater's at home, recovering, not… not dead. I shudder despite the heat.

"Hey, you know what? We can get those cute little fairy figurines, and they even have, like, little barbecues and little ice cream stands and all this stuff," Kendall says. "Have you seen that kind of thing?"

"Not really. I've mostly been focused on the doors."

"Oh, yeah," she says. "There's like a whole fairy world out there. You can buy a lot of it at Michael's. It's super cute."

"You think older kids would like it?"

She shrugs. "I don't see why not. I mean, I like it and I'm… quite a bit older than the kids."

I chuckle. "Fair enough."

When we reach the second and final door I've placed near the intersection of Peach Grove and Laurel, Kendall squats to get a better look. "Wow, I love this!"

"Thanks," I say, catching up to her and pushing the stroller onto the grass next to the door.

"Did you do this yourself, or did you buy it?"

"Huh? I painted both doors all on my own," I say, brows wrinkling. She knows I painted those doors. Does she think the job is so good, it must be store-bought?

"No, this," she says, pointing to a miniature wreath hanging on the door.

My bladder seizes as I study it. 'Wreath' is too generous a term for what this is—a tightly woven circle of spindly twigs, the ends violently splintered. My bladder pulses urgently as a full-body shiver courses through me.

"No, that wasn't me," I croak. "Oh, wait. It was you, right? I mean, it's cute. How did you know the door was here? Did you find it accidentally?"

Kendall cocks her head and puts her hands up. "Wasn't me."

The pain in my bladder recedes enough that I no longer think I might wet myself. "Right, right, sure you didn't. It was the fairies, huh?" I waggle my fingers at her.

"No, I mean—this seriously wasn't me."

We stare at each other. "Then who?" I say.

After a beat, she laughs, the tension draining from her face. "It was probably one of the Yoga Moms, trying to one-up us."

I laugh too, but it's not that funny. Even though I know she's probably right—I mean, of course someone had to put that wreath there, and a Yoga Mom is as good a guess as any—something's off. A Yoga Mom surely would have done something with that wreath, something whimsical—painted it pink, hot-glued fake flowers to it, sprinkled it with glitter, something.

As is, the wreath is... dull. There's no real cuteness to it, despite what Kendall thinks. My bladder pounds again, my head swimming with the heat.

"Yeah, probably," I say, turning away from the horrid little thing. "Let's head back."

Around us, the undeveloped lots are abuzz with life—droning cicadas, chirping red-winged blackbirds, croaking frogs. Overhead, the sun is hot and bright, and there's not even the slightest hint of that heavy silence that descends when I'm alone out here. Despite all that, I'm scared. Or, rather—I remain scared. I've been scared since I saw the double line on the pregnancy test, since my first ultrasound, since my first contractions, since I held newborn Holly in my arms, since Cash and I brought her home from the hospital and looked at each other in abject disbelief, thinking, 'How did they let us walk out with a baby? We have no idea what we're doing! Where are the real adults?' I've been scared since I mistook Holly's smattering of baby acne for a life-threatening allergic reaction. Since the first time she cried uncontrollably, and there wasn't a damn thing I could do to make it stop. Since I saw a diaper full of frothy, green poop that left me reeling and wondering if I should bag it and take the smelly evidence to the doctor. Since she fell asleep in her bassinet, and I checked over and over and over, my finger under her tiny nose, to make sure she was still breathing.

So, yes, I'm scared, but I don't tell Kendall any of this. Why? I don't tell her because, quite simply, suffering is boring. Suffering is monotonous—there's no levity, no break. And while it's perfectly okay to be a mommy drunk, a hothead, even an insufferable Instagram tradwife or a multi-level-marketing schemer pushing low-quality leggings or stinky essential oils, God forbid you commit the cardinal sin of being boring.

In a world where every aspect of everyone's life is mined for 'content,' being boring is a death sentence. So, even though Kendall is my best friend here and I've been suffering for so long, I don't tell her about what's really going on—in my home, in my marriage, or in my head.

CHAPTER TEN

Whatever Lives There Is Doing a Whole Lot of Killing

The air is hot and clammy against my skin, but I know there's cool respite ahead. The hidden trail opens up like a flower, beckoning me. I don't want to go, but my feet insist, and then I'm in the clearing. The poison ivy-choked tree with its stout trunk and thin, reaching branches, spindly as a spider's legs, greets me. The door sits at ground level, corrupting the atmosphere. It shouldn't be here. I shouldn't be here.

Why am I here?

The creak of tiny hinges rips the silence apart, and the door opens a crack. Minuscule fingers, thick and blackened as if with soot, creep around the edge of the weathered wood, pushing it wider, wider…

An angry wail pierces the atmosphere like a missile, and I bolt upright, nearly falling out of my bed. Cheesy-smelling sweat coats my body, and my heart pounds.

I look around, catching my breath. I'm at home. I'm safe.

It was only a dream.

When I lay Holly back down after her feeding, instead of collapsing back into bed, I linger over her bassinet, watching her, reluctant to step away, even though my bed is only a few feet across the room. I don't want her out of my sight, nor do I want the nightmare to come back. Whenever I manage to snatch a few hours of thin sleep, the nightmare envelops me.

I grow more and more terrified that this time, Holly won't wake me up, and I'll have to see what exactly is living in that tree.

* * *

"That's the problem, Mom. I obviously love Holly more than anything, but nobody tells you how supremely boring newborns are," I say, pressing the phone to my ear as I lie prone on the ground, patting Holly's back during her tummy time.

"I don't remember you ever being boring," she says. "But, that was a while ago."

"Rose-tinted glasses," I say, running my fingers along the back of Holly's soft little hand. Her sweet baby smell wafts toward me, and I breathe deeply.

"I suppose," she says. "So, what else is going on?"

"Ugh," I sigh, weighing how much to tell her. The dead squirrel? Tater's bone vomit? The creepy door? I don't want to scare her, especially since there's little she can do from across the country, so I settle for a piece of the truth. "Cash and I are… not doing so hot."

"Oh, honey," she says. "What did he do?" My entire body unclenches. I needed the reminder that there's someone irrevocably, one hundred percent on my team, no matter what. My husband should be like that too, right?

"Well… we can't seem to get on the same page," I say, rolling onto my stomach to mimic Holly. My still-healing abdominal muscles groan in protest.

"I can understand that," she says. "Having a new baby is hard on a relationship."

"But shouldn't we be stronger than that?" I blurt. "I mean, we've been married for four years already. Shouldn't we have… I don't know, figured things out more by now?"

"That's not how it works," she says. "A baby changes everything."

"Does it really?" I mutter sarcastically, thinking about Cash's consistently well-groomed appearance, his return to work, the way he spends his afternoons playing golf on the Agua Roja course while I try futilely to nap.

"Let me clarify. A baby changes everything… for you. For the mother. A baby doesn't always change much for him."

I breathe out, relishing the pressure of the floor on my stomach, when for so long I had to lie on my back like a beached whale. "That's so true!" I yell, startling Holly. She whines and turns her attention back to her play mat.

"The fact is," my mom goes on, "there will be times in your marriage when you're closer, and there will be times in your marriage when you're farther apart. Yeah, you'd think a baby would make you closer, but that's not always the case. Ask any couple that has gotten pregnant to try to save the marriage. It simply doesn't work that way."

"Our marriage isn't in trouble," I stammer, hoping I'm telling the truth. "We're… in a tough place right now."

"Of course," she says. "I adore Cash. You know that. You telling me whatever you need to tell me doesn't change my opinion. Unless he hit you or the baby, of course. If that happened, I'd cut his balls off with a rusty kitchen knife and not feel bad for a single second."

I laugh, even though I know she's not kidding. "Thanks, Mom."

"Sure."

There's a beat of silence, and then I reveal another piece of the truth. "I'm just so tired, Mom. All the time. All the time."

"I know," she says. "I wish I could be there more, to help you out."

"Me, too," I say.

"That's the hard thing about being a mom," she says. "It's a twenty-four/seven job with no holidays, no paid time off, no sick leave, no vacation. The work is never, ever done."

"Ugh," I groan.

"Don't get me wrong. It's one hundred percent worth it, one thousand percent. One million percent. But that doesn't mean it's not really, really hard. Especially in the beginning. You're learning how to be a mom, he's learning how to be a dad, and you're both learning how to be parents, together. While also navigating how to be a husband and wife. And employees, and friends, and everything else you are, everything else you do."

"Yeah," I say, my eyes prickling with tears, something that has more or less become a reflex by now.

"I think it might be harder for you, too, because you didn't grow up around other little kids. Cash probably has a leg up on that, growing up with all those brothers and sisters."

"Yeah," I repeat. "I mean, I absolutely love being a mom, I can't imagine my life without Holly, but… I'm not the kind of person who ever wanted to hold a random baby. I don't think I ever even babysat."

"Maybe once," she says. "Linda Lawson's daughter."

"Oh, yeah," I say. "But she was, like, what? Ten? When I was fifteen? That's different. That's not a baby. That's not even a little kid."

"True," she says. "But I know you, sweetie. You're kind and generous and big-hearted and smart and resourceful. You're a wonderful wife, and you're already a wonderful mother."

"Thanks," I say, flipping onto my back, but that doesn't relieve the growing tension in my guts. I haven't told her about the times I've screamed at Holly to shut up when she won't stop crying, or about how I considered driving back to the hospital, shoving Holly into the nearest nurse's arms, and begging them to take her back. I haven't even told Cash about any of that. Not for the first time, I wonder if I need help—real, professional help.

"You're strong," she says. "Stronger than Cash."

"I don't know about that."

"I'm sure he thinks you're strong, too, but he doesn't know what to say. He doesn't always understand what you need, especially when you don't tell him. He can't read your mind."

"I know."

"Talk to him," she says, her voice gentle. "He's a good man, even if he does have the emotional intelligence of a mosquito. Tell him what you need from him."

"I guess."

"I mean it. I know he's back at work now, but he can take an afternoon off from golfing to watch the baby so you can nap. He can pick up a pizza so you don't have to cook dinner every night. He can make his own sandwiches so you don't have to drop everything and bring him lunch. You're doing too much, sweetie. That would be hard on anyone, much less a new mom."

"Yeah," I say, staring at Holly. She's looking back at me, her green eyes so like Cash's, it's as though he's the one looking at me, eavesdropping on my conversation. "I… I don't want to upset him."

"He should be worried about upsetting you! Your feelings matter, too."

"Right," I say, but I'm not sure I believe her. Cash has shown no compunction about hurting my feelings in the past; even worse, he's communicated in a thousand different ways how much he needs me to be okay. My feelings matter, only as long as they're good ones.

"Okay?" she says.

"Okay," I say, a small part of my soul withering. How many times will I be forced to say I'm okay when I don't mean it?

"So," she says brightly, moving right along. "What else you got for me? Any gossip?"

Before I can stop it, or maybe because I want to test the waters, or maybe because I'm too tired of holding it in, the story—or, rather, parts of it—comes tumbling out. The trail, the clearing made of tiny bones, Tater choking…

"Huh," she says. "It's probably an owl, sweetie."

"What?" I say, snorting.

"My book club is reading this entire book about owls. To be frank, it's a bit of a snooze fest, but parts of it are interesting. Apparently, owls love hollow trees, and they eat all kinds of rodents and small animals, and then they spit up the bones in these little pellets after they've digested the good stuff."

"Oh," I say. "Interesting. But…" But these bones weren't buried in pellets. The clearing looked more like the site of a massacre than an owl's litter box.

My palms grow slick as I stare up at the ceiling, memorizing the chips in the paint. I want to tell my mom about the door, but I can't have her thinking I'm crazy. She's too far away to do anything about it, and she'll only worry. That won't do either of us any good. Worse, she might try to talk to Cash about it.

"But what?" she asks.

"There… there were too many bones," I finish, my voice cracking on the last word.

"Well, whatever lives there is doing a whole lot of killing," she says. She means it in a lighthearted, silly-spooky sort of way, but the words send a spark of fear jolting through my nerves.

"Right," I say.

"Really, sweetie. I'm sure it's just an owl."

"Yeah. You're probably right."

There's a muffled sound on the other end of the line, then she says, "Hey, sweetie? I'm so sorry, I've got to go. I love you!"

"I love you, too, Mom."

"Give that baby a kiss for me. And give your husband one, too. When you feel angry for no reason, a little kindness, even—no, especially—

when you don't feel kind can go a long way. You guys are a team, and you need to remind him of that."

"I will," I say.

"Bye, sweetie!"

"Bye, Mom."

Maybe she's right. I should take her advice, try to reinvest in my marriage in some small but meaningful way. I should ask for a little bit of help here and there, instead of assuming he won't give it. Truth be told, I haven't asked him. I've been sitting here, stewing in my resentment because he can't read my mind.

I roll Holly onto her back when she starts to make frustrated grunts. I brainstorm nice things to do for Cash.

I try to ignore the fact that the bones around that tree weren't encased in owl pellets. That they were, in fact, scored with tiny teeth marks. That they had blackened edges, as though they'd been cooked over a fire.

CHAPTER ELEVEN

Sucky Offerings

My thighs are chafing something awful, but I walk this morning anyway, because that's what I do. Up ahead, a chubby brown squirrel squats in the street, looking at me. Reflexively, I look around and say, "Tater! Go get him, boy!"

Then, of course, I remember. No squirrel-chasing for Tater, not for a few more weeks, at least. And definitely no squirrel-eating, ever again.

As I cross to Sweetgum Street, I feel naked. Without Tater Tot sniffing around at my side, I'm unprotected, vulnerable to attack. But come on, who's going to attack me in the middle of this posh neighborhood? Jessica, in her hot pink athleisure set? Mandy, her neon yellow bike shorts and matching top stretching to accommodate those massive fake breasts she got as part of her not-so-secret mommy makeover? Tiffany, her fingers weighed down by her wedding ring and three others, each one a ridiculously expensive and showy push present from her husband for birthing their children?

I almost laugh, but then my lip curls involuntarily, remembering a conversation I'd had with Cash. I was pregnant, lying on the sofa and looking at jewelry on my phone.

Cash came in, decked out in a pink golf shirt and striped shorts.

"How's it going?" he asked.

"Good," I said. "Just, you know… doing some research."

"Research on what?" He crossed into the kitchen and pulled a can of Spindrift from the fridge. He cracked it open and drained it in two loud gulps.

"Have you ever heard of a push present?" I asked.

"No. What's that?"

"You know, after a woman has her baby, and she had to push so hard, she gets a present from her husband. For all that hard work."

Cash frowned. "Why would you get a present for having a baby? Isn't the baby the best present you could get?"

I rolled my eyes. "I mean, yes, of course, but still. Being pregnant isn't easy. I can't imagine giving birth is a cake walk, either."

"I don't know. What do you want, exactly?"

"Well…" I angled my phone so he could see my screen. "This David Yurman diamond necklace would be the perfect piece for everyday wear, and it's so timeless, and it's not even that expensive…" I trailed off when I saw Cash's face, his frown deepening into a scowl.

"Come on, Sadie," he said. "Push presents"—he crunched his fingers into harsh air quotes—"sound like a stupid invention by the jewelry industry to sell more overpriced rocks."

"I—"

"And again, you want to have kids too, right? Why would you get another present when you're already getting exactly what you want?"

I nodded and shoved my phone behind a couch cushion. "I need to take a nap," I said. I waited until Cash went back to work before I let the angry sobs out.

Now, scraping my fingers over my bare throat, I wish I'd pushed harder for that present. Pun intended. I deserved it—nine and a half months of discomfort and then all of this that comes after, and Cash only put in thirty seconds of work in the beginning, and not much more than that once we brought Holly home.

A bird—possibly a chickadee—trills as Holly and I reach the first fairy door. I let out a breath I didn't know I'd been holding when the door appears, exactly as I left it. No ugly wreath, no bones. Thank God.

"Look, Holly!" I say, my voice Day-Glo bright. I shift the stroller so she can, theoretically, see the door. At three months, I still don't think she's capable of seeing that far, but whatever. "It's a fairy door!"

Holly looks up at me, a slight frown creasing her perfect little face.

"Fairies live in there," I say, forcing a smile onto my face. "Maybe one day, we can do a little craft project and leave some tiny furniture here for the fairies!"

Holly blinks, then a sweet, gummy grin breaks over her features, as beautiful as a sunrise.

"On to the next!" I say, shoving aside thoughts of the necklace I didn't get, jubilant despite the pearls of moisture rolling down my back. Sweat has become a fixture of my postpartum body, along with the leaking nipples, the spit-up, the bleeding, and the watery baby poop. I'm fairly certain John Mayer wrote "Your Body Is a Wonderland" about me.

As we continue to walk down Sweetgum before turning onto Peach Grove Court, my mind drifts back to Tater Tot. I can't help imagining what it would be like to throw up bones. Bones, of all things. Wouldn't a splintered bone slice your esophagus? Wouldn't a hard chunk cut off your air supply? If any of it did manage to make its way into your intestines, wouldn't the shards stab your bowels full of holes?

I suppress a gag.

"Enough of that," I say out loud, and Holly coos at me, as though she agrees. It's times like this, when she's calm and happy and I'm not actively crying, that gratitude overwhelms me. She is a wonderful little girl, and I'm lucky to have her. In fact, I'm lucky for everything I have, Cash included. It can be hard, in the thick of all the chaos, to remember that simple fact.

We're halfway down Peach Grove Court when the hairs at the back of my neck prickle. Is this a new postpartum symptom nobody told me about? It seems as though everything strange about my body can be attributed to pregnancy, in some way.

But this feels different, I have to admit.

As I approach the next fairy door, goosebumps break out on my arms like sores, despite the heat of the morning. A cloud passes over the sun, and by the time my eyes adjust, we're standing in front of the door. I squint, making out the horrible little wreath, and force myself to sound chipper. "Look, Holly! There's the other door!"

Holly's little brows knit, and a low, keening moan escapes her lips.

"It's okay, it's okay!" I say, but I'm not sure if I'm talking more to her or to myself at this point. I push the stroller into the grass by the door and crouch down, ready to give it a playful knock.

That's when I see it—or, I guess I should say, see *them*.

The corpses.

The carcasses of roaches, palmetto bugs, and quarter-size beetles surround the door, their bodies sucked dry and withering in the heat. There's a tiny rib cage, cracked open at the sternum, with a tuft of gray-brown fur still stuck to it. My eyes dart over the scene, nearly shaking in their sockets. It's exactly like the hidden door in the woods, the one that oozes wrongness from every moss-covered inch…

"No, no, no, no," I moan, shooting up to my feet and backing away. There's no confusing it this time—this was no Yoga Mom trying to one-up my fairy doors. This was no person, period—it couldn't be. My mind flashes back to my nightmare, to the miniature, blackened fingers that reach around the door in the clearing right before I wake up…

"No!" I yell, and Holly bawls in response.

I wobble over to the stroller on legs as sturdy as Jell-O. "It's okay, baby, it's okay. We're fine." Without glancing back, I shove the stroller onto the road and head back down Peach Grove, the way I came.

Turning ahead onto Laurel Lane would be faster, but I can't make myself do it. I don't want to see that trail entrance, don't want to suffer the inescapable tug pulling me toward the tree, toward the door, toward whatever lives behind it.

Toward whatever did this.

"It's okay," I say again to Holly, who is calming down with every step I take toward Sweetgum Street. Gradually, the mantle of panic lifts from my hunched shoulders, and I take a deep, lung-clearing breath.

"It's okay," I repeat. "That was probably natural, right? I mean, how often do I seriously look at the ground, especially around all those trees? The ground is probably covered in dead things. It's wild, after all. Animals everywhere. Bugs everywhere. Right, Holly?"

Holly's cries lapse into silence, and she stares at me, her eyes wide.

We turn onto Sweetgum, and I begin to relax, the tension uncoiling between my shoulders. The closer I get to home, the more ridiculous I feel. Of course all those dead bugs, those little ribcages, were normal. I've watched enough Planet Earth to know nature is brutal. Cash and I used to watch it together. If he were here, if he saw those bugs, he'd say the same thing: *Don't worry about it, Sadie. This is what happens. It's natural.*

I sigh. When was the last time Cash and I watched anything together? Since Holly's birth, I've barely wanted him to be in the same room with me, much less touch me. It's as if my body is rebelling against him for the trauma it put me through, what with pregnancy and labor and everything. That's another thing the other mothers don't tell you—giving birth is absolutely a trauma. Sure, it's great and empowering and beautiful and whatever, but it's also traumatic, and you don't simply get over it. The pain doesn't disappear in the afterglow of new motherhood.

Or, at least, it didn't disappear for me.

Not for the first time, I consider the possibility of reaching out for professional help. At least as far as I know, none of the women in my family—aunts, cousins, sisters-in-law—have suffered from postpartum depression. Why would I be any different?

As I reach our front porch, my stomach growls so loudly it sounds like an animal. How can I be hungry at a time like this, after finding all those tiny corpses? I shouldn't be, and yet I am. After all, the parenting books told me breastfeeding burns six hundred calories a day.

"I'm starving. What about you, Hols?"

I answer myself in a cutesy baby voice. "I'm hungry too, Mama!"

"What can I get you?"

"I want… cookies!"

"Mmm, cookies sound great," comes a deep voice somewhere to my right, making me scream.

"Sorry," Ron Callahan says, leaning out of his golf cart. "Didn't mean to startle you!"

"It's fine," I say. Oh God, how much of that embarrassing conversation did he hear?

Ron carts over to me and stops. "Where's my best buddy?"

As if on cue, Tater Tot's furry head pops up in the front window. "He's not allowed to go on long walks right now," I say.

Ron's bushy white eyebrows hike up to his hairline. "Why's that?"

"He… uh… he swallowed some bones, and then one got stuck in his throat. The vet got it out, but he's got a lot of bruising. He's on a soft-foods-only diet for a while, and short walks only."

"Yikes. That's no fun," Ron says, giving Tater a wave. "Can he still ride on the golf cart?"

"For sure," I say.

"You don't mind if I take him out on a few rides every now and then?"

"Not at all. That would be amazing, actually."

"Happy to do it! I don't want him getting lonely while he's recovering." Ron's smile is infectious, and I find my own face mirroring his.

"You're his best friend, you know," I say. "I think he'd happily run off with you any day of the week."

"He's a good boy," Ron says, his radio announcer voice echoing throughout the block. "And how's that little girl doing?"

"Great, great," I say. Looking down at Holly, I can't help but see her through Ron's eyes. He's a devoted grandfather, and ever since we moved here, he's kept me up to date on the lives of his four grandchildren. Even though I've never met them, those kids, and Ron's relationship to them, reminds me what I'm working toward, the sort of family I'm trying to build.

"She's such a sweet thing," he says, reaching down to tickle Holly under her chin.

"We're very lucky to have her," I say.

Ron nods. "And this neighborhood is lucky to have y'all. I thought that place would never sell."

"Oh? Why not?"

His eyes slide away from mine. "Well, there was some unpleasantness with the former owners. Nothing you need to know about."

"Unpleasantness?"

Ron waves a hand in front of his face. "Nothing to concern yourselves over. We're all so glad to have you here, have some youngsters around to liven the place up."

"But—"

Tater Tot barks so loudly we can hear it through the glass. "I should take Mr. Tot out for a ride, don't you think?" Ron asks.

"Yeah," I say. "Definitely."

I leave Holly with Ron and run up the steps to open the front door. Tater comes barreling out and leaps into Ron's golf cart, immediately sitting upright like a person, his tongue covering Ron's white beard with dog spit.

"Tater, stop that!" I say.

Ron laughs. "Oh, I don't mind one bit!" He scratches Tater behind the ears. "Let's go see what trouble we can get into, huh?"

I want to ask him again about the former owners of our house, but now is clearly not the time. "Thanks again, Ron," I say.

"Anytime," he says. "Oh, and I was reading this wonderful article in this week's Book Review about the newest horror books coming out this year. I'll stick it in your mailbox this afternoon."

"You're the best, Ron!"

"I do what I can." He winks, then speeds off, Tater still licking his face.

"At least we have one awesome neighbor," I tell Holly as I push the stroller up onto our walkway.

My stomach growls again as I put Holly on the play mat of her activity center. I hum as I walk into the kitchen to preheat the oven. Cookies—that is something I can do, something that will make everybody happy, that will help me wipe the strangeness of today off my skin like dirt. I should give some to Ron, too. He's earned them.

Now that I think about it, this is the first time I've even turned the oven on since I brought Holly home from the hospital. We've been eating mostly simple stuff—hummus and crackers, sandwiches, pasta, defrosted leftovers I stockpiled during my nesting phase. The week after we got home, Jessica even brought over what she called a 'healing salad.' The gesture was sweet, I guess, but the Tupperware full of undressed kale, edamame, shredded carrot, and chunks of rubbery feta was mostly inedible. I'm not proud to say I was secretly pleased to find she was a terrible cook. The beef jerky Ron brought us from the local butcher was much, much tastier.

Listening for any sounds of distress from Holly in the other room, I gather the cookie ingredients from the pantry. Even after months of not baking, I remember the recipe by heart.

I combine the butter and sugar, creaming them with my electric hand mixer. When they're adequately integrated, I add the dry ingredients. Baking powder, salt, flour—

A cranky squawk from the other room interrupts my concentration.

I drop everything and rush to the other room to find Holly on her back, off the play mat.

"Wow," I say. "Did you get over there all by yourself?" I didn't even know Holly could roll over, much less scoot herself any perceptible distance. Cash needs to know about this—it's probably time to invest in one of those playpens, or get the pack and play we received for our baby shower all set up. The last thing we need is Holly scooting herself right into the fireplace, or into an electrical socket, or into a solid chair leg.

I pick up Holly and reposition her on the mat. "No funny business," I say, trying not to let the resentful little voice in my head pipe up that Cash will, inevitably, ask why I wasn't watching her when she scooted off the play mat.

"Stop," I breathe, closing my eyes for a moment. "Just stop it."

Holly looks up at me, all innocence and baby fat. "Be chill," I tell her, then rush back to the kitchen to finish the batter so I can get back to Holly before she does something else I didn't realize she could do.

I scoop spoonfuls of dough onto a cookie sheet so fast wet drops of batter splatter the counter. The dough is a bit runny, but—Holly whimpers from the living room, her cries threatening an explosion, like a ticking time bomb. When my cookie sheets are full and my dough is used up, I pop everything in the preheated oven, set the timer, shove all the dirty equipment into the sink, and scamper back to Holly.

Thank God, she hasn't moved. She's staring up at a purple monkey dangling from her activity center, transfixed.

The couch cradles me when I collapse into it, utterly exhausted, trying not to think about the dead husks of insects or the crunch of tiny, broken ribcages.

A yawn escapes my throat, and the thought of closing my eyes is so tantalizing I drool. I've never been a big sleeper—I mean, I need my seven and a half hours, sure, but I could never understand my friends in school who, when given the opportunity, would happily sleep until one in the afternoon. That sort of excessive sleep seems like such a waste of time.

Now, with hours upon hours of sleep debt accumulating and threatening to crash over me like a tsunami, I spend an inordinate amount of time fetishizing sleep—how it smells to lay down in a freshly made bed, the scent of lavender detergent washing over me. How my body creates a comforting divot in the mattress. How my silk sleep mask slips delicately over my eyes. How…

"Sadie?" Cash's voice jerks me awake. So, the temptation overcame me. Why did he have to wake me up at all? And what's that smell—

"Agh!" I blurt, leaping off the couch and scrambling to the oven. Miraculously, there are still two minutes left on the timer. All is not lost.

"Sadie?" Cash repeats, perfectly groomed eyebrow arching. "You alright?"

"Yes!" I say, ping-ponging around the kitchen—cleaning, rearranging, washing. "Great!"

"It smells awesome in here," he says from the other room. When he pops his head in the kitchen, he's holding Holly, and a broad grin is creasing his annoyingly handsome face. Seeing them together, their physical similarity hits me like a punch to the gut. I wonder for the millionth time if I contributed any genetic material at all.

"I made you a surprise," I say, biting my lip. Might as well kill two birds with one stone—feeding myself and making Cash happy. Didn't Mom say I should do something to show Cash I care?

Cash tickles Holly, and she giggles, the sweetest little burble of joy. "Wow," he says. "Is it—"

Before he can finish the sentence, the oven timer beeps. Opening a drawer, I grab a pair of oven mitts and slip them over my hands. Cash isn't wrong, the smell is delicious—sugary, warm, with a hint of vanilla. I know I need to 'get my body back'—ugh—sooner rather than later, but I won't be able to resist the siren call of those cookies, I know it. And why should I? Breastfeeding makes me ravenous.

A plume of steam escapes the oven as I pull it open. When the cloud clears, I feast my eyes upon…

Vomit.

That's what it looks like. The cookies are wide and thin, the chocolate chips suspended in puddles of chunky beige soup. They may smell good, but they couldn't look more heinous.

Cash comes up behind me and peers into the oven. "Oh," is all he says.

"Fuck," I mutter. What happened? "I added the butter and sugar, and the vanilla and…" Oh. Of course. "The flour," I whisper. I was adding it when Holly cried out.

"Are they supposed to look like that?" he asks, and I want to smack him, because of course they're all wrong. Anybody could see that—does he need to rub my face in my failure?

"No," I say through gritted teeth. "I think I forgot to add the second cup of flour."

The oven is still ajar, pumping heat out at us. "Take them out anyway," Cash says. "I'll still eat them."

Mechanically, I do as he says. When the trays are resting on the cool stovetop, I close the oven, turn it off, and toss the mitts aside, my face burning from the oven's blast.

"See? They don't look so bad," Cash says.

"Uh-huh," I say. "Right."

Still holding Holly, he reaches out for one.

"Don't!" I say. "They're super hot."

"I don't care," he says, his fingers alighting on the firmest-looking cookie of the bunch. As soon as he makes contact, he squeals and yanks his hand away. "Ow!"

"I warned you," I say, trying not to indulge the little voice of guilty joy, which is insisting that Cash never listens to me, so he deserves what he gets. Briefly, I consider telling him about the mass grave around my fairy door, but why? If he didn't believe me about the dead squirrel that

Tater literally puked up, why would he believe that?

"You were right," he says, the grin back on his face. Despite myself, I smile back, pleasantly shocked.

"I'm going in again," Cash says, and I don't try to stop him this time.

He grabs the same cookie that burned him before, and it's just firm enough that it doesn't melt in his hands. Without waiting for it to cool off any longer, he stuffs the entire thing in his mouth.

"Mmmmm," he says, chewing thoughtfully, letting little periodic puffs of heat escape his lips.

He swallows, then smiles again. His teeth are covered in chocolate, and goo lines his gums. A guffaw spews out of my mouth.

"It's so good to hear you laugh again," he says, and before I can respond, he points at the cookie sheet. "Can I have another?"

The front door opens, and a bellowing voice announces, "Sir Tater Tot has had quite the adventure!"

Tater sweeps into the room, absolutely beaming. "Thanks so much, Ron!" I say.

"Like I said, Sadie—anytime." If Ron hadn't found his niche as a successful dentist, he could have made a killing as an audiobook narrator.

"Have a lovely evening, Hansens!" The door closes behind Ron with a bang.

Cash looks at me, head tilted.

"Ron's going to get Tater out on golf cart rides while he's healing."

"Ron's a good dude," Cash says. He grabs a second cookie and eats it slowly, taking his time. I can't imagine these failures are any good, but he's savoring his cookie like it's the best thing he's ever eaten.

"Have as many as you want. I made them for you. I was going to save some for Ron, but..." I wave a hand at the unappetizing mess. "Not sure he'll want these. I need to do something nice for him, though."

"It'll come to you," Cash says through a mouthful of cookie.

Holly looks from Cash, then to me, then back to Cash, following our conversation like it's a tennis match. When Cash finishes his second cookie, she burbles happily.

My eyes well with tears, but they're the happy kind. This—this is what I wanted. A husband who loves me, a child who is happy and healthy, a home that is warm and welcoming and filled with the smell of fresh-baked cookies.

As Cash reaches for a third cookie, I grin.

If he asked me right now *Are you okay?*, I'd be able to answer 'Yes' and mean it. My whole body is lighter, more springy.

Best of all, at Holly's next check-up, I won't have to lie on that ridiculous postpartum questionnaire, because I'm fucking finding joy.

CHAPTER TWELVE

Shit Eating Grin

"Let's go for a walk," Cash says, polishing off the last cookie. He grabs his taut stomach. "I need to work this off."

"Work what off?" I laugh, nibbling on a slightly stale granola bar and a small plate of everything bagel-flavored hummus, crackers, and sliced cheddar. It's a girl dinner that absolutely hits the spot.

It's only six-thirty, and the sun won't set for at least another hour. It's a mild September evening, puffy cumulus clouds floating like marshmallow fluff high in the deep blue sky.

"We could both use the exercise," he says. "You've got to heal sooner or later."

"Mmm." My grip on my dirty plate tightens as I rinse it in the sink.

"Just a short one," he says. "We can bring Tater. I know he's still not back to normal, but he needs to get out."

Hearing his name, Tater Tot sidles into the kitchen, big fluffy tail wagging.

"Okay," I say. "Sure."

"It's so nice out," Cash says, walking to the living room to get Holly. "What about you, Hols? You want to go, too?" Holly gurgles, then laughs in great, hiccuping bursts as Cash holds her tight and spins. He's done this before, and it always makes me anxious. What if he spins too fast, and she gets whiplash? What if he trips and falls on top of her? What if he loses his grip and she falls to the ground and breaks something? What will the doctors at the emergency room say? Will they call Child Protective Services? What if—

"You coming?" Cash says, interrupting my doom-spiral inner monologue. I look over at the two of them, my husband and my tiny daughter, wrapped in an embrace. She's fine. He's fine. Everyone is fine.

Why don't I feel fine?

"Yep." I wipe my hands on a dish towel and follow them out the door.

We load Holly in the stroller and head down the road, Tater Tot trailing at our heels. Anybody passing by would probably think we look sweet, as long as they don't get close enough to see my milk-stained shirt or the greasy roots of my hair, in desperate need of a color touch-up.

"Hey, want to show me those fairy doors you painted?" Cash asks, looking at me sideways. "I bet they look awesome."

My chest tightens. "Yeah, sure."

When we reach the first door, nailed to the maple on Sweetgum Street, a whoosh of air escapes my lungs and my fists unclench. No wreath adorns this door; no graveyard of bones surrounds this tree.

Cash makes a big show of bending down to take a closer look. He knocks gently, his fingers rapping the thin plywood. "Hello? Any fairies in there?"

Holly giggles from her stroller, and a shiver of gratitude runs down my spine. Even though she's too young to understand, she's lucky to have a father like Cash, someone who isn't afraid to be silly, to get down on her level. I have to force myself to act that way, but to Cash, it's completely natural. It's one of his most admirable qualities.

Straightening up, Cash grins. "I've got to admit, this is pretty cool," he says. "Where's the other one?"

"On Peach Grove," I say, reluctantly. Will he still think the doors are cool when he notices all the dead things?

A tiny part of my mind whispers, *Wouldn't it be so much worse if he didn't see the dead things at all?*

"Let's check it out!"

"Wait," I say, tension coursing through my jaw. "Don't you think… that's a bit too long of a walk for Tater?"

Cash shrugs. "He'll be fine. It's not that far."

"I don't think—"

"Sadie, come on! Live a little!" He claps his hands and pushes the stroller toward Peach Grove, leaving me no choice but to follow in his wake. My heart beats quicker with each step, my entire body waiting for that blanket of silence to envelop us, but it doesn't come. Frogs chirp, birds squawk, and bugs buzz, completely unperturbed.

When we finally reach the second door, my palms are sweating so heavily, moisture is dripping off the tips of my fingers, turning the Band-Aid covering my hammer wound into mush.

I force myself to look at the door. Like before, Cash hunkers down, unbothered by the dead bugs crunching under his feet.

The weathered wreath is still there, but something's different. The ends of the little twigs are coated in something dark and sticky-looking. Oh God, is that—

"Knock knock!" Cash says, reaching out to the door.

I want to scream at him to stop, to pull his fist back, to stand up and run away from here, but I'm paralyzed with fear, my feet rooted to the ground. How can he not see the Lilliputian bones scattered around the door? How can he not detect the crack of chitin from all the bugs under his soles?

Cash's knuckles make contact with the door, and he raps once, twice, three times.

Silence.

Then, something knocks back.

"Jesus Christ!" I yell, falling back a few steps, my whole body tingling. "What was that?"

Cash's face crumples into confusion. "What was what?"

"Did you not hear that? That knocking?" I'm backing away faster now, standing next to Holly and Tater Tot, who has kept his distance from the door.

Cash laughs. "Honey, that was a woodpecker."

"I heard—" I stop, his words penetrating my frantic thoughts. "A woodpecker?"

"Yeah," he says, standing up and coming over to me. "Just a woodpecker."

"I thought…"

"You thought what? That something was knocking back?"

I force a laugh and shake my head. "No." My voice sounds tinny and strange. "No, of course not."

We turn right onto Laurel Lane, heading home. My breath comes in sharp, painful bursts. Cash is talking, but I'm not hearing him. Perspiration pours down my face, obscuring my vision and making my eyes burn.

Tater growls, low in his still-healing throat. The corners of my mouth tremble.

"Easy, boy," Cash says. "What's got you all riled up?"

We're right next to that trail, but of course it's not there. I don't know if I should be relieved or terrified.

Tater glares at the curtain of vines where the trail entrance should be, ears pressed against the back of his head.

I tiptoe past the spot, willing myself to keep going, to get past this, to get home.

"Tater, come on!" Cash calls, and after one more menacing rumble, Tater follows us. The rest of the way home, Cash natters on about work, something a colleague said that annoyed him, but I'm not listening. I can't stop hearing the sound of that knock. Could it have been a woodpecker?

I want so badly to believe that's all it was, but my thoughts won't stop spinning, reminding me that woodpeckers don't dismember mice. Woodpeckers don't suck roaches completely dry.

Woodpeckers don't hang tiny wreaths, edges tacky with dried blood.

* * *

"Can you get the bath ready?" I say as we walk into the house, Holly wriggling in Cash's arms. Tater Tot limps in behind us. He looks as exhausted as I feel.

"On it," Cash says, heading toward the baby tub in our bathroom.

Tater collapses into his bed, panting.

"You okay, boy?" I squat down to pet him. My lady bits are heavy and hot, and I try not to squirm. The only thing that will make me feel better is rest. I'm guessing Tater feels the same, because he gives a halfhearted tail wag and then leans his head back.

Despite the heat, my skin is peppered with goosebumps, and I fight the urge to chew my lips to shreds. Hearing the sound of running water, I head back to our bathroom to help Cash with Holly. I'm sure he doesn't actually need my help, but it seems lazy to ask him to do something when I'm perfectly capable. I can't imagine what it would be like to lie on the couch, watching an asinine reality TV show, while Cash does the heavy lifting with Holly.

As soon as the thought arrives, I have to blink away resentment. Isn't that exactly what Cash does, every time he heads to the golf course while I stay behind, breastfeeding and changing diaper after diaper? I've heard him say far too many times that 'Golf is good for business, babe! I have to keep my skills sharp!'

In the bathroom, Cash hovers over Holly, who's staring up at him from the newborn sling in her baby bathtub. The water level is a bit high for my comfort, but I don't say anything. I don't want to give Cash a reason to never help me out here again.

Cash glances up at me. "That was a nice family walk, huh?"

"Yeah," I say, trying to morph my twisted grimace into a smile. I want to lean in to the 'wholesome family' environment he's trying to create here, but between my pain, exhaustion, and the sense of wrongness about what's in the woods that I can't seem to shake, I'm on the verge of a breakdown.

He takes a step toward me, leaving Holly in her tub. "You okay, babe?"

A sigh burbles up my throat at this maddening question, but I push it back down. Really? We have to play this game again? There's only one acceptable answer to this question, as always, and I give it without too much hesitation. "Yeah."

"You sure?"

I sigh as quietly as possible. "Yeah. I'm sure."

"Okay," Cash partly singsongs, still looking at me. His gaze makes me uncomfortable; I don't want him to look at me so intently. He might not like what he sees.

There's a delicate splashing from the baby tub, and Cash turns back around. Our whole exchange couldn't have lasted more than thirty seconds, but apparently, that's all the time Holly needed.

The once-clear bathwater is now a slimy yellowish-brown, and Holly has slipped down just enough in the newborn sling that her perfect little lips are touching the fouled surface.

"Christ!" Cash yells, lunging toward her. He grabs under her armpits and pulls her higher, separating her face from the poo stew she's now bathing in. I expect Holly to cry, but she doesn't.

I've never fully understood the phrase 'shit-eating grin' until this moment. Her chin still coated in liquid feces, Holly's gummy mouth stretches into the largest smile I've ever seen her make.

Cash, hands still under her armpits, laughs, which sets Holly off into a fit of musical baby giggles.

I want to laugh, too, but I can't seem to form the right sounds. Anger bubbles up in my stomach like acid reflux. This should be funny, I know, but the humor has evaporated, because all I can think about is everything I'll now have to do that I wouldn't have if Cash had been watching Holly instead of asking me stupid questions. I'll have to give Holly a second bath in the real tub, which is much harder, then I'll have to strip out that newborn sling, hose it off, wash it in the machine, then disinfect the rest of the plastic baby tub—and all of that needs to be done tonight, before the filth dries. My stomach sinks all the way into my bowels.

Cash and Holly are still giggling at each other.

"Why weren't you watching her?" The words are out of my mouth before I can bite them back.

Cash stares at me, confusion and hurt twisting across his handsome features. "What?"

"You should have been watching her the entire time!" Tears pool in my eyes as my anger melts into despair, as it so often does these days. "I can never leave her with you!"

"Seriously, Sadie?" Cash says, inflating with the anger that just departed from me. It's like we're on some sort of tragic emotional seesaw—when I'm up, he's down, and when I'm down, he's up. We haven't mastered the balancing act that will keep us both on an even keel, that will allow us to communicate effectively with each other instead of hurling anger or insults.

The tears overflow, coating my cheeks with sticky salt. "Now I have to wash her and clean the tub and disinfect everything and I don't have time to do all that before she needs to eat!" The words come out in a rush, like angry river rapids.

"Well, Jesus," Cash says. "If this is how you act when I try to help, I get it. I won't help with this anymore. Fine. You get your wish."

"You're such a child!" I say.

"Wow, Sadie, just wow—"

From the other room, Tater Tot barks—boisterous, angry, hoarse howls.

Because it can't rain without pouring around here, Holly starts to wail.

Cash stares at me, his gaze flat and hard. Without a word, he thrusts the screaming, poop-coated Holly at me and stalks out of the bathroom.

What choice do I have? Holly's hungry, and I can't keep her waiting while I sanitize everything to my satisfaction. Her cries pierce my eardrums like tiny daggers, so sharp and shrill.

My own tears are now coming as fast and hard as hers as I slump down on the floor and unhook the flap of my nursing tank top. Holly finally quiets when I put my cracked nipple in her mouth, and I can make out Cash murmuring lovingly to Tater Tot in the other room: "You're such a good boy, Tater, you're so good. Did you have fun with Ron?"

I try to ignore the searing pain in my breast. The tile floor is cold and hard under my butt, and my back aches holding Holly up without my nursing pillow. She's still covered in poop, the cloying smell coating the inside of my nostrils. I'll have to wash her, and take a shower myself, and clean my clothes… oh fuck, this is my last clean nursing tank top. I'll have to dig a less-dirty one out of the hamper, then do laundry first thing tomorrow.

Did any of the Yoga Moms ever have to deal with this kind of shit? Try as I might, I simply can't picture Jessica shoveling feces out of her child's mouth with a perfectly manicured fingernail.

Now that I think about it, are any of the Yoga Moms as good as they make themselves seem? Do they have the perfect kids, like Instagram would want me to believe? Do they have the most equitable, caring marriages? There's Heather's juvenile delinquent kid, of course, and then there's a rumor floating around that Mandy's husband is sleeping with the babysitter, as cliché as that is. None of that is going on Instagram.

Ugh. What kind of person thinks that way? My own schadenfreude disgusts me. I wouldn't wish the trauma of infidelity on someone else's family, someone else's kids.

The tears keep coming, even harder and faster. I'm a worthless excuse for a human being.

I unlatch Holly and switch her to my other breast. A bright red trickle of blood drips from the nipple she vacates.

Great. There's definitely still poop on her mouth, and on top of everything, I'm probably going to get some sort of bloodborne infection.

Would that be such a bad way to go, all things considered?

CHAPTER THIRTEEN

Upping the Ante

Minuscule femurs and papery husks crack beneath my bare feet, sending bolts of tension sparking through me like live wires. The tree squats ahead of me, the mossy door stuck to its surface like the last rotten tooth in a gummy mouth.

Stop moving, I tell my feet, but they don't listen, carrying me closer to the door. Each crunch underfoot, the only sounds in the fraught silence, makes my fists clench tighter, my nails digging into my palms. Why can't I stop?

A hollow knock cleaves the atmosphere, and my feet finally freeze. There's another rap, and I know it's coming from inside the little door, and I'm rooted to the ground, all alone, paralyzed by fear.

My neck shakes, my head a fragile flower on a flimsy stalk. The door creaks open, one millimeter at a time. As I watch, unable to shift my gaze or even blink, those chunky fingers slither around the doorframe like gray worms. The miniature nails are chipped and blackened, tipped with rusty half-moons. The fingers creep farther and farther around the door, exposing one gnarled knuckle, then another, then the back of a dirty hand.

I jolt upright, nearly toppling off the bed. My entire body is soaked with foul-smelling night sweat. The blast of the overhead fan makes me shiver as I gasp for breath as silently as possible so I don't wake Holly.

My fingers find my eyes in the dark and rub. *I can't keep going on like this.*

Every night, the dream goes on for a little longer. Two nights ago, I saw the sliver of a nail. Last night, the first finger joint. And tonight… that horrible hand…

"Go back to sleep," I hiss to myself, trying to swallow down the metallic aftertaste of my fear. But who am I kidding? If I close my eyes again, what will I see? Can I bear it when that hand becomes a forearm, or that forearm becomes a bicep, or that bicep becomes…

"No," I say aloud, shuddering, and now there's late afternoon sunlight filtering through the windows and the couch cushions are too soft against my back. How did I get here?

Holly's on the play mat in front of me, face down, trying to roll. She glances at me, big green eyes full of concentration, and burps. A thin stream of watery spit-up drips onto the mat.

My nails press into my palms, making me gasp. I unfurl my fists to find four bloody crescents on each hand.

"It's okay," I say, squeezing my lids shut. "It's okay. Keep going."

My head swims when I stand, and I breathe through a wave of dizziness before heading to the changing table for a wipe. The package crinkles as I tug out the last one. I'll need to resupply before I have to change Holly again—the last thing I need is to be wrist-deep in poop before realizing I'm out of wipes.

Holly grunts from the play mat.

"I'm coming, I'm coming," I grumble, but I head to the closet instead. If I don't refill those wipes soon, it'll be a literal shitshow.

The door opens with a squeal, and for a moment, I'm not in my home anymore. I'm back in that clearing, frozen in place as I watch the tiny door creak...

"Stop!" I yell. I shake my head so violently pain shoots through my skull. Pain is fine. Pain I can handle.

The extra packages of wipes are on the shelf directly in front of my face. I step forward to grab one, my bare toe connecting with something thin and coiled, oh God—

Before I can choke it down, the scream erupts from my throat and I shrink back against the open door, cowering and covering my face. It's not until Tater Tot rushes over and licks my finger that I finally peel my hands away.

For the second time in what feels like as many hours, my mouth floods with bitterness as my heartbeat slows. There are no snakes in my house, no skulking, slithering things, no piles of carcasses. There's just a tangle of cords resting on the floor.

Tater follows my gaze and moves to investigate, pawing at the pile. His nails connect with something hard and plastic, raking it closer to me.

It's the handheld baby monitor my sister-in-law gave us for our baby shower. The casing is smooth and solid, nearly slipping out of my slick fingers. I turn it over in my hands, letting my breathing slowly return to normal.

The monitor is battery-powered and video-enabled. My sister-in-law told me it has the longest range on the market. Perfect for keeping watch over the baby…

…or something else.

I shoot up off the ground, startling Tater, the monitor clutched tightly in my hands. If I don't do this now, I'm going to lose my nerve, and I can't take another sleepless night.

When I get back to the living room, I find Holly on her back. She must have rolled over while I was gone, but I barely stop to do more than give a lackluster cheer.

"That's great, Hols! But now, we have to go do something important, okay?" My lips tremble and my face feels puffy. "You're coming with Mommy."

Tater nudges my knee, whining. “Sorry, boy,” I say, patting his soft head. “I wish you could come, I really do.”

He slinks to his bed in the corner and collapses into a sulky heap.

I’m almost out the door when I remember to check the batteries. I set Holly down, pop open the back of the monitor’s camera unit, and find four fresh AA batteries. My right eye twitches, and a grin that’s definitely more manic than happy breaks across my face.

I load Holly into the stroller and shove the monitor into the stroller’s storage compartment. My legs pump as quickly as my healing body will allow.

A voice in my head pipes up, *What are you doing?*

“I can’t lose any more sleep, I can’t. I can’t I can’t I can’t I can’t,” I singsong to Holly, who doesn’t want to look at me. “I can’t I can’t I can’t I can’t—”

“Hey, mama!”

My words die in my throat, clogging it. I whip around to find Tiffany jogging toward me.

“Motherfucker,” I hiss around the smile forming reflexively on my face. Then, more loudly, “Hey, Tiffany!”

She closes the gap between us and stops next to Holly, veneers gleaming in the morning sun. “It’s a beautiful day, huh?” she says.

“Gorgeous,” I say, reaching behind me to peel the back of my shirt off of my sweaty skin.

“And how’s this little sweetie doing?” she asks, bending over Holly’s car seat. Holly grins, all gums and dimples, the little traitor.

“She’s great,” I say. “We’re both just so, so great.”

“Motherhood is such a gift,” Tiffany says. This is the first conversation we’ve had beyond a wave and a hello, and the pressure to make a good impression fills my stomach with bubbles.

“Ain’t that the truth.” An acrid burp makes its way up my throat, insistent and indefatigable, and I have to let it out—

Carrie Underwood's 'Jesus Take the Wheel' explodes into the air, hiding the sound of my burp. Tiffany scrabbles at her waistband, then pulls out a phone with a pink glittery case.

"Hello?" she says. I can't make out what the person on the other end is saying, but whatever it is, it isn't good. A new layer of wrinkles garlands Tiffany's perfect nose with each passing moment, and her lips curl into a scowl. She turns away from me, but she doesn't make any effort to lower her voice. "How do you know the other boy didn't hit him first? It's not always Kayden's fault." Tiffany listens, her shoulders rising to meet her ears. "Please. It's not like a pencil could do that much damage, even if it was sharp. It's a pencil, for God's sake!" Tiffany's face grows redder as she continues to listen. "Fine. I'll come pick him up in fifteen minutes." Tiffany ends the call and shoves her phone back into her waistband before turning to face me again.

"Everything… okay?" I ask.

Tiffany's mouth wobbles before she wrestles it back into an Instagram-ready smile. "Absolutely. You know, I'm so sorry, but I've got to run."

"Okay, sure—"

"Oh, and you might want to put down the shade for her," Tiffany says, nodding at Holly. "And maybe a fan? It's a bit hot for babies this morning."

My lips stretch so tight, they might split from grinning. "Oh, for sure," I say. "You're so right. Thank you! I appreciate it!"

But Tiffany's already jogging back the way she came. "You're doing great, mama!" she calls over her shoulder. I watch her perfectly sculpted butt, encased in aquamarine leggings that leave nothing to the imagination, until she's nothing but a blue speck.

"Doing great, my ass." At least I'm not the one picking up her bully of a child from school.

With damp fingers, I pull Holly's stroller shade down. The fan is tangled up with the monitor, and it takes me far too long to extract it. It clips into place with a satisfying thump, blowing the heavy air into Holly's face.

As soon as the blue speck of Tiffany's backside blinks out completely, I turn the fan toward myself and start walking.

* * *

We reach the intersection and take a right onto Laurel. Cicadas hum all around us, and somewhere deep in the foliage, a small animal squeals—perhaps in pain.

"You don't own me," I say. "You don't own me, you pesky fucker." My pictures of the door might not have turned out, but I'm going to get some undeniable proof, one way or another.

As if it's been waiting for me, the trailhead appears on my right. Without hesitation, I push Holly's stroller onto the grass and underneath the hanging canopy of grapevine. Tall stalks of switch cane wave as I pass by. The deeper I go into the woods, the more I sweat. Who needs a sauna when you can simply step outside?

Even though I'm expecting it, the sudden silence that engulfs us sends a bolt of anxiety through my brain.

Maybe this isn't such a good idea.

Before I can change my mind, we arrive at the clearing. The stunted, misshapen tree juts out of the earth like a zombie's arm, scrabbling around to escape the grave. I pinch myself, letting the pain confirm I'm really here.

I grab the baby monitor and clutch it to my chest like a rosary. My sneakers—no bare feet, I'm not dreaming, I'm not—step around the stroller, bringing me squarely in front of the tree. My eyes travel down its knotted trunk to the nasty little door, which, mercifully, is firmly shut.

But, wait—what's that? Oh, God.

Directly in front of the door lies a lump of light brown fur. Droplets of crimson decorate its long ears like a Pollock painting. Steam rises from the fresh corpse.

The marsh rabbit is tiny, barely more than a baby.

"Christ," I whimper, and then I shake, because this is too nightmarish to be real. My feet are rooted to the spot, exactly like in my dreams, and am I even awake at all? Yes, the rabbit is dead, but no flies are buzzing around it, and what could possibly be horrible enough to keep flies away from a hot, fresh kill?

Holly cries, cutting through the silence and wrenching me from my paralysis. I still don't know if I'm awake or asleep. In a trance, I squat down, my lady parts protesting, and press the base of the monitor's camera unit into the dirt, aiming it at the door. Part of me wants to abandon the whole thing, turn and shove the stroller out of here as quickly as possible, but I know that won't solve my problem. If anything, it'll only get worse; now, I have more nightmare fuel.

When the monitor is situated just right, I flick it on and check the corresponding handset still clutched in my quivering fist. The image quality is far better than I expected; it's black-and-white, but I can make out the clumps of moss on the door, the ridges of the tree's bark, the crisp tendril of a dead vine, the dark spots of blood on the rabbit's pelt...

And then I'm doubled over, retching; at the same time, my weak pelvic floor can't hold things in any longer, and warm urine dribbles down my legs, pooling in my socks.

"No!" I yell, because if I were asleep, then I'd be waking up now in my bed, but I'm not, I'm still here in the woods, and then, because the silence of the clearing presses down on me like a physical weight, I scream. My throat is raw from stomach acid, and it hurts, but I scream again, unintelligible, incoherent, a raving lunatic.

When I can't scream anymore, I stand up, heaving. I toss the monitor handset into the stroller and barrel back the way I came. I don't want to be here any longer, and I definitely don't want to be here when whatever murdered that rabbit comes back to feast on its kill.

* * *

Holly is crying softly by the time we emerge back onto Laurel Lane, and with each soggy step, my toes squish in my urine.

A sigh rattles from my mouth. At least I'm awake, right? I don't know if that's better, but it's definitely not worse.

"Everything is going to be okay." I'm looking at Holly, but I'm talking to myself. I did what I set out to do, and now all that's left is to watch the monitor. It has a motion-sensing function that will beep anytime something moves in the camera's range. Even if all I ever see is a vulture ripping the rabbit apart, I'll have peace of mind. A vulture is expected. A vulture is normal.

"Sadie, hi!" comes a too-chipper voice from behind me.

Come on. Seriously?

I turn to find Jessica, head hanging out of her black Tesla. Her matching athleisure set is the color of ripe tangerines. I don't think anyone else could pull off that color. Except Tiffany, or Heather, or Mandy, or… any of the other Yoga Moms. Fuck.

"Hey," I say, weakly.

She slows the car to a stop next to me, and I hope she's not close enough to smell the stomach acid on my shirt, or the urine in my shoes.

"How are you doing?" she asks, and I want to scream. Do all the Yoga Moms read from the same playbook?

"Fine," I say through gritted teeth, trying to make myself small. Maybe she won't notice my stained shirt, my wet shorts, my ragged nails, my frizzy, uncombed hair, or the dark bags under my eyes. I know I don't look good, but standing next to her, with her coiffed sheaf of shiny hair, her perfect makeup, her fitted athletic wear, and her candy-colored nails, I feel as attractive as Jabba the Hut.

"You've got a little…" she points at my hair, gesturing vaguely.

"What?" I say, hands flying to my head.

"It's only a leaf," she says, smiling as my fingers locate the crispy brown foliage and yank it out of my hair so hard I wince.

"Thanks," I say, because what else can I do?

"Sure," she says. "Have you been… hiking or something?"

"No," I say, too quickly. "Just walking…" my voice trails off as I gesture at the opening in the grapevines, but of course, it's not there anymore.

Jessica looks back where I'm pointing, and for a second, her golden tan evaporates, and her contoured pink cheeks go an unfashionable shade of pale. There's a flash of fear in her eyes, or of something more akin to pain, I'd swear it. But then it's gone, and she shakes her head. She turns back to me, and her expression morphs into something darker, more uncertain. She opens her mouth, sucks in a breath, then closes it. Her gaze makes me sweat even more than I thought possible. What is she thinking? Does she know about the path, too? Or is there something in my teeth, on top of everything else that's wrong with me?

"What?" I finally ask, a bit too sharply.

Jessica sighs, then leans a bit closer through her car window. "You know, Sadie, I wasn't going to say anything, but I want you to know it's okay."

My eyebrows shoot up. "What's okay?"

She smiles, but it looks more patronizing than kind. "It's okay to get some help."

Help with what? I could definitely use more child care, but that's not happening right now, so…

When I don't say anything, she goes on. "I don't want to be nosy or anything, but I don't like to see a fellow mama in need. A lot of mamas suffer from postpartum depression."

There it is. The words hang in the air like a bad smell. In fact, Jessica even wrinkles her nose. She should have slapped me; it would have been less excruciating.

"Oh," I choke out. "I'm not—I don't—"

"It's not a big deal," Jessica says. "But you should definitely get help."

"I don't—"

And then, so softly I almost don't catch it, she adds, "While you still can."

Without waiting for me to respond, she gives a dismissive little wave, rolls up her window, and drives off.

As I walk back home feeling like a total basket case, my urine-soaked shoes completely forgotten, I wonder how long it will take until Tiffany and Jessica compare notes and all the Yoga Moms start gossiping about me, the 'bless her heart' sentiment echoing in the caverns of their wineglasses.

CHAPTER FOURTEEN

Now You See Me

By the time I get home, my entire body is wet, the perspiration mingling with the urine to the point that I can't tell which is which. I shuck off my shoes and put them outside to dry, but I don't make any real effort to clean myself beyond a cursory swipe with a towel. What's the point of showering? I'm going to get sweaty all over again, and I'm fatigued beyond measure, as though I've descended into a new sub-basement of exhaustion. Somehow, I summon the energy to feed Holly—I'm so tired I don't even wince when she latches onto my still-wounded nipples—and put her down for a nap.

While she's sleeping, I take Cash's advice for once: I try to nap, too.

Our couch was an expensive housewarming present from my parents, but it's decidedly uncomfortable. Every time I shift, trying to find a sleep-inducing position, the fabric of my nursing bra chafes and burns my wrecked nipples.

I tell myself it's the couch that's keeping me awake, or my breast pain, or the ever-present ache in my lady parts, but that's not actually it.

The baby monitor handset is sitting innocently on the carpet in front of the coffee table, out of Cash's sightline on the off chance he makes an appearance. Every time I'm about to drift off, I imagine the rustling of dead leaves, the squeal of a dying rabbit, the creak of a tiny door.

"Ugh," I groan, turning onto my back, eyes squeezed shut. All I want to do is sleep, escape into oblivion, but nothing is working. Maybe I should turn the monitor off; after all, what was I thinking? Animals die in the woods all the time—that rabbit didn't mean anything. I'm not going to catch whatever I think is in that clearing on a stupid baby monitor, because there's nothing to catch.

But then I think about the look in Jessica's eyes, as though she knew exactly what trail I was talking about.

"Get a grip," I tell myself, squeezing my head between my hands, trying to massage some sense into my brain. All this sleep deprivation, this pain and responsibility and isolation, it's too much. It's too much for me, and I have all the privileges in the world. How do other moms do it?

The baby monitor crackles to life.

For a second, I tense, preparing to get Holly, but then I realize what I'm hearing isn't coming from her.

It's coming from the woods.

I fall off the couch in my haste to grab the plastic handset off the floor, clutching at it like I'm drowning and the monitor is a life—or sanity?—preserver.

Something triggered the monitor.

And I'm finally going to see what it is.

I squeeze the monitor, riveting my focus to the tiny black-and-white screen. A rustling sound pipes out of the monitor's speaker, and there's a ripple of movement near the dead marsh rabbit. Something small and feisty is disturbing the layers of leaf litter and carcasses, rocking the rabbit to and fro. I force air into my lungs and try to slow my racing heart. It's probably just a vulture or snake, some animal come to claim the meal.

At the very edge of the monitor's view, the rabbit's haunch jerks. The fur is so thick that whatever is grabbing it sinks deep into the plush, rendering it nearly invisible.

"Come on, motherfucker," I whisper.

The rabbit shakes like it's possessed, its body jittering this way and that, all at the hand—beak?—of this unseen predator. It's definitely being torn apart, that much is clear. I don't want to see the gore, but I have to know. I have to be sure about what's in that clearing, or else I'll never sleep again, and if I never sleep again, I won't be a good mom, a good wife, a good anything, and Cash will divorce me and Holly will disown me and I'll end up in a gutter on the street since I can't seem to do anything right.

Stillness on the screen. The rabbit stops seizing, and there's no crackle of dead leaves, either.

I hold my breath.

What happens next is so fast I'm not sure I can trust my own senses.

In the top right corner of the screen, directly next to the rabbit's long foot, a tiny face appears. It's haggard, ghoulish, and I know that even if I saw it in full color, it wouldn't look much different. The thing edges around the rabbit too softly for the monitor to pick up the sound, never taking its eyes off the camera, off of me.

It's in front of the rabbit now, and I can make out a stocky, powerfully built body in miniature. Darkness steeps in the crags of its face as it creeps toward the camera, studying it. Slowly, its features contort into something like a grin, its mouth full of sharp, pointed teeth. It's impossible to tell if those teeth are blackened with rot or with blood.

My lungs are burning, but I've forgotten how to breathe. There's no way the thing can actually see me, of course, but I can't shake the conviction that it's staring through the camera and into my soul, taking in everything there is to know about me. It's not studying the camera.

It's studying me.

All at once, the thing rushes at the monitor, too fast for me to make out any additional detail. There's a loud crack, and the screen goes dark.

As if it's on fire, I throw the monitor handset across the room. The breath whooshes out of my lungs, leaving me panting and heaving on the floor.

"What the fuck?" I whisper. "What the fuck what the fuck what the fuck?"

I curl up into a ball. What did I see? How is it possible?

Dread pools in my stomach, because no one will believe me. I'm not even sure I believe me. The monitor doesn't record, after all, and I'll never be able to get more proof like that.

Or can I?

I shoot to my feet, standing so fast I get assaulted by a wave of dizziness.

I have to get the monitor—or what's left of it—from the woods. I need to know what happened to it. That could be proof enough that something is out there, something… more than an animal.

I ram my feet into a pair of slip-on shoes and run to Laurel Lane. The ache between my legs fades into the background; in fact, the pain has become so normal, I don't remember what it was like before. I'm sure my OBGYN would have things to say about me running full-out at only three months postpartum, but my OBGYN isn't here. Even if she was, I hardly think the running would be the greatest of her concerns. I still haven't changed out of my urine-stained shorts.

My legs are shaking when I get to the trail, but I push on, barreling into the tunnel of foliage, hardly registering the silence that descends over the thicket the closer I get to the clearing, to the tree, to the door.

The clearing looms ahead, and then my feet crunch on desiccated bugs. Out of the corner of my eye, I catch the long spiral of a snake spine, sucked clean, the ribs as bare as toothpicks. I rip my gaze away and hunt for the monitor, wanting—needing—to get this done as quickly as I can before whatever destroyed it comes back.

There—near the beginning of the tree line: a shard of white plastic. I rush over and squat down, pawing through the dead leaves like I'm searching for buried treasure.

I unearth two more pieces of plastic, the bits smeared with sticky scarlet, then the camera lens, which is spiderwebbed with cracks. Tiny shards of white litter the area like glitter.

The monitor has been absolutely pulverized.

Oh, God.

How could a creature so small do something like this?

CHAPTER FIFTEEN

The Golf Cart Chainsaw Massacre

A carpet of enormous dead horseflies is laid out like an offering in front of my pink fairy door. I slam my lids shut and count to three, but when I pry them back open, the flies are still there.

I grit my teeth and keep walking, pushing the stroller with one hand, my phone gripped tightly in the other. All of the Google results for 'postpartum hallucination' are bad. Postpartum psychosis? Delusions? Seeing and hearing things that aren't there? Thoughts of self-harm or harming the baby?

I take no comfort in realizing I'm not the only mom to deal with this, because what happens to moms who see things? Who hear noises that aren't there? Who believe in evil little creatures that live in a hidden tree in the woods that no one else seems to be able to see?

Those moms get their babies taken away. Their husbands leave them. They lose their houses, they lose their jobs, they lose their families. They lose their friends. They lose their dignity.

They lose their freedom.

I have too much to lose.

I haven't told Cash about the baby monitor. He didn't believe me about the dead squirrel, or the trail, or the door or the tree or the bones.

He'd say it was obviously an animal, or, more likely, he'd chastise me for ruining an expensive gift for no good reason.

My eyes roam the Google results page against my will, and I want to throw my phone to the ground. Instead, I quickly close that tab and open a new one. This time, I try something else: 'evil little woodland creature.'

"I'm not crazy," I say to Holly, who keeps her gaze trained on the sky above her. "I'm not."

Google gives me Reddit posts about rogue raccoons stealing garbage and chipmunks chewing through someone's new fence. That's not right, either. There's no way a raccoon or a chipmunk pulverized my baby monitor.

I keep walking, looking off into the distance, trying to find the right words. Maybe I should call it what I think it is, however ridiculous it may sound.

It lives behind a little door in a tree deep in the woods, after all.

With some trepidation, I Google 'evil fairy.'

Am I actually entertaining this impossible, silly idea? Do I truly believe there's a nonzero chance that a creepy flesh-and-blood fairy is living in the woods near my house like some suburban Rumpelstiltskin?

I look down at my screen. The webpage is packed with websites, links, photos… but come on, come on. Fairies aren't real, goddammit!

An Instagram notification pops up, breaking my concentration: @JessicaMama414 liked your photo.

A bolt of adrenaline shoots through me. Jessica liked my photo? What did I even post? Probably something stupid about how pretty the scenery is while I'm walking with my perfect little baby, or something equally vague and completely devoid of my true feelings at any given point. I hate how excited I am that Jessica noticed me, took the time to click the heart icon on my photo. It's not like she actually likes me.

Or does she? Could she?

Come on. Fairies aren't real, but I believe in all sorts of things that aren't real. The Yoga Moms aren't real. Everything funneled through the lens of social media is definitely not real. The illusion of the perfect marriage is simply that—an illusion.

If I can believe in all of that, is it too much of a stretch to believe in fairies, too?

I navigate back to my Google search page, correcting myself at the last moment to keep from careering off the road. I have to sift through fantasy websites about the Fae and plenty of references to fairy tales, but I eventually find something that seems legitimate. It's a list of evil fairies from around the world. Apparently, evil fairies are quite prolific in the United Kingdom, and many of them have impenetrable names I have no idea how to pronounce. There are vampire fairies, shapeshifter fairies, sadistic fairies, mermaid fairies, and, most disturbing of all...

...fairies who kidnap babies.

I examine the silly illustrations accompanying each fairy type. I don't have a photo of what I saw on the monitor's screen, of course, so I have to keep pulling up the memory, an ever-present tab in my mind that refuses to close.

None of these fairies look like what I saw. And what the hell is going on in the United Kingdom to attract all these awful creatures?

This is ridiculous. "Fairies aren't real," I tell Holly. Should I go ahead and tell her now that Santa Claus isn't real, either? The laugh that burbles up out of my throat burns like strong alcohol.

And yet... I saw something in those woods. Something put up that fairy door, and there's no longer any possibility it was a Yoga Mom. Mandy doesn't go anywhere where wine isn't present. Tiffany probably doesn't know how to hold a hammer. Even though there was something in her expression the other day, I don't think Jessica would deign to ruin her nails.

At the intersection of Sweetgum and Peach Grove, I'm so focused on my phone that I don't notice the maintenance golf cart as it swerves in front of me.

There's a screech of tires, and when I do look up, heart hammering, there's a rattle and snap, and then a chainsaw is hurtling through the air straight at me.

* * *

I can barely hear screaming over my pulse pounding in my ears.

I don't remember closing my eyes, but when I open them, there's Holly's face, her cheeks bright red, her mouth open so wide I can see the back of her throat.

Oh God, is she hurt?

I run my hands along her body, quick, fluttery motions. There's no blood, nothing's broken.

But she's not the only one screaming.

In front of us, the maintenance golf cart is stopped in the middle of the intersection, and the young guy—no more than a teenager—who was driving stands next to the cart, wailing and wringing his hands on a dirty red bandanna.

"Oh God, oh Jesus, oh Mother Mary, are you okay?" He's blubbering, his shoulders shaking in enormous heaves.

The chainsaw rests in the street, about three feet away from the front of the stroller.

I ignore the dude, take one, two, three deep breaths, then smile down at Holly. "It's okay, baby, it's okay," I coo, but she's inconsolable. She couldn't even see the chainsaw since she's facing me, but she can sense the panic in the atmosphere, the near miss, the kiss of proximate death.

"I swear I tied it down, I did. I don't know what happened. Somebody must have untied it. Oh, God. I'm so sorry, I'm so sorry," the teenager says, still twisting the bandanna into tight knots.

"It's fine," I shout over Holly's cries, even though it's absolutely not. Is this the kind of careless kid Agua Roja is hiring to transport dangerous machinery? What if I'd been walking even the tiniest bit faster, or his reaction had been even the tiniest bit slower?

"What's going on here?" that radio announcer voice cuts through the noise like a sharp knife through butter, and then Ron pulls up beside me in his golf cart with a squeal of brakes. Tater's perched in the seat next to him.

"It was an accident, I didn't mean to, please don't tell my supervisor, I'm so sorry—"

"Hush, now," Ron says to the kid. He climbs out of the cart, Tater at his heels, and puts a hand on my shoulder.

"You alright, Sadie?"

At his question, a wave of sudden, crushing terror washes over me. My first instinct is to bolt, but I've been doing way too much running lately. The pain in my lady parts is agonizing, but right now it's mostly overshadowed by the cold rush of adrenaline.

"Sadie?" Ron says, bending down to look at my face. Tater Tot nuzzles at my hand.

My mouth opens and closes, but nothing comes out.

"Let's get you home," Ron says. With expert finesse, he unsnaps Holly's car seat from the stroller and places it on the seat of the golf cart. He folds up the stroller like he's done it a million times, wedges it into the back of the cart, then steers me gently away from the chainsaw and the whimpering teenager whose negligence could have killed me.

Tater hops in the middle of the golf cart's front seat, and I sit next to him, pulling Holly's car seat into my lap, my fingers squeezing the handle like I'm trying to juice it.

"Get your act together, young man," Ron booms at the kid, who still hasn't moved. He scoots into the driver's seat, the four of us packed in there tighter than sardines, but I've never felt safer.

"I'll give Dale over in maintenance a call," Ron says in his version of a whisper, which is still loud enough for the kid to hear. "This won't happen again."

We ride back to my house, the warm wind whipping my face. "And then McKenna told her brother to swing the bat harder if he ever wanted to hit anything, and God bless him, the boy swung harder than ever. Unfortunately for Rachel, the boy missed the ball and hit the glass coffee table, which shattered into a million pieces." Ron chuckles, and even though I haven't been able to utter a single word since he whisked me away, I find myself laughing hoarsely along with him.

"I always hated that coffee table. That's why we let Rachel have it when we moved. Nobody was hurt, so it's no big loss, I suppose."

We come to a stop in front of my house, and the words finally make it to my tongue.

"Thank you, Ron," I say, emotion clogging my throat. "Seriously."

"It's no problem, Sadie. I mean it."

I'm sure we must look like some sort of preppy clown car: Ron unfolds himself from the cart first, followed by Tater, and then I peel myself off the plasticky seat, carrying Holly's car seat in the crook of one arm.

Ron lifts the stroller out of the back and snaps it into its ready position with a resounding click. "Here she is, all ready for you."

"You're the best, Ron."

"The worst part is, I know it!" Ron cackles, and I'm sure the neighbors on the next block can hear him. I bet they laugh right along with him.

"I'm sure you have better things to do than rescue me nearly every day."

"Nonsense." Ron waves a hand in front of his face. "I was going to go to the pool, but Tracy Roosten told me it's closed for the day."

"Closed? Why?"

Ron sighs. "It was probably an accident, but the pool chemicals are all out of whack. Tracy's husband Bob—he's all but lost his sense of smell—got into the water this morning and nearly coughed up a lung. If he could have given it a sniff, he'd have known something was off. Tracy had to call an ambulance because Bob couldn't catch his breath."

"Seriously?"

"Seriously. Let's hope there's no permanent damage, for Bob and for the neighborhood's sake. That's a lawsuit right there."

"That's terrifying."

"These things happen, I suppose. Someone isn't trained well—think about what just happened to you, dear—and they mix in the wrong chemicals." Ron pats me on the shoulder. "But don't you worry, Sadie. Everything will be fine. You rest up now."

"I will," I say, and then Ron's gone, zipping off in his golf cart.

Cash is in the kitchen, cracking open a can of La Croix, when I stumble through the door with Holly and Tater. My armpit sweat stains reach down to my sagging belly button, and my hair has come loose from my bun in wild, frizzy tangles, the ultimate contrast to Cash's crisp, clean golf shirt and perfectly coiffed hair.

Taking in my appearance, his eyes bulge and jaw drops. It's not an attractive combination, and for the briefest, pettiest of moments, I'm gratified to see Cash looking less than handsome.

"Sadie," he splutters. "What happened?"

Bouncing Holly on one hip to quiet her down, I'm too tired to sugarcoat anything. "I was out walking with Holly. And… oh, God… and this maintenance cart was going too fast, and when it stopped in front of us, a freaking chainsaw flew off it and almost hit us."

His eyes bulge even farther, which I didn't think was possible.

"Jesus Christ, Sadie," he says when I finish, the torrent of words leaving me breathless. "Why weren't you being more careful?"

My mouth falls open. "What? It was a freak accident—"

Cash cuts me off. "What if that chainsaw had hit Holly? I can't even… I would never get over it!" Now he's the one panting. His frosty can of La Croix lies untouched on the kitchen counter. I wonder, absently, if he's going to drink it, or if I can swipe it from him. I'm pretty sure it's the last one, and I'm so fucking thirsty.

"Why aren't you worried about me, Cash? That thing could have hit me, too! Or would that be much easier to get over?"

He shakes his head. "Were you sucked into your phone again? Were you on Instagram?"

I bite my lip so hard I taste blood. Where's the compassion, the warm hug, the comfort? Where's the understanding? Ron didn't ask questions, he didn't chastise me, he didn't try to make me out to be a bad mom. He was just there for me, and he didn't make it look difficult.

How many times has Cash done silly, stupid, avoidable things, and I play the role of good wife and pat him on the back, telling him everything will be okay?

"You have to be more careful, Sadie! I need to know Holly is safe with you!"

I don't want him to see me cry, but he's gone for the jugular, and I feel like I'm bleeding out. "You want to know the truth? I was researching the evil fairy in the woods, Cash! Because you don't believe me! Because you aren't worried about *me*!"

As soon as the words leave my mouth, I regret them. That's the last thing I need—Cash worrying about my mental stability. I don't need to give him another reason to worry about Holly being safe with me. Of course she's safe with me!

All the rage melts out of Cash's body. He looks wrung out, defeated. He sighs. "Of course I'm worried about you, Sadie. You're all I'm worried about, lately."

Holly lays her head on my shoulder. All the excitement has worn her out, too, and her wails have tapered off into frustrated whimpers.

"Jesus," I say, my eyelids so heavy it hurts to keep looking at Cash. I don't want to fight in front of my child. I don't want to have angry conversations around her that will make her think her home is unstable, insecure. I don't want to give her a reason to suspect she can't count on me. All my rose-tinted visions of future motherhood, of the kind of parent I would be, feel like pipe dreams right now, and shame washes over me once again, as painful as a full-body cramp.

His voice low, Cash says, "Something is up with you, Sadie. This is not normal."

Of course it's not normal! I know that! But I also know I'm not crazy. He didn't see the exploded shards of the baby monitor, the offerings of dead things. He's never even seen the trail, or the clearing, or the tree, or the door, for God's sake!

"Right," I whisper. All the fight has gone out of me. All I want is to put Holly down for a nap and curl up on the couch with some terrible reality TV and forget all of this ever happened.

Cash takes a few steps toward me. "I've been reading about… about postpartum depression," he says. Ugh—those words again. Has he been talking to Jessica? Did she say something to him in the guise of being a 'good neighbor?'

When I remain silent, he continues. "You're—you're not doing well, Sadie. I mean, fairies in the woods? Come on, babe. You're imagining things. That's a classic sign. It's not healthy for you or for Holly to keep going on this way without help. I mean, what if something really bad happens next time? This can't… this can't go on."

Is this the same speech husbands give their wives before they have them committed? How would Cash transition Holly to formula while I'm in a mental institution? Maybe he'd finally understand how hard it is to be at an infant's beck and call 24/7. Actually, being institutionalized might not be so horrible… I'd finally get a good night's sleep, if nothing else…

"Sadie?" Cash is in front of me now—when did he get so close? I can smell his woody aftershave, the mint of his toothpaste. "Sadie, are you hearing me?"

"Yes," I say, because, more than anything, I want this conversation to be over. "I hear you."

"Will you talk to your doctor?" His eyes have de-bulged, and he's back to his annoyingly handsome self.

"Yes," I say, but I don't know if I'm telling the truth. I don't want to go on drugs. What if I take them, and they turn me into a zombie, erasing my entire personality? What if they're not safe for breastfeeding, and I have to give Holly formula instead? What if she hates it, or it gives her painful gas, or she doesn't get all the natural antibodies from my breastmilk and she gets sick every month?

Cash envelops me and Holly in a too-warm hug, but I'm stiff against him. He doesn't seem to notice.

"I'm proud of you, babe," he says. "For getting the help you need."

Slow down, dude, I haven't even called the doctor yet. "Yeah," I respond, my face crushed against his chest, my nose completely filled with that cologne, along with his natural, earthy scent lurking underneath. What do I smell like? Probably anxiety-induced body odor and spoiled milk.

Cash takes Holly from me, and she slumps into his arms, beyond tired. "I'll put Holly down," he says. "Why don't you go call your doctor and then take a nap?"

A marvelous idea. Well, the nap part at least. "Thanks," I say.

Cash disappears with Holly into our bedroom. I head upstairs to the vacant guest room and collapse onto the bed, which smells musty.

As I lie there staring up at the ceiling, I can't help but think about Mike the headless chicken. I read about Mike a few years ago, stumbling across this circus sideshow creature on some Wikipedia rabbit hole or Buzzfeed listicle, I can't remember now. Basically, Mike was a chicken who lived for eighteen months without his head. His owners, back in the 1940's, had decided they felt like chicken for dinner, but when they lopped off Mike's head, he didn't die. The blood loss didn't kill him, and apparently his brainstem was still intact, so he simply… kept on living. They cleaned out mucus from his open throat hole and dripped food down it with an eyedropper.

New motherhood and Mike the headless chicken have so much in common. A part of me has been extracted, but yay, I didn't die from blood loss! Now I'm surviving, and everybody is so happy for me—look at this brand new, brave mama!—but I'm hardly thriving. My brainstem is active, but that's about the only thing keeping me going.

Did Mike the headless chicken have to deal with postpartum depression when he lost his head?

It's too ridiculous, and I can't help it—I giggle. And as I giggle, I begin to thaw.

Cash might be right about a few things, but he's wrong about me being abnormal. Postpartum depression, I learn as I take out my phone to Google it more in-depth, couldn't be more normal. I read article after article, carefully avoiding all mentions of 'postpartum psychosis,' sticking to the depression information only.

Eventually, I fall into a thin, dreamless sleep.

CHAPTER SIXTEEN

Even Yoga Moms Get PPD

"It wasn't even that close, Mom. Seriously." The sun pierces my retinas, and I shift my chair farther back on the porch, trying in vain to find a patch of shade.

"I don't care, honey. No matter how you describe it, 'almost getting hit by a flying chainsaw' is a phrase I never want to hear." My mom's voice flows out of the phone's speaker, soothing despite the way it hitches with concern.

"Please don't worry, Mom."

"I'm your mother. That's what we do. We worry about our kids."

The wood of the Adirondack chair is burning my thighs, but I don't move. The pain feels good, enlivening. It's a pain I can control.

"I know," I say, sighing. "I don't want to worry you, though. I don't want to worry anybody."

"Oh, honey, I know," she says. "What did Cash say about all of this?"

"He totally freaked out," I say, shuddering. "He… he told me to go see a doctor."

"What for?" she asks. She works from home, and the sound of shuffling papers comes from the background. She's probably sitting in the guest room she uses for an office, filing invoices or opening mail.

"Are you listening?" I ask, unable to keep the whine fully out of my voice. I want to tell her everything Cash said to me, but I want her full attention. There's nothing worse than being vulnerable, flaying your body and mind open to another person, only to have that person shake the daze from their eyes and ask, 'What was that?'

The shuffling stops. "Of course I'm listening."

"Cash… he told me I should see a doctor about postpartum depression."

There. I said it. It's out there now, and there's no taking it back.

"Oh," she says. "That's it?"

"What do you mean, 'That's it?'" I splutter.

"Honey, postpartum depression is incredibly common. Hell, I even had a touch of that after you were born, although in those days, everybody called it the 'baby blues' and there wasn't treatment like there is today. Back then, we had to get through it as best we could. Now, you can go to your doctor, get a prescription, and get back to feeling like yourself."

"Huh," I say. "You never told me that before."

"Why would I? It didn't seem relevant. Until now, I guess."

"Yeah."

There's a beat of silence, then Mom says, "I have to say, I think Cash is right. Have you called your doctor yet?"

"No," I say, and my cheeks burn the same way they did in high school when she'd ask me if I'd finished my homework when I hadn't even started it. "I did a bunch of Googling and reading about it. I… I don't want people to think I'm crazy."

"You're not crazy," Mom says. The heat on the porch is too intense now; I heave myself out of the Adirondack chair, thighs scorched, and head back inside.

"Thanks," I say.

"Go to your doctor, honey. You'll be so glad you did. If you don't want to do it for you, do it for Holly. For Cash. You need to be the best person you can be, for them."

I flip on the overhead fan, letting the cool air wash over me. "I know you're right… but I hate the idea of being on drugs."

Mom snorts. "These days, everybody takes medication for something. Don't fret over it—they'll be able to prescribe you something that's still safe for breastfeeding. Another thing they didn't have when I was your age."

"Okay, okay," I say, lying down on the floor and stretching out my aching back. "I'll call."

"You will?"

"Honestly, I will. As soon as we hang up."

"Good," she says. "Then, in that case, bye! Call me tomorrow, baby."

There's a soft beep, then she's gone.

I drop my phone onto the carpet beside me and hug my knees to my chest, relishing the flexibility after so many months of barely being able to see my legs around the bulk of my pregnant belly.

After a few moments of blessed stillness, I pick my phone up and call Dr. Tallis.

* * *

"How would you describe your mental and emotional state since you gave birth?" Dr. Tallis asks me. I'm naked, swathed in a blue paper gown and sitting on the exam bench. It's so cold my cracked nipples poke at the thin paper of the gown, even that tiny amount of friction causing ripples of pain throughout my breasts. I cross my arms in front of my chest.

"Um," I say, swallowing the sour lump in my throat. "Not great?"

Dr. Tallis nods. "Can you be more specific?"

I gulp again, trying to keep my voice level. "Well, I don't think I'm healing as quickly as I should—physically, I mean—and my nipples hurt all the time, and breastfeeding is super painful, and… I guess I've been kind of moody, too."

Dr. Tallis nods again, her face stoic. I'm sure she's heard all of this hundreds, probably even thousands, of times before. The lump in my throat starts to dissolve.

"Have you had any thoughts of harming yourself or your baby?"

Well… my mind flashes back to Holly at two weeks old. She wouldn't stop crying, and I stood in my bedroom, glowering at the bassinet and its red-faced occupant, screaming at her to shut up. When she didn't, I'd shoved her bassinet with one foot, rearing back to kick again before I came to my senses.

Then, when she was three weeks old and sleep was even harder to come by than it is now, I found myself standing over the stove, the gas burner roaring, wondering what it would feel like to place my hand over the flame and hold it there until my fingers curled into a charred claw.

"No," I answer.

Dr. Tallis cocks her head. "Would you say your mood swings are triggered by anything in particular?"

"Lack of sleep," I answer instantly. Then, after some more thought, "Anytime my husband asks—no, tells—me to do anything. And breastfeeding, to some extent."

"I see," Dr. Tallis says. "Are you experiencing any other physical symptoms besides the vaginal pain and the breast pain?"

"No," I say.

"What about any other mental or emotional symptoms?"

Should I tell her about the trail in the woods only I can see? Or the dead squirrel stuffed in my mailbox? Or about Tater Tot throwing up bones? The offerings of dead flies, the broken tiny ribcages, the horrible tree with its nightmarish door, the pulverized, blood-spattered monitor?

"Nope," I say. I lower my head, hoping she doesn't notice my cheeks flush with guilt at the lie.

"Alright," she says, snapping on a pair of blue nitrile gloves. "Why don't you lean back and scoot your bottom to the edge of the table. Let's take a look at how you're healing."

I stare up at the drop ceiling, faint outlines of water damage forming strange patterns, and try to ignore her probing fingers reaching deeper and deeper inside of me. After what seems like an eternity but has probably been no more than thirty seconds, she leans back. "Everything looks good here," she says. "There's a bit of swelling still, but I think with some more rest, you'll be back to normal before you know it."

"Great," I say, sitting up and yanking the gown over my knees. I haven't shaved my legs in ages, and the dark hairs carpeting my skin make me look like a Sasquatch. I bet Jessica shaved her legs, even at nine months pregnant. Hell, I bet she got a Brazilian wax right before her induction.

"Now, let's take a look at your breasts," she says, rolling her stool to my side. She gently lowers my paper gown and inspects my cracked nipples.

"It hurts every time she latches," I say.

"Hmm," Dr. Tallis says, prodding one breast with a gloved finger. "There does seem to be quite a bit of tissue damage around both areolae. Have you had your baby checked for a tongue tie?"

"Yes," I say. "The pediatric surgeon snipped one millimeter of tissue from under her tongue before we even left the hospital."

"Ah," Dr. Tallis says. "Well, here's what we're going to do. For the lingering vaginal pain, let's say no vigorous exercise or sex for another two weeks, and try taking Epsom salt baths. For the breast pain, I'm going to prescribe ointment—it's over the counter, but I'll call it in to make sure you get the right one. I also recommend buying a pair of silver nipple cups. Take the ointment, spread it around the inside of the cups, then put them over your nipples and wear them whenever you're not breastfeeding. That should help you heal pretty quickly."

"Thank God," I say, relief flooding through me.

"As for the mood swings, it sounds to me like you might have a borderline case of postpartum depression. I'll go ahead and prescribe an antidepressant that's safe for nursing mothers. It's one pill, once a day. Give it some time—it can take a few weeks to really kick in."

This time, a veritable tsunami of relief crashes through me. Dr. Tallis isn't treating me like a mental patient, she isn't holding me at arm's length, nor is she acting as though I am in any way abnormal. Along with the relief comes a bloom of hope. Why didn't I seek out this solution earlier?

If Dr. Tallis is right, and the pill and the ointment can make me feel like myself again... maybe...

Maybe I won't see the trail in the woods anymore.

The possibility is almost too wonderful to contemplate.

"Thank you, Doctor," I say.

"You can buy those silver cups on Amazon. Make sure you get pure silver."

"Alright." I make a mental note to fill my Amazon cart with razor blade refills and shaving cream, too.

"Is there anything else I can help with?" Dr. Tallis asks, typing notes into my computerized medical record.

Again, I think about the horror of the past few weeks. Should I tell her everything? She's seen it all, heard it all. Would she balk at my story, or would she tell me what I'm going through is totally normal? Would she believe me, or would she tell me it was all in my head?

I shove down the words thumping at the back of my throat. There's no need to tell Dr. Tallis, not yet, anyway. Let's see how those pills work before I open myself up to further scrutiny.

"No," I say, plastering a smile on my face. "Thank you so much."

"I just sent the prescriptions to your pharmacy. They should be ready soon. Be sure to call our office if there's anything else you need," she says, rising and heading to the door.

"I will," I say.

When the door closes behind her, I waste no time getting dressed. I'm shivering, and I hate being so exposed, from my Sasquatch legs to my flabby stomach to my traumatized vagina to my chewed-up breasts.

There are no mirrors in the exam room, but I am all too aware of how I must look. I need to focus on taking care of myself so I can be the person my family needs.

So I can be the person I need.

Lacing up my shoes, I try to picture any of the Yoga Moms with postpartum depression, but it's impossible. All I can imagine is a perfect Instagram grid reflecting their size zero-Lululemon-wearing, smoothie-drinking, Bible-thumping, wine-swigging brands.

Thirty minutes later, when I get home with my prescriptions, I find Cash in the kitchen eating a banana.

"Where's Holly?" I ask.

"I put her down ten minutes ago. She seemed tired."

The rage that scalds my throat is inappropriate, but that fact doesn't make the anger any less intense. "I have to feed her before she goes down," I say through clenched teeth.

"Oh," he says, shoving the last of the banana into his mouth. He tosses the peel in the trash and shrugs. "How was the doctor?"

I walk past him into our bedroom. "It was fine," I call over my shoulder, heading for Holly's bassinet. She's still awake, her tongue making little searching, darting motions. She's hungry. How does Cash not understand her schedule by now? She never goes to bed without eating first!

I return to the kitchen, Holly clutched to my chest.

"Did you get any prescriptions?" he asks, and even though I know he's not trying to be an asshole, it's like he wants to cross my mental health off of his to-do list. Deal with crazy wife? Check.

"Yes," I say, moving to the couch and strapping on my nursing pillow. Holly latches on immediately, greedily, and I wince yet again. The silver cups I ordered while waiting in line at the pharmacy won't be here until tomorrow night. At least I'll have the ointment in the meantime.

"Everything else okay?" he asks, and I'm not sure if he means with my body, with my mind, or with our relationship. Maybe it doesn't matter.

"Peachy," I say.

When I don't elaborate, he says, "Okay, well… I guess I'll go back to work, then."

"Great."

His hand is on the doorknob when he turns back to face me. "Sadie?"

"What?"

"Have you taken your new pill yet?"

I want to say *Mind your own business and stop trying to tell me what to do.* Instead I say, "Not yet. I was going to, but then I realized you'd put Holly down already and I needed to feed her first."

"Hey, I was engaged with her for the entire time you were gone. I wore her out." Cash's handsome face has melted into a scowl. Jesus, the bastard looks good even while scowling.

"Yep," I say. Then, because I can't help myself, "Must be really hard to have to babysit your own child."

Cash's mouth opens, then closes, then opens again, like a hungry fish. Finally, he says, "I hope the meds kick in fast." He yanks open the door and hustles down the stairs, off to go do whatever it is he does while I'm caring for our child.

I switch Holly to my other bruised, broken nipple. When she's done, I lay her in the bassinet, her eyes already closing.

In the kitchen, I tear open the paper bag with my pills and ointment. The pea-size amount of goo I rub into my nipples is greasy and smells like clean linen. I wipe my fingers on my shirt, ignoring the stain.

It takes me a few tries to open the childproof cap of the orange bottle, the contents rattling inside. When I wrestle it open, I shake a pill into my palm and stare at it.

Mom's voice is in the back of my mind, telling me I need to get myself right not only for me, but also for my family.

I slurp the pill out of my hand and swallow it dry.

CHAPTER SEVENTEEN

Get Your Body Back

"Good morning!" Cash says, far too chipper for six a.m. A frizzle of pain shoots through my brain.

My jaw cracks as I yawn. Eyes still half-closed, I rummage through the cabinet, looking for my favorite mug, the handmade blue one with the wide handle. The crockery clatters against each other as I sift through the contents of the shelf. I know it was clean last night, I saw it in here…

"Good morning," Cash repeats, this time with less enthusiasm.

I glance over at him, sitting at the breakfast bar, scrolling on his phone and periodically slurping from a bowl of beige, watery oatmeal that looks shockingly similar to the contents of Holly's diaper. Is he trying to broadcast how overtly helpless he is?

"Morning," I mumble, and that's when I spot my favorite blue mug, right there on the counter next to Cash's nasty breakfast. Oblivious, he reaches for it and takes a loud gulp. Irritation pricks me like a thousand needles. Why does that happy pill have to take weeks to kick in?

"How did you sleep?" Cash asks. "Did the pills work?"

"Good," I answer, hoping that will suffice for both questions. I don't feel like telling him the pills could take weeks to make a difference. It would be one more thing he could complain about.

"You okay?" he asks. If I had a dollar for every time he's asked me that… I'd be rich enough to afford a full-time nanny, thus preventing Cash from needing to ask that question ever again.

"Yep," I say. "Still waking up, that's all."

Cash gulps the last of his oatmeal, his spoon clanking loudly against the bowl. "Not the best meal ever, but it'll do," he says.

If I stay quiet, he might get the hint and leave me to the blessed, luxurious silence I crave.

I select an inferior mug from the cabinet, fill it with water, and pop it in the microwave. My nursing-safe herbal tea doesn't have much kick, but at least it's soothing.

Cash's lips are moving, but it takes me awhile to tune in. My brain is heavy and waterlogged, as though it's been pickled in brine. "What?" I ask, cutting off his monologue.

Cash clears his throat. "I wanted to tell you I'm proud of you."

"For what?" Thirty seconds left on the microwave.

"For being open to treatment. For getting on the meds."

"Oh. Yeah." Ten seconds left.

"I mean, this is the first step to getting your life back. To getting your body back, too."

The microwave dings, but I barely notice. All I hear is 'get your body back.' Where does he think my body went? I never lost it, asshole!

Every hair on my supposedly lost body bristles, like an animal sensing a predator. I know I'm a pale, blobby wreck, while Cash is still tan and chiseled. He goes to the gym every morning, chugging a Blender Bottle full of protein on the way. Meanwhile, I'm stuck taking gentle walks that barely elevate my heart rate. That is, when I'm not running for my life. All the sprinting I've been doing lately—from the trail, from the chainsaw, through the rain—probably slowed down my healing, making this process of 'getting my body back' take even longer. How lovely.

"Sadie?"

"What?" I say, my voice on the bleeding edge of a snarl.

"Um… your water is ready. For your tea."

I yank open the microwave and grab the mug. With my teeth, I rip open the paper packaging on the teabag, then dunk it into the water.

"Everything okay?" he says slowly.

My internal scream is so loud, I'm certain he must be able to hear it. But when I turn to face him, one side of his mouth is quirked in a half-smile, his hands up to placate me like I'm an unfriendly dog.

I grit my teeth, say "Yeah, totally." Would he be asking me that constantly if I looked normal again? If I were pretty and thin? There's the unspoken agreement that if you're beautiful, you're beyond reproach, all of your transgressions automatically forgiven.

After all, that's how the Yoga Moms get by with being raging bitches.

I sip my tea, even though it's too hot and the water scalds my tongue and burns my throat, settling like a hot stone in my stomach.

"Well, I'm going to work now," Cash says.

I nod, staring down at my slack belly. I know how it is—if you're bloated, your hair's frizzy, and you've got bags under your eyes, you can go to hell as far as most people are concerned.

When Cash tells me I can 'get my body back,' he's demanding I get skinny so I can have value again. So I can be loved. So I can be believed.

"Bye," I say, taking another too-hot sip. The damage has been done; my mouth feels numb and slippery, burned beyond sensation.

* * *

Holly wakes up right as my antidepressant glides easily down my throat with my last sip of tea.

I change her diaper. I feed her. I take her on a walk, far from Laurel Lane. I put her down for a nap. I try to nap myself, without much success. I make lunch. I feed Holly. I change her diaper. I put her down for her second nap. I try to nap again, and again, have no success. I feed Holly. I change her diaper. I make dinner.

Cash drones on at the kitchen counter, Holly wedged in his arms while I do the dishes. "And then Jason, that asswipe, emailed me the brief and it's beyond horrible. I can't send that kind of shit to a client. The dude has zero grasp of basic grammar, which is crazy, because he went to Purdue. Purdue, of all places!" He lifts Holly up, bringing her to his face. "Hols, maybe no Purdue for you. Not if Jason is the kind of graduate they churn out."

There's burned cheese on the bottom of my skillet. My wrist aches with the effort of scrubbing, but no matter how hard I press the brush into the crispy blob, the skillet gets no cleaner. Sweat breaks out on my forehead, and I press harder, harder, harder—

The head of the dish brush snaps off in a shower of white plastic shards. The skillet clatters into the sink along with the remains of the brush, and my shoulders shoot all the way up to my ears, my entire body stiff as I hunch over the mess.

"And get this—Mr. 'I Went to Purdue' signs off his emails with 'Cheers.' The guy is from rural Indiana, not Great Britain. Honestly, it's embarrassing. I wonder if I should tell him that."

The broken end of the dish brush gleams in the light, a series of jagged points sharp enough to draw blood. If I slashed it across my wrists, how long would it take for Cash to notice?

"You know what? I think I will tell him. The guy should know. And I kind of see him as my protégé, in a way. Yeah, he's got a lot to learn, but he's not a bad guy. I shouldn't be so hard on him."

Saliva pools in my mouth, thick and bitter. My body is numb; will it stay that way when the blood starts flowing?

"Sadie?"

My fingers creep toward the dish brush.

"Sadie?"

The handle is firm and cool against my palm.

"Sadie!"

"What?" I snap, the brush dropping back into the sink. "What?"

"I asked you how's day two of the meds?"

I pull in a ragged inhale, forcing my shoulders back down. What was I thinking? If I'm going to hurt myself, I can't do it in front of my baby.

"Fine," I say, finally turning away from the sink to face him. "All good."

"Awesome," Cash says. "So, you ready to give Holly a bath?"

My jaws are locked so tightly together, I'm amazed I can get the words out. "Can't you do it tonight?"

"Aw, sorry babe—I've got to finish up an email for work. I want to put this Jason stuff out of my mind, you know, so I won't be stressed tonight."

My right eye twitches. "Got it," I say.

He stands, lifting Holly above his head and making airplane noises. "Zoom.... zoom... and the Air Force Holly is cleared for landing!" He plops Holly into my arms, my hands still dripping with dirty dishwater. Holly squirms, and Cash plants a kiss on her chubby cheek. He gives me one, too. I wait until he leaves the room before wiping it off on the inside of my shirt.

In the living room, the sounds of Cash's favorite show, *Breaking Bad*, erupt from the TV. It blares throughout Holly's bath, as I change her diaper, as I give her one final nighttime feeding. My rage slowly softens like candle wax, melting into a pool of exhaustion. Is this how the happy pills work, even though it hasn't been that long?

At least the ointment Dr. Tallis prescribed is helping, and the silver nipple cups arrived today. Whether the twinge in my breast as Holly feeds is actually lessening or simply wishful thinking, I can't tell. Not that it matters, anyway.

Holly finishes suckling, and I snap my ugly nursing-accessible tank top back into place. The TV is still echoing throughout the house, even with the closed bedroom door, but mercy of mercies,

Holly falls asleep almost instantly.

I snap off the light, and Tater Tot jumps up onto the bed, curling into a furry ball. I slip between the covers next to him, my body sticky with dried sweat and old milk. Despite my filth, the sensation of lying down is so delicious I almost drool…

Right as I'm about to drift off, there's an explosion from the TV and the sound of Cash hooting in delight. Tater Tot shifts at the foot of the bed, then collapses back with a breathy groan. My eyes pop open, burning with fatigue.

I cover my head with my pillow, pressing my skull into the mattress. My rage is solidifying yet again, lodging in my esophagus, a lump I can't seem to choke down and digest.

What else is there to do? I ignore the old adage. I go to bed angry.

* * *

A rumble splits the air and I jerk awake with a snort. I'm already unsnapping my nursing tank top when I realize the sound isn't a Holly hunger cry.

It's Tater Tot.

The growl is low and guttural, coming from deep in his throat. He sounds like a cross between a broken air conditioner and someone choking to death.

"Shhh," I hiss, as quietly as possible. If he wakes Holly, I'll have to feed her, because that's the only surefire way to get her back to sleep, and it'll throw her schedule completely off, and my breasts badly need a break…

As my vision adjusts to the darkness, I study Tater. His furry hackles are raised, and he's staring at the open doorway leading to the bathroom, an even darker rectangular abyss.

A film of panicky sweat glazes my skin.

A faint light appears, glowing softly from down the hall. It's the motion-detecting nightlight… so it could be Cash back there?

But I don't honestly believe that.

Goosebumps prickle across my arms. The sound conditioner is loud, but it doesn't completely drown out a faint pitter-patter, like a scampering mouse.

Oh God, do we have a rodent problem on top of everything else?

Abruptly, the motion-sensing nightlight snaps off. A primal fear grips me, something possessive and atavistic. I want to leap out of bed and run to Holly's bassinet so I can cover her with my body, protect her.

Protect her from… what, exactly? A mouse?

The pitter-patter comes again. It's fainter, but Tater's growling takes on an even more menacing timbre. If he ratchets it up any more, he's going to wake up Holly, no doubt.

I can't let that happen.

To shut him up, I jump out of bed and rush into the dark hall as quietly as possible.

My eyes roam over what little is illuminated by the thin glow of moonlight.

There's nothing here.

When I tiptoe past the nightlight, it comes to life, illuminating the hallway with a soft glow.

And then I see it.

In the corner between the end of the hallway and the bathroom door, there's a pile of… something. I don't want to move, but my feet bring me closer, closer, until I'm nearly on top of the thing. Squatting down, I can make out every detail.

I wish I couldn't.

Bugs, mostly cockroaches, lie in a heap, some still twitching. A furry piece of some small mammal, coated in something dark—blood?—tops the pile like a heinous crown. The death throes of the insects make the repulsive pyramid shift and creak, like tree branches in a storm.

"No," I say, too terrified to keep my voice down. "No, oh Jesus no."

It's the thing from the woods, the creature with the pointy teeth and bloodstained fingers—it's been in my home, it's been near my sleeping baby, it's left me this pile of suffering as a warning, and I'm not crazy, I'm not—

From the bedroom, Holly starts crying, her hunger howls filling the room, overpowering my panicked thoughts. I rush to her, yank her from her bassinet, and lift her to my nipple, still slick with ointment.

When she's latched, I collapse into my nursing chair, heart pounding. Does the rapid beating of my heart make the milk pump faster? Will Holly choke?

Tater Tot leaps from the bed and creeps toward the bedroom doorway, filling the room with that gravelly growl.

"No," I moan. Holly whimpers, and I look down at my fingers, white from squeezing her too hard. The blood rushes back into my hands with a prickling tingle as I slowly release my grip. Why couldn't this be another one of my nightmares? I can escape nightmares; I can't escape reality.

Well, I can't escape reality and still live my normal life. Reality escapees don't get to be mothers and wives. They become inmates and patients.

Holly finishes with a burp, and I lower her gently back into her bassinet, my arms shaking.

My bed is right there—I could slide back between the covers, put on my sleep mask, cover my head with my pillow, and pretend none of this is happening. My right foot is perched on the mattress, my body aching for rest, when the rustle-crunch of the dying insects overpowers the sound conditioner.

No matter how hard I press my pillow over my ears, I won't be able to drown out that sound.

The wood floor is hard and cold against my bare feet. Tater pads after me, teeth bared. The pile is still there, pulsing and writhing and shifting, shiny insect bodies glinting in the faint moonlight. How do I even go about cleaning this up? The thought of touching any part of that squirming mass makes me gag. Do I get a bucket? A garbage bag? Do we have rubber gloves? If I sweep them up, won't they all get stuck in the broom's bristles?

Tears spring to my eyes. Tater creeps closer, and I have to jerk his collar back to keep him from snapping at the bugs. Then again, what if I let him at it? He'd be much faster at cleaning all that up than I ever would…

Or what if I didn't clean it up at all? I could leave it for Cash to find. Maybe then he'd finally believe me about everything. After all, seeing is believing, right?

Tater Tot edges around me, licking his teeth with a slurp. "No, Tater," I whisper. Tater ignores me, stretching out his neck, his nose quivering wildly, his body coiled to dart forward, and now he's springing—

The motion-detector nightlight flares to life, bathing us in a warm yellow glow. Tater lunges into the corner, hitting the wall with a thud, snapping at the ground, jaws gnashing at…

Nothing.

The corner is empty, the spasming pile gone, as though it never existed at all.

CHAPTER EIGHTEEN

If You Want It Done Right, Do It Yourself

Sleep eludes me for the rest of the night. I lie in bed, staring up at the ceiling, Tater Tot shifting restlessly at my feet. My bladder pulses painfully, but I refuse to leave the room. It's not safe. What if the thing that left that pile of death breaks in again? What if it comes back for me?

Oh, God. What if it comes back for my baby?

When the first hint of daylight filters through the curtains, I have no choice but to get up, or else I'll wet the bed.

I creep to the doorway, dizzy and unsteady on my feet. Tater leaps to the floor and passes by me, his head down. My pelvic floor is still unsettlingly weak, and the weight of my full bladder is agonizing. As quickly and quietly as I can, I close the bedroom door and scramble to the bathroom with my gaze trained ahead of me, barely making it in time to unleash a torrent.

When that's taken care of and I'm no longer in danger of wetting myself, I stumble back into the hall.

The corner where I swear I saw the pile of twitching bugs is still empty.

A bitter taste fills my mouth. Maybe it was all a dream? God knows I've had some vivid nightmares since giving birth—*the trail, the clearing, the tree, the door… and what lives behind it…*

My entire body quakes. What's more likely, though? That I dreamt I saw a pile of half-dead, seizing insects, or that a malevolent, evil little imp from the woods broke into my house, left me that horrible offering, then spirited it away after he was sure I'd seen it?

Then again… something left a dead squirrel in my mailbox. No matter what Cash thinks, I didn't dream that. Is it really so crazy to think whoever—whatever—killed the squirrel also left the bugs? And then took them away to fuck with me?

My open palm connects with my cheek, hard. *Stop it, Sadie. You can't go on like this.*

I slap my other cheek, twice as hard. Of course it was all a crazy dream, and if I don't get a better grip on things, I'm going to have to increase my antidepressant dosage. That's the last thing I want to do. I already feel foggy enough as it is.

There's a crunch near the floor. Tater lays at my feet, jaws working.

"What do you have?" I say. I squat down next to him, my thighs screaming. He gives me the side-eye.

"Give it up, Tater." I wedge my fingers into his mouth and open it wide. When he shakes his head, the object of his interest falls to the ground with a tiny click.

It's light brown, almost the same color as the hardwood floor, and it would have been easy to miss if Tater hadn't snagged it.

It's an insect wing.

Shiny, chitinous, crispy-looking.

Oh, God.

Instead of standing, I fall onto my butt and backpedal away from the corner, from the crunchy roach piece that the thing from the woods left behind, a high keening sound ripping out of my mouth.

"Sadie! What's going on?" Cash kneels beside me, his hands pressed against my shoulders. "Sadie?"

I turn and look into his bright green eyes, threaded through with streaks of red.

"I—there—" I point toward the corner, and Cash's eyes follow my shaking finger.

"What?" he says. "What is it?"

Cash moves to the corner to investigate and I clamp my lips shut, stifling a sob. What can I say? I can't tell him what I saw—or thought I saw—in the middle of the night. He'll tell me I was dreaming, he'll tell me my body is still adjusting to the antidepressants, he'll tell me—

"This?" Cash says. Something crackles in his hand.

"No—don't touch it!" I yell, covering my face.

"Sadie? Sadie!" Cash crouches next to me. "Sadie, open your eyes!"

I ignore him, my body curling into a fetal ball.

"Look!" Cash demands. "It's just a leaf, Sadie!"

My eyes pop open and land on what is, undoubtedly, a dry leaf. "What? No, I saw… it wasn't…"

What's the point? He won't believe I saw a pile of half-dead things in the corner, especially now that he thinks I was reduced to a quivering mess by a leaf, of all things. He didn't believe me about the trail, or the door, or the horrible tree, or the squirrel… and if I tell him about last night, he won't think I'm in danger.

He'll think I'm crazy.

"I had a nightmare," I finally choke out. The worry line between his brows smooths, and he puts his arms around me, dropping the leaf to the floor. His face is close to mine, his sour morning breath filling my nostrils.

"Oh, Sadie, I'm sorry. I've been reading up on it, and apparently vivid dreams are super common in postpartum moms. And they can also be a side effect of antidepressants," he says slowly and meaningfully, like he's speaking to our baby.

He stares at me, smiling. Is he waiting for me to thank him? Should I be impressed that he bothered to do a few halfhearted Google searches that probably started with something along the lines of 'What's wrong with my wife who just had a baby?'

"Yeah," I say, my mouth squished against his shoulder. "You're probably right."

"Of course I am," he says, and now I can taste his breath, and I've never wanted to gargle mouthwash more in my life. "You okay?"

"Yep," I say, lying through my teeth, trying gently to push him away. I'm okay enough to get up, to get dressed, to make him breakfast, to feed Holly, to go about my day, sure. But am I okay enough to sleep at night? To walk outside without anxiety dragging me down like an anchor? To tell the horrible truth to my patronizing husband?

Not in the slightest.

Cash doesn't take the hint; he keeps his arms around me, suffocating me, as though he can squeeze all the madness right out of me with the force of his grip and the stench wafting out of his mouth.

Cash can't protect me, and since he won't believe me about what's actually threatening our family, he can't protect Holly, either.

I'm the only person who truly sees what's going on here, which means I'm the only one who can keep us safe. My body tenses, not from anger or fear, but from resolve.

When he finally lets go and helps me up, I have my plan.

That piece of fairy-tale shit from the woods has invaded my home, threatened my family.

At my sides, my fists squeeze into tight balls. I refuse to be the blubbering mess Cash thinks I am. I refuse to be the easy target this evil troll thinks I am.

Everybody always says a mother can do impossible things when her child is in danger, like lifting a car to free her baby or taking down a man twice her size.

As for me? I'm going to fight an impossible thing.

And I'm going to motherfucking win.

* * *

I wait until Holly's morning nap. Cash is off doing Cash things, which suits my purposes perfectly. I don't want him to try to come with me—if he does, the trail will hide itself, and I won't be able to do what I have to do.

Tater whines as I leave the house. "Not today, buddy," I say. "It's not safe."

He whines again, pawing at the air. "Don't worry. I'll be okay. I need you here to watch over Holly."

Tater snorts and lies back down in his bed.

In the garage, there's a stack of miscellaneous tools in a rusted, ancient toolbox Cash has been toting around with him since college. He fancies himself some sort of fix-it man, the kind of guy who can look at a clogged toilet or a sticky door or a loose shutter and put it to rights with a wave of his tools. In reality, he can barely change a lightbulb, and so the tools and their box remain largely undisturbed—by him.

Me, on the other hand—I'm the one who built the dresser-cum-changing table from IKEA at seven and a half months pregnant, particle board slats spread out in front of me on the floor like giant puzzle pieces, groaning over my unwieldy bump. I'm the one who put some WD-40 on the squeaky door hinges so Tater Tot wouldn't bark every time someone entered or exited the house. I'm the one who stripped, sanded, primed, and re-stained the most gorgeous end table after finding it in a secondhand shop in downtown Savannah.

It was during my refinishing of that end table that I found the hidden compartment in the tool box—and the knife.

I lift the guts of the tool box out and place them on the floor as quietly as possible. My fingers find the secret latch, and the false bottom pops up like a jack-in-the-box, revealing the wicked-looking blade. At the end of its hilt is a ring, and if I hadn't done some Googling the first time I found it, I would have thought it was one half of a scissors.

Instead, I know what this actually is: a SOCP dagger made for self-defense. I dig it out of the box and squeeze it in my hand, my fingers fitting into the grooves on the handle as if this dagger were made specifically for me.

If this thing could gut a mugger, which I believe it absolutely could, then prying off a minuscule fairy door from a dying tree should be child's play.

I sheathe it and tuck it into my waistband, where it creates a narrow bulge. I stride out of the garage, shoulders back, and head for Laurel Lane.

The atmosphere grows hotter and heavier with each step, as though I'm descending into some fetid swamp. By the time I take the right onto Laurel, my scalp is drenched and my armpits have created wings of perspiration so massive they touch in the front.

Dear God, I hope none of the Yoga Moms have chosen this moment for a stroll.

I must look like quite the picture of insanity—sweaty as all get-out, hair a frizzy mess, eyes most likely bloodshot, a scary-ass knife tucked into my shorts. Jesus, I'd probably call 911 if I saw me on the street.

There's one harrowing moment where a car rumbles behind me. I dart to the side of the road, scooting as close to the wall of vegetation as I can without immersing myself in poison ivy. The car, a black Escalade that could very well be the one Mandy drives, comes to a stop at the intersection of Sweetgum and Laurel. I hold my breath, praying she doesn't turn onto Laurel, doesn't see me standing here like a maniac from a slasher film.

When the car continues straight, I finally let myself exhale. That was too close of a call; I need to get a move on.

I cover the last few yards at the fastest scrabbling power walk I can manage, ending up in front of the parted curtain of grapevine, trumpet flower, and Virginia creeper. The leaves drift lazily in the moist breeze, as if beckoning me deeper into the sylvan labyrinth.

Grappling for my knife and pulling it from my waistband, I plunge into the abyss.

Everything is the same. The silence descends like an itchy blanket, the Virginia creeper gives way to tangled snarls of red-stemmed poison ivy, the trail widens into that awful, death-carpeted clearing.

There, directly in front of me, is the evil-looking tree, stunted and horrible. At its base clings the fairy door, moss-covered and decrepit. The sea of small corpses and animal bones is deeper now than it was the last time I was here, as though the evil asshole living here has grown hungrier.

"Oh," I whimper, ice cubes of fear slipping down my spine to cool my rage. What if that thing shows up while I'm here? Or, worse, what if it's lying in wait behind the door, ready to strike at any sign of attack? What if this is all a trap, and this is exactly what it wanted me to do from the beginning? Is this why it filled my head with those nightmares?

My palm is so wet the knife feels impossibly slippery in my grasp. I slide it back into the sheath and wipe both hands on my shirt; since the cotton is already soaked, the drying effect is pretty much nonexistent. I tug the knife back out and grip it even harder, finger curled in the ring at the end of the hilt, willing myself to stop sweating.

You know how your mind can play tricks on you when it's too quiet? You might imagine you hear music from far away, or a basketball being dribbled in the driveway, or the low wail of a hungry baby. There's a name for that type of auditory hallucination—paracusia. I remember reading about it in one of the articles Ron saved for me. The murmur of imagined sound, of something right at the edge of perception, is making my ears itch.

"No," I say aloud, trying to shake myself out of this terror-induced torpor. This is all part of its game. It wants me to be petrified, immobilized. It wants to play with me before it pounces.

"Not today, asshole," I say, and I take a step forward, into the clearing.

Dead bugs and small bones crunch beneath my feet, but I ignore the disgust creeping up the back of my throat. If I'm going to get this done, I need to get my rage back, let the anger boil over and displace the fear.

Scared people make mistakes, but angry people do what needs to be done.

Five steps are all it takes to bring me directly in front of the door. This close, I can make out the individual wisps of Spanish moss on the weathered wood, the white-green bloom of lichen.

I gulp. It needs to be done now. If I wait any longer, I'm going to lose my nerve.

I raise the dagger, squat down, and do what I came here to do.

The first stab of the blade into the door is cathartic, like plunging a steak knife into a particularly juicy and well-cooked piece of meat. I pry it out, the brittle wood giving little resistance, and stab it again. I'm going to get rid of this little portal to hell, right here, right now. I stab and stab, hack away at the glue or hinges or whatever is holding this thing to the tree. My vision blurs, and I become a machine, raising the knife and bringing it down over and over with the repetitive necessity of a factory assembly line. The clunk and thud of the knife breaks the oppressive stillness, and I don't slow down. I keep going, over and over, my shoulder and fingers aching, my wrist vibrating with fatigue. When I eventually stop, not due to a lack of resolve but due to bodily exhaustion, I rock back on my heels and take a look at my handiwork as my left eye twitches in tiny spasmodic jerks.

There are ugly gashes like knots of scar tissue in the door and the surrounding bark of the tree, sure. But other than that, there is zero evidence of my murderous rampage.

The door hasn't budged, not even the tiniest bit.

As I watch, the shallow but splintery slashes from my knife start to bleed a dark, thick pus that oozes from the wood like plague sores.

My scream cleaves the charged atmosphere, echoing around the clearing. My cramping hand can't hold on to the knife anymore, and the ring at the end of the hilt slips off of my finger, the blade falling to the ground. I don't bother to scoop it up; before I fully comprehend what's happening, I'm fleeing that evil place, more drops of salty perspiration streaking down my face like tears, my legs and lungs burning with fatigue.

I don't slow down until I'm turning off of Laurel and back onto my street. Those scratches and pops of sound at the very edge of my auditory range follow me all the way home.

I fling open the door and collapse onto the floor, Tater Tot running over to lick away my sweat.

I think I forgot to take my pill this morning.

CHAPTER NINETEEN

Lost in Reality TV Land

My hands are still shaking but at least my left eye has stopped twitching by the time I lay Holly down on her play mat. I shuffle into the kitchen, filthy and exhausted. It takes three tries before I successfully open my bottle of pills. I pluck one out and squeeze it between my fingers, my sweat turning the chalky outer layer into paste.

Go on, take it, Cash's voice whispers in my head. *Sadie, you need it.*

"I don't need it," I say, even as the pill edges closer to my mouth. This close, its acrid smell burns my nostrils—or is that the scent of my own body?

Take it, Sadie. Do it for Holly. Do it for me. Do it for yourself.

"Why should I?" I hiss. My fingertips tingle from the effort of squeezing the pill. The damned things make me feel foggy and out of touch, and I can't afford to be either if whatever's out there in the woods comes back…

No. I can't think that way. That's the sort of thinking that put me on the pills in the first place, right? If I want to stay off of them, I have to purge all that absurdity from my mind. Right?

There is no fairy in the woods, Sadie, Cash answers. I hope the medication will excise him from my head like diseased tissue. The pill inches closer to my lips, my tongue flicking out to grab it…

The image of the creature's ghoulish face, scowling and miserable and, above all, hungry, explodes in my brain and I recoil, dropping the pill on the floor. I fall against the kitchen counter, heaving, waiting for Cash's voice to pipe up in the recesses of my brain.

He stays silent.

I throw the soggy pill into the trash, cap the bottle, and put it back in the cabinet.

In the living room, Holly scoots around on her play mat, burbling contentedly. Her chubby cheeks jiggle with each movement, and I fight the urge to reach out and pinch them. I read about this phenomenon once—it's called 'cute aggression,' when a creature's unbearable cuteness stimulates the impulse to squeeze or even eat it. Hansel and Gretel must have been absolutely adorable for the fairy-tale witch to go to such great lengths to lure them into her oven. Oh God, is that what the thing in the woods wants to do to my baby?

The forest imp's face flashes in front of my eyes again, and before I can wipe the image from my mind, its dirty little fingers are reaching out, wiggling, searching, grasping…

"Stop!" I yell, startling Holly. Her face scrunches up, readying herself for a cry. I hold my breath, but after a tense moment, she lets out a massive burp instead.

"Excuse you!" I giggle. Holly smiles up at me, and my heart is so full, so unbelievably heavy, I fear it might drop right through my weak pelvic floor.

"You can get through this, Sadie," I whisper. "You need to get your mind right."

I'm strong—barely three months ago, I pushed a whole-ass human out of my body, and I survived.

What happened in the woods did not happen.

I am not crazy.

What happened in the woods did not happen.

I am not crazy.

I repeat these mantras over and over in my head as I watch Holly coo and roll. I'm like the school troublemaker, forced to write 'I will not do bad things' over and over on the chalkboard.

The evil creature's face dances into my field of vision again, and this time it's even closer, dear Jesus—

"No!" I shout, and then I'm fumbling for the TV remote. I need to lose myself in something mindless, to fill my head with images that don't threaten my sanity—something low-stakes and flashy. I turn on the TV, find the trashiest reality show, and burrow deeper into the couch.

The nine women on the screen competing for one loser's love don't hold my interest for long. They're on some sort of group date that involves camping, and there's no escaping the dark trees, the curtains of leaves...

I pull out my phone and navigate to Instagram, letting the TV blather on mindlessly.

There's a photo of my childhood neighbor's goldendoodle, then a shot of my college roommate's massive plate of brunch waffles, smothered in syrupy strawberries, then—

Ugh.

I followed Jessica on Instagram when we first moved here. I thought we'd become friends in real life, and I'd eventually end up making an appearance in her photos. Since that has yet to happen, I've been sort of lurking, seeing what she's up to, trying to understand what makes her tic, who the real Jessica is beneath the blowout and the eyelash extensions. I'm still not sure, to be honest.

Jessica posts pretty much everything—everything that makes her look good, anyway. Fancy dinners she's cooked, date nights with her husband at expensive restaurants, her children in immaculate church clothes, her new manicure.

Oh, and all of her parties with the Yoga Moms.

Of course, this isn't the first time I've come across photos of all of them at a party I wasn't invited to. This isn't even the second time, or the third, or the fourth. Every time I see that group of ten or so hamming it up at one of their stylishly decorated houses, playing Yahtzee or Cards Against Humanity, glasses of wine in hand, I feel diminished, and yet—I keep looking. This digital voyeurism does me no good, but at least right now, it's stopped me from thinking about the woods, about what may or may not live there.

The same old questions cycle through my head. Why don't they invite me? Why aren't I good enough? Are they talking about how much they hate me?

"Stop it, Sadie," I hiss, digging my nails into my thigh. I know these thoughts aren't rational, but how else am I supposed to feel when these women post pictures of things I was deliberately not invited to?

Tater comes up and nudges my leg, moving aside my digging nails. "You know, Tater, they don't need to post all this shit. Those pictures from 'the best night ever' can easily be sent in a group text. Forget about me—I'm sure Grandma Mabel doesn't care about seeing her granddaughter getting drunk over cards that say things like 'Pixelated Bukkake.'" Tater stares at me, big brown eyes luminous. He cocks his head. "No, Tater. They post these photos so everybody else can feel less than. Uncool. Uninteresting." Tater snorts, spraying my leg with snot.

On the TV, Tawny B. is yelling at Matty, telling him he shouldn't have kissed Greta if he wanted to ever touch her double-D's again.

On Instagram, Jessica, Mandy, Tiffany, and the others are all holding up long-stemmed glasses almost full to the brim with scarlet wine, wearing headbands that say 'PARTY HARDY.' All of their Chiclet-like veneers are on full display behind filler-enhanced lips. No frown or smile lines mar a single face. The caption reads, 'Celebrating Heather's birthday in style. Love these ladies so much! #happybirthdayheather #blessed #wineoclock #partyhardy #bestfriendsforlife #mamabesties'

The post is so cringeworthy I want to throw up, but I also want to cry because I was left out. Even though I simply cannot imagine myself in that photo, holding a goblet of wine and smiling like an idiot, I'm still hit with intense and excruciating FOMO—fear of missing out. Besides Kendall, and Ron to some extent, I don't have many real friends here. Imagining all the fun I could be having if I were a different sort of woman, even if it's only half-real, hits me right where it hurts the most.

"Could you turn off the TV if you're not watching it?"

A breathy little scream escapes my throat. I didn't even realize Cash had come into the house, I was so absorbed in hate-scrolling on Jessica's Instagram.

"Sorry. Didn't mean to scare you," Cash says, walking into the living room and plopping down onto the opposite end of the roomy sectional.

"It's okay," I say.

When I don't say anything else, or move to turn off the TV, Cash says, "Did you hear what I said? Maybe we turn off the TV?"

I don't want to turn off the TV; in fact, the combination of mindless background noise and scrolling, even though anxiety and resentment nip at me like two fighting puppies, has formed the kind of heady cocktail I need to shove everything that happened in the woods out of my mind.

"I'm watching that," I say, setting my phone down next to me.

"I thought you were on your phone," he says, and it sounds like an accusation.

"Just checking something," I say, trying to keep my voice level.

"Well, TV is bad for Holly's brain while it's developing, you know. Could you do something else with her?"

My eyebrows skyrocket into my hairline. Did he seriously say that? He has no idea what it's like to hang out with a newborn all day. The unrelenting, brain-cell-killing, personality-sucking, mindless hours of boredom. Yes, she's sweet. Yes, she's so cute it almost makes me angry. Yes, I obviously love her. But is she exciting? Not in the slightest. Why don't more new moms talk about the boredom?

"Like what?" I say, but it's more of a snarl. I can't help it.

"Read her some books?"

"Cash. She's three months old. She can barely see the pictures, much less understand even one of the words." My voice is flat, but that's better than angry. My teeth press together so hard I wonder if they'll explode into sharp shards at any moment.

How dare Cash try to dictate how I spend my time? I'm not thriving here, I'm barely surviving. I am entitled to any coping mechanism I need to get me through the hell of new babyhood, especially when he's not helping. He doesn't know anything about babies, anyway.

"But that doesn't mean we can't start early. You know, with the reading. Didn't you tell me reading to babies is great, no matter how old they are?"

I dimly remember telling him that early in my pregnancy, before I'd been beaten down by exhaustion, nonstop crying, and evil fairies in the goddamned woods.

"Mmm," I grunt.

Cash sighs, opens his mouth, then closes it. Without another word, he scoops Holly up off the play mat—where she was quite content, I might add—and lifts her up high. Before I can say anything, he tosses her lightly into the air and catches her.

I'm off the couch and by his side before Holly's fully back in his grasp. "Cash! Stop! You can't do that!"

He gives me a look like I'm the crazy one, the unreasonable one. "What do you mean? I'm playing with her." Holly giggles. "See? She loves it!"

"Cash, it's not about that—she's only three months old. You can't be so rough with her. You could give her whiplash, or a neck injury, or something!"

Cash presses Holly to his chest and narrows his eyes at me. "Chill, Sadie. Seriously."

"No, you chill, Cash. You can't be throwing a three-month-old baby into the air! She's not big enough for that!"

"You know what? Fine. If you won't even let me play with my own daughter, then I'll go somewhere else."

"Oh, so you're going to punish me by helping even less?" The words are out of my mouth before I can stop them. Oh, God. This is not going to end well.

"Even less? Are you kidding me, Sadie? Do you have any idea how hard I work to provide for this family?"

The anger is rising inside of me again, the tide of rage so high I'm choking on it. "Do you have any idea how hard I work, Cash? I'm bored and exhausted and in constant mental, emotional, and physical pain and you still have the gall to try to tell me what to do?"

Cash splutters, spittle landing on Holly's head. "The pressure is all on me, Sadie! I'm doing all this work to provide for us, financially. We would not be able to live here on the few thousand you bring in every month!"

That stings. "At least you get to clock out! I'm always on the clock, twenty-four seven, and I never get paid for anything I do. Think about that, Cash. Just think about that for a second. You think you'd be happy working all the time with absolutely zero compensation? You think we couldn't live without your salary? Try living without everything I do!"

Cash is still clutching Holly, and she's staring at me, her mouth a perfect O. Cash's face is a ripe tomato, his eyes narrowed with anger and hurt. We're both panting, like animals in heat. We've never fought like this before. I never thought we would.

The TV is still on in the background, and Tawny B. is making out with Matty's best friend Dominic.

Cash finally breaks the fraught atmosphere, his voice soft but cold. "It's like you're a different person."

I sigh, letting some of the furious breath out. All at once, I'm completely worn out, a limp dish towel of a human being. "I'm not a different person," I say. "I don't have the time to sugarcoat everything or stroke your ego like I used to. I'm not focused only on you, not anymore."

"Who are you focused on, then? Your scrolling? Your TV? What were you paying attention to when that chainsaw almost hit Holly?"

Anger animates me once again, my lips twisting and quirking until my teeth are bared. "That was a freak accident, Cash," I say, my voice shaking with the effort of maintaining control. "That was not my fault."

"Are you sure? Well, how does it feel to be blamed for something that was clearly an accident? Like when Holly ate her own shit in the bathtub?"

My mouth falls open. "That was—"

"An accident, yeah? But you blamed me!"

"That was different!"

Holly senses the electricity in the air, and lodges her protest—a high-pitched, ear-splitting wail. Cash thrusts her at me, disgust etched all over his face. "If you're going to play the martyr, then go ahead, take her. Have a good night."

It's only three o'clock, but his threat couldn't be more clear. He's going to punish me by helping even less, after all.

Oh, well. I guess that means I'm off the hook for feeding him dinner.

As the slam of the door echoes throughout the house, I can't help but wonder if marriage is nothing more than a seething undercurrent of growing resentment, flowing into a river of hostility, tumbling into rapids of hatred, culminating in a waterfall of pure odium that dashes both spouses against the rocks over and over and over until they're nothing more than bloody chunks of meat.

CHAPTER TWENTY

It Wants My Baby

A rattly growl invades my dreams after what feels like mere seconds of sweet, deep sleep. For a few terrifying moments, I try to move, to open my eyes, to investigate, but I'm paralyzed. When the spell breaks, I shove the covers off.

Tater Tot is at the foot of the bed, snarling and gnashing his teeth, exactly like the other night.

Dear God, please no. No.

Part of me wants to leap off the bed and go catch this evil little thing from the woods right now, to grab it by the scruff of its neck and hold it up to the searing light and look it right in its nasty, bloodshot eyes, to shake it until all its limbs are broken and it's nothing but a flesh sack of splintered bone.

The other part of me wants to pull the covers back up over my head and burrow deep into the bed until the thing leaves and Tater Tot stops growling and I can pretend none of this is happening at all.

A sharp cracking sound from the hallway makes my decision for me. Tater Tot lets out a single, strangled bark, and if I don't get up and investigate, he's going to wake up Holly.

"Hush," I whisper at Tater, then, before my rational brain can stop me, I head out into the short hall leading to the bathroom.

In the silvery moonlight filtering through the blinds, I don't see it until I'm nearly upon it.

My knife is back.

A 5x7 framed family photograph perches on our console table. Even though I couldn't close the top button of my jeans postpartum, I had insisted that the three of us plus Tater Tot get a professional family photo taken when Holly was seven weeks old. The photoshoot itself was a mess—Holly spit up on my shirt, which meant I had to change into something less flattering, the sky was constantly threatening rain, and Tater Tot kept chasing squirrels. In the final photo, discomfort is plainly evident in the lines etched into my face, and Cash's thin smile is little more than a scowl. Holly, pink-cheeked and plump, looks sleepy. Tater Tot didn't make the final cut. In the end, I spent nine hundred dollars on a terrible photograph and an exasperating experience, but instead of admitting defeat, I framed the photograph and stuck it resolutely on our console table.

The SOCP knife is sticking out of the center of the photo, its tip poking through the glass, positioned squarely between the grimacing face of my husband and the puffy cheeks of my baby. Cracks spiderweb out from the wound, rendering the photo kaleidoscopic.

My entire body goes cold, and terror hardens like a stone deep in my viscera. This can't be happening, it simply can't be happening. I left that knife in the woods, I dropped it after I tried to hack off that door… but that wasn't real, was it? What happened in the woods did not happen!

My fingers, against my will, reach out to touch the ridged handle of the knife, but before they can make contact, I yank them back. The thing in the woods came into my home again, destroyed my picture-perfect family.

My breath is harsh in my lungs, each breath on the verge of a hysterical sob. Oh, Jesus. It wants my family, doesn't it? It wants my baby!

A strange moaning sound fills the hallway, and for a second I'm worried Holly is waking up, but it's not Holly. The moan, panicky and ragged, is coming from my own throat. I press my lips together, trying to get ahold of myself.

"Deep breaths, Sadie. Deep breaths," I whisper.

The words don't help. My breath is rapidly escalating toward hyperventilation, and my vision swims. Like in the woods, faint sounds tinkle at the edge of my hearing, and I whip my head this way and that, trying to understand where they're coming from.

I know I didn't stick a knife in the family picture, of course I didn't. This is evidence, solid, tangible proof that there's a sentient creature who wants to harm me, to harm my family. There's something dangerous out there, but what can I do about it? I tried to go after it, but I only made it angrier.

I should tell someone, but who? My mom? Cash? God, nobody will believe a word I say. They'll think everything I tell them is the result of my out of whack hormones, or, God forbid, postpartum psychosis, then they'll think I'm a threat to my baby, and they'll cart me off to a mental institution and then what will everybody say about me? Will the Yoga Moms say I went crazy? Will they make fun of me at their little book club, call me pathetic and psychotic? Weak and fragile? The kind of dangerous that is pitiable instead of sexy?

No, no. I can't tell anybody. It's not worth it.

I slump to the ground and Tater presses his furry warmth against me. After a minute, my breathing gradually slows down. Standing, I grit my teeth and pluck the knife out of the glass. I bury the ruined picture under crumpled tissues in the bathroom trashcan.

Holly continues to sleep soundly as I shove the SOCP knife under my pillow. I'll be prepared the next time that thing comes to threaten my family.

CHAPTER TWENTY-ONE

What If I Can Only Save One?

When a few fingers of light creep into the room, I pull off the covers, sleeplessness sending spikes of electrical pain through my brain. I shove the knife deeper under my pillow and tiptoe out of the room on trembling legs, gently closing the door behind me.

Thirst claws at me, desperate and frantic. Rivulets run over my chin and down my damp neck as I chug a glass of water, then another. I set the glass in the sink with a clunk and lean over, panting.

What happened last night was an obvious threat, one that only I can defend against. A dizzy spell washes over me and I fall against the counter, steeling myself.

The clouds shift outside, and a watery ray of sunlight illuminates the orange bottle of antidepressants Cash keeps helpfully placing front and center on the kitchen counter.

"Fuck that," I say, grabbing the bottle and shoving it deep into the back of the medicine cabinet.

Seconds later, Cash wanders into the kitchen, rubbing his face and yawning. He drops his balled fists, revealing a pair of bloodshot eyes.

"Good morning," he says slowly, turning it into more of a question than a statement.

"Morning," I mumble. I hope he didn't hear the rattle of the pill bottle—or me talking to myself.

"Did you have a good night?" he asks.

"It was fine," I lie, my hand yearning for the comforting grip of the SOCP knife.

"Good, good," he says. "I slept like dog shit."

The silence stretches between us for far too long before I respond, "Oh. Sorry."

Blood rushes to his cheeks. "Yeah. It's my own fault, though."

"Why?"

He rubs the back of his neck with one palm. "It's nothing."

My teeth find my bottom lip and bite down, hard.

"I'm just gonna… okay then," he finishes, then heads off for the bathroom. Why can't he use the one upstairs? If the toilet flush wakes Holly up, I am going to throttle him, because who has to deal with her then? Not Cash, never Cash. Me. Always me.

Before the tinkling of running water or even a toilet flush breaks the silence, Cash comes striding back into the kitchen with newfound purpose.

"Sadie," he says slowly. "Um, what happened to the picture?"

I force myself to smile, and my left eye twitches. "What picture?"

"You know, the family picture. From the table in the hall."

"What about it?" My teeth find the inside of my cheek and dig in, like I'm chewing a tough steak.

"Um… well, I found it in the trash. The glass is broken."

I release my bruised cheek. "Oh, that, right. It fell. I found it like that."

Cash's red-tinged eyes search my face for the lie. I smile, lips closed, and my left eye twitches again.

"Are you taking your pills?" he finally asks.

"Of course."

He nods, but those searching scarlet orbs, the irises like green bullseyes in the centers, don't leave my face. After a moment, he says quietly, "You can ask me for help, you know."

I cock my head. "Help?"

He shrugs. "Yeah. You know, with Holly. I know you've been under a lot of stress."

I squint. What is he really saying? Does he think I can't take care of my own baby?

"Yeah," I say simply, mirroring his shrug. The two glasses of water slosh around in my stomach.

"Everything okay?"

God, I am so beyond tired of this question. He wants to know if everything's okay? He wants to help? Fine, then.

"Actually, I could use some help. I have at least three loads of laundry to do. Can you take Holly this morning so I can take care of all that? An hour or so, maybe two?"

Cash's handsome face twists into a grimace. "Oh, Sadie, um… this morning's not good."

I grin, my left eyelid fluttering. "It's not? Why?"

He slides his palms over his scratchy stubble. "Dude, I told you I barely got any sleep last night. I'm exhausted."

The smile is still on my face, but my body goes rigid, and I might explode if someone doesn't prick me with a needle soon and let all the boiling-hot air out. "Yeah, you mentioned that. Why?"

His fingers move from his eyes to his forehead, then to his temples. "Don't know," he mumbles, but he won't meet my gaze.

"Mmm," I say. My mind races, thinking of all the times I've done everything for him, for Holly, for everyone, even though I'm tired to the point of sickness. Who said mothers have to be selfless, anyway? Why is that a virtue? After all, if I keep giving away pieces of myself, there's going to be nothing left. Nobody praises fathers for being selfless. No, they get praised for making something of themselves. Mothers get praised for unmaking ourselves. Why can't we incorporate motherhood into our selfhood instead of letting it swallow us whole?

I shake my head and poke at my left eyelid, urging it to be still. It doesn't work.

"I'm sorry, Sadie. Truly," he says, and then he yawns, and it seems so theatrical, so rehearsed, that I stifle a bitter laugh.

I do everything because I have responsibilities, and those can't be ignored for something as trivial as being tired, or feeling cranky, or having a headache. Doesn't Cash get it? Doesn't he understand how things have changed?

Clearly, though, he doesn't get it. The reality has yet to sink in. He's still thinking about taking care of himself first, meanwhile I'm taking care of everybody else, all the time. I bet he's tired because he golfed all day yesterday in the hot sun, or stayed up late playing games on his phone, or something equally self-serving and meaningless.

"Sure you are," I manage to say.

"I love you," he says, but it's more of a plea.

I take a deep breath. "You, too."

If it comes down to it—if we're actually in danger and I could only save one of them, Holly or Cash, who would I save?

Cash would save Cash.

I would save the baby. Of course I'd save the baby.

CHAPTER TWENTY-TWO

A Distant Star in Another Solar System

"Carol keeps sending me these stupid calendar invites for 'weekly huddles,'" Cash says between bites of pasta, the marinara sauce collecting in the corners of his mouth. "It's so annoying. Does she really think I have time to check-in every week? And for a whole hour?" Cash shovels in more pasta, sauce flying off his fork and onto the counter. Does he even taste his dinner? It would be so easy to blend something dangerous into a casserole, or grind something poisonous into a burger. He eats so fast and so mindlessly, he wouldn't even notice a weird flavor or a strange texture.

I shake the thoughts away and focus on my own food. The pasta tastes gummy and acidic on my tongue, but I force it down anyway. I have to eat to keep my breastmilk supply up. I'm not eating for me, not anymore—I'm eating for her. Everything I do is for her.

"Carol also won't shut up about 'rap sessions,' and she uses all this weird business lingo that is at least two decades out of date. I don't understand why James hired her."

"Maybe he's fucking her," I say, mashing a noodle to pulp between my molars.

"Um," Cash says, his gaze darting to Holly, contentedly lying on her back on her play mat. "I doubt it."

"Oh," I swallow another mushy lump of pasta and try not to grimace. Do postpartum hormones mess with your taste buds, too? I wouldn't be surprised.

When I look up, Cash's green eyes, no longer bloodshot, bore into mine. "What?"

"It's just..." He winces. "We shouldn't curse around the baby, right?"

I want to tell him it doesn't fucking matter because she's an infant who can't understand us, but I don't. All I say is, "Yeah, fine."

Cash smiles, then finishes his dinner with a slurpy flourish, making me instantly lose what little appetite I had.

"Thanks for dinner, babe," he says. He scoots his chair back, stands, and stretches, his spine popping like Fourth of July fireworks. "I'm gonna go meet the guys for a quick round. Only nine holes."

He does not put his plate in the sink. He does not offer to change Holly. He does not ask for my permission. He doesn't even wait for my response.

He gives a quick wave and then heads out, humming, pasta sauce still caked around his lips.

I wait until the sound of the golf cart backing up echoes from the driveway before I start wailing. Eventually, Holly joins in.

I leave his dirty plate out on the counter. I hope it attracts every bug in the neighborhood.

* * *

"Then he left. Walked right out the door to go play golf, leaving me with the baby yet again. And it wasn't like he asked me if it was okay. He told me what he was doing, right before he did it. It's like he's completely oblivious to the fact that we have a child, and he can't do whatever he wants, when he wants." I'm pushing Holly's stroller, Tater Tot at my side, my phone on speaker sitting in the stroller's cupholder. Sweetgum Street is deserted, exactly how I like it.

"Did you say anything to him?" my mom asks over the clatter and thud of her making dinner in the background. Cash must be on the third hole by now, unless he's playing with Josh Kramer and Griffin Howser, in which case they're probably still cracking open beers on the first tee box.

"No," I say. "He didn't give me any time. He told me where he was going, then he left."

Mom sighs on the other end of the line. "Men are oblivious, you're right about that. You have to spell things out for them, even if you think it should be obvious. To Cash, he's probably thinking that he has some time, so why not go golfing since you've got the baby and don't have any plans anyway?"

"It's so shitty," I say, putting extra emphasis on the curse word, defying Cash even though he's not around.

"It is shitty," Mom agrees. "But if you want things to change, sweetie, you need to change them. Talk to him."

I reach the end of Sweetgum Street and turn right onto Peach Grove. "What do I even say?" I ask, my voice jumping an octave into a whine.

Pots clank in the background. I'm sure she's making something much more palatable than boxed pasta with sauce from a jar. For a searing, painful moment, I wish I were a kid again, my mom cooking me a delicious homemade meal, something nutritious, tasty, and from-scratch. My sinuses start to burn with unshed tears.

Before she can answer, I blurt, "Ugh, Mom. I get it now. Everything you had to do for me. I don't think I appreciated it enough when I was a kid. How did you even get through it? I'm not even a single mom and I'm struggling so hard I don't know how I'll make it through the end of the day."

The clanking stops. "It was all worth it, sweetie. A million times over."

My hands ache from gripping the stroller so hard, and I exhale slowly as I flex my fingers.

"You'll get through this, no matter what. But it'll be a hell of a lot easier if you tell Cash the truth," she says.

"The truth? That I'm bored and lonely and wish he would be around to help more without me having to spell everything out all the time?"

"Yes," she says firmly. "That's what you tell him." She sighs. "He's not your enemy, sweetie. He's your husband. He loves you. He wants to be with you. He just doesn't understand what you need, and even though you think it's obvious, if you don't tell him then he'll never know, and he'll never change."

Now it's my turn to sigh. The conversation she's describing sounds so mentally exhausting, I can barely imagine myself having it. "Right," I say.

"Is the medication helping?" she asks.

"Sure," I say, guilt settling in my stomach at the lie.

"Good," she says. "Things will get better. I promise."

"I hope so," I say, instinctively doing a one-eighty with the stroller before coming to Laurel Lane. I'm not going down that road again, figuratively or literally. Tater Tot pads softly beside me, head swiveling in all directions.

"It will," she says, and the clanking of pots resumes. "Listen, sweetie—I've got to go. Dinner's almost ready. I love you, okay?"

"I love you, too," I say. At least that's not a lie.

* * *

"Jessica posted another photo from that party last weekend," Kendall says, wrapping a length of red twine around a cardboard letter 'K.'

"Yeah, I saw," I say, winding spangled white yarn around a cardboard 'H' for Holly. I've already done S and C, then T for Tater Tot. Kendall saw this tutorial for Christmas ornament letters on Instagram, and it seemed easy enough that even we could master it. So far, my letters look more like a child's amateur alphabet project than any sort of art, but whatever.

"Did you hear anything about it?" Kendall asks, tying a knot and holding the K at arms' length, scrutinizing her handiwork. Hers looks better than mine; then again, she's spent the past hour of our crafternoon on a single letter, while I've cranked out nearly four of them.

"Not much," I say. "It was for Mandy's dog's birthday or something stupid like that, right?"

Kendall laughs. "Worse. I think it was for Mandy's god-dog's birthday."

"What the hell is a god-dog?"

Kendall laughs again, harder. "I think it's like… a godchild but a dog? Like, if the dog's owner dies, the dog will go to Mandy?"

"Okay… but who is the god-dog's owner?" I'm laughing now, too, and it makes my entire body tingle.

Kendall shrugs, and she's now laughing so hard tears are sliding down her face and pooling in the corners of her mouth. "Oh, my God, I think it's Mrs. Essner."

"Nancy? Um… why would Nancy name Mandy her dog's godparent? And, more importantly, was Nancy invited to the party?"

Kendall pants, trying to catch her breath. "I don't think so!"

"There are too many questions!" I yell, then grimace, hoping I didn't wake Holly sleeping in the room down the hall.

"So many questions!" Kendall agrees.

My ribs hurt, but I relish this kind of pain. When we're both able to breathe properly again, I say, "Okay, let me get this straight. The Yoga Moms threw a party. For Mandy's god-dog. Who is Nancy Essner's actual dog. But they didn't invite Nancy."

Kendall wipes tears from her cheeks. "I think that's right."

"Was the dog even there?"

This question sends Kendall into a fit of fresh giggles, and soon I'm joining in again, too. The laughter is therapeutic, cleansing—instead of staring through the small square of an Instagram photo into a party like a digital peeping Tom, I can laugh at the absurdity with my best friend.

In this moment, I'm not thinking about how often I see myself through the Yoga Moms' distorted lens, how often I imagine peering out from between their eyelash extensions and finding myself inevitably coming up short. I mean, Jesus Christ, I still have my natural, stubby eyelashes and my nails are never painted, much less garnished with clickety-clackety acrylics.

"This neighborhood is going to hell," Kendall says, her breath hitching. "First Yoga Moms, now goddamned god-dog birthday parties."

"Ridiculous," I agree, trying to ignore the twinge of hurt at not being invited to the stupid event, even though I can't truly picture myself there, eating bone-shaped cupcakes and singing happy birthday to Nancy Essner's schnauzer, surrounded by moms in matching skirt sets getting day-drunk.

My left eye flutters. As I finish my 'H' for Holly, Kendall finishes her painstaking 'K,' and then it's nearly time for Holly's afternoon breastfeeding.

"Anyway, Nancy better keep a tight leash on that schnauzer of hers," Kendall says.

"Why?"

"You didn't hear?"

"Hear about what?"

"Oh my God, I can't believe we haven't discussed this already," Kendall says. "Apparently, Rich Sawyer's cocker spaniel was killed by an alligator last week."

"What?" I gasp, clapping a hand to my mouth.

"Yeah," Kendall says, nodding gravely. "Rich let the dog out to pee early in the morning, when it was still dark, and when the dog didn't come in after a while, he went outside with a flashlight, and…"

"And what?"

"And he found the dog in the middle of that little pond behind his house."

I squint. "Maybe it drowned?"

Kendall frowns. "It was in pieces, Sadie."

"Jesus!" I say.

"Definitely an alligator," she says. "Nothing else could do that."

"That's horrible," I say.

"Yeah," Kendall agrees. "Rich is completely torn up about it. I know Tater's much bigger than that cocker spaniel, but definitely stay vigilant if he's near the water."

"I will," I say, mentally tallying all the weird things that have happened lately. Too many, that's for sure. Besides the fairy—obviously—there's been the dead squirrel, the chainsaw, and now this gruesome alligator attack…

"You okay?" Kendall asks as she gathers her craft supplies. "I mean, for real?"

There's that question again, but this time, it doesn't bother me as much. When Cash asks it, it's a warning—'You have to be okay, you have no choice.' When Kendall asks it, I can tell she genuinely wants to know if I need anything, if there's any way she can help. Even though my mouth wants to form the words 'Actually, no—I'm pretty sure there's a carnivorous woodland fairy sneaking into my house and threatening me at night, and I've stopped taking my antidepressants and I think I might be going crazy,' I keep my true feelings to myself. Instead, I hear myself say, "Yeah. For real."

I don't know when I became such a liar. Was it when I got married, and I had to pretend I loved cooking for my husband, day in and day out with no relief? Was it when I got pregnant, and I had to pretend I was overjoyed to be a mother instead of terrified of the changes happening to my body? Was it when I became a mother, and I shifted irrevocably from the center of my own universe to a distant star in another solar system?

Kendall stands up and hugs me. "You know you can ask me for help, right?"

Again, so similar to Cash, and yet so different. I know she means it.

"Yeah," I say. "I know."

Kendall gives my shoulders a squeeze, then lets herself out. I stand at the window, watching her retreating golf cart, her clubs jangling in the back, until Holly's hunger cries echo from the back bedroom.

That night, I clutch the knife under my pillow, my ears itching to hear even the slightest growl from Tater Tot. I'm ready for a fight.

Nothing happens, and in the darkest, loneliest depths of the night, I wonder, hopefully, desperately, if this could be the beginning of the good times, at last.

CHAPTER TWENTY-THREE

The Widowmaker

"Christ, Holly," Cash says, his voice bellowing out from the back bedroom into the kitchen. "What have you been eating?"

I laugh, nearly choking on my yogurt. To Cash's credit, he doesn't call out this time and ask me to come help with Holly's diaper change. Could it be possible that he's finally understanding what I need from him? I swallow my last spoonful of yogurt as Cash emerges with Holly, a look of disgust on his face.

"That is truly awful," he says, nose wrinkled.

"I don't know," I say. "I've gotten used to it. Breastmilk poops aren't that bad, anyway. They kind of smell like milkshakes."

"Sick," Cash says, frowning even harder.

"Just wait until she starts eating real food."

"Ugh." He turns Holly to face him. "You're a stinky girl, aren't you?"

Holly responds with a burbly burp, which launches a jet of milky spit-up onto Cash's clean shirt.

"Argh!" Cash screams, nearly dropping Holly.

Laughter grips me, deep in my belly, and I double over. "Oh my God. She got you good."

"Yuck." He rips a paper towel from the roll and dabs at his shirt.

"Won't be doing that again," he mumbles.

While he's distracted, I rush into the bathroom to give my teeth a better brush than they've had in months, comb the knots out of my hair, and put on some mascara and blush. When I look in the mirror, I look a bit more like the person I was before motherhood broke the solid core of my self-identity and replaced it with a gooey infant.

"Sadie?" Cash calls from the living room. "You almost done in there?"

"Yep!" I holler back, pulling on a pair of only slightly stretched-out leggings and a short-sleeved pink top. My stomach jiggles, and I yank the leggings up higher. My belly button looks like a collapsed eye socket, wrinkled and cavernous and droopy. My bikini-wearing days are over, that's for sure.

What would you give to have it all back? Your mind, your time, your body?

I recoil. Where did that come from?

"Sadie?"

"Coming!" I lace up my tennis shoes, my fingers clumsy and slow.

Back in the living room, Cash sits on the couch, scrolling on his phone. When I come in, he looks up and gives me an approving smile.

"You look nice," he says. "Like your old self."

I know this is a compliment, but it makes me bristle instead of beam. Is it impossible for me to look nice as my new self, this self that is a mother? This self that has gone through a serious trauma, no matter how quotidian it might be? This self that provides one hundred percent of the nutrition another human needs to survive and thrive?

"Thanks," I say. He's already turned back to his phone, so he doesn't notice the sour grimace on my face, my lips pulled a bit too tightly over my teeth. Am I too young to get lip filler like Jessica?

"What are you going to do with Holly today?" he asks, attention still glued to his screen.

"What I do every day," I say, shrugging.

"And what's that?" Still with the scrolling. Is it too much for me to ask him to look at me while he's talking to me? Would he even notice if I remained silent until he had the common decency to look up and engage with me the right way? For God's sake, he was on my case not that long ago about my own phone usage.

I clamp my lips shut and stare at him. The seconds tick by, one, two, three, four, five, six, seven… when I get to fifteen in my head, he looks up at last, as if startled out of a trance. "What's up?" he asks, those green eyes glazed.

"Oh, you know," I say, shrugging, frankly amazed at his ability to ignore simple social cues. Was he always like this? Would I have married him if he were?

"Sounds good," he says, but his attention has already wandered back to his phone. On the ground, Holly hiccups, the precursor to crying.

Tater Tot rushes to the front door, ready to get a move on. I round up the baby and the dog and exit the house. Cash doesn't notice until we're outside and the door is an inch from closing. "Bye, girls!" he calls.

I don't bother saying goodbye back.

* * *

The air is a bit less humid today, the temperature a touch cooler. I can tell Jessica has taken this into account as she walks toward me. Instead of bike shorts and a matching crop top, she's wearing ankle-length leggings and a short-sleeve shirt, her taut belly rippling with every step. The outfit is traffic-cone orange, and on anybody else, it would be preposterous, but on her, it looks sleek and stylish, fun and flirty. It makes her look like the kind of person whose approval you desperately crave, but you try to hide that craving just as desperately because you don't want to look like a try-hard loser.

Rosie the Shih Tzu isn't with Jessica today, so Tater Tot runs up and sniffs a human butt instead of a dog butt. Jessica chuckles uncomfortably and pushes Tater's nose away.

"Sorry about that," I say as I get closer, the stroller crunching over loose chips of gravel. "He's been cooped up for a while. I think he forgot his manners."

"Don't worry about it," Jessica says brightly, but there's still a faint hint of distaste evident in the twist of her lipsticked mouth.

I bring the stroller to a stop next to her, my heart beating fast. Thank God I put on makeup today. "How have you been?" I ask, at the same time she says, "How's the baby?"

We both chortle, then Jessica bends over to take a look at Holly in her stroller. My shoulders relax when Holly coos adorably and bats her eyelashes.

"She's so sweet," Jessica says, gently probing Holly's toe with her orange-shellacked nail. God, even her nails match her outfit.

"She's a pretty easy baby," I say. "I got lucky."

"You sure did," Jessica says. She shifts her attention from Holly to me, her eyes lingering on my face for a beat longer than usual. She's probably surprised to come across me looking put together for once.

"How've you been?" I repeat.

"Great," she says, still studying me. "I love your blush. What is it? Clinique?"

"Oh, thanks," I say. Then, a bit sheepishly, "It's NARS. Orgasm."

"Oh, my God, I love Orgasm!" she squeals, and I wonder what a passerby would think of this conversation, someone older like Nancy Essner. Would they think we were swapping sex tips?

"Really?" I blush, deepening the color of the Orgasm.

"Oh, totally," she says. "I like to play with my look, so I'm constantly switching brands, but I should go back to NARS. It looks fantastic on you. Love the little hint of glitter." She puts her hand casually on my arm, and a frisson of electricity rips through my body.

"Thank you!" I say, too quickly. Calm down, Sadie. Is this all it takes to get this sort of response from a Yoga Mom? A bit of mascara, some blush, a comb through the hair? Do I look enough like one of them now to be treated like a human being instead of an obstacle to move past as quickly as possible?

"Say," Jessica says, withdrawing her hand and moving it to her chin, which she taps with one neon fingernail. The style, long and pointy, is stylish but wildly impractical. How does she wipe her butt with nails like that? Maybe she has someone to do it for her. I bite the inside of my cheek to keep from laughing. "Some of the other neighborhood moms and I are getting together tonight. Just a casual thing, some wine, some snacks, you know how it is. You should come!"

The laugh dies in my throat, and my lungs refuse to expand. Am I actually getting invited to a coveted Yoga Moms gathering? Will they judge me if I don't drink? Does Jessica legitimately think I 'know how it is,' when I absolutely, completely do not? What in the world will I wear?

"Wow." I suck in a ragged breath and manage to stammer, "That would be great!"

"Awesome," she says, flashing her Chiclet-size veneers, so white they're almost as blinding as her neon orange outfit. "It's at Mandy's house. You know where it is, right?"

"Sure," I say, my body fizzing like a shaken soda. Everybody knows Jessica is the alpha. If I'm in with Jessica, then I'm in with them all.

"Great! It's going to be so fun! You need a night out, mama," she says, still smiling. It's a bit unnerving, that smile with all those teeth, like an uncannily realistic dental dummy.

I don't even cringe when she calls me 'mama.' Instead, I blurt, "Should I bring anything? What's the dress code?"

"No need to bring anything, only yourself. And it's casual, don't stress!"

I want to ask for more clarification—is what I'm currently wearing okay, or is this a sexy pajama thing, or are we wearing cute sundresses?—but I don't want to risk telegraphing my uncoolness. Now that I've secured an invite, I can't risk blowing it by asking too many stupid questions. It's a girls' night, after all. Shouldn't I know how to dress for a girls' night?

I'm floating on a cloud of bliss, scented by Jessica's floral perfume, and then I remember: Holly. Oh no.

"Oh," I say, more to myself than Jessica.

"What is it?"

"Oh, nothing," I say, waving my hand and smiling. "I'll have to leave Holly with Cash. It'll be fine."

Jessica squints, then nods. "Oh, that's right," she says. "I keep forgetting you don't have a night nurse. I was able to have lots of me-time after Chesley was born thanks to Irma. Henry was totally useless with the baby, but Irma was a godsend."

"Right."

"He'll be fine," Jessica says, waving her hand as if this declaration will make it so. "He's a smart guy, right?"

"Yeah," I say, without a ton of conviction. How often have I had to tell him where the diapers are, or help him locate a clean onesie, or instruct him how to hold Holly so he's properly supporting her head? A pit of anxiety opens up in my stomach, but I try to drown it with a Jessica-inspired wave of my hand. It doesn't quite work.

"Well, see you tonight! Around seven o'clock, okay?" She brushes past me without waiting for my response. I look around for Rosie before remembering she must have stayed at home today.

Rich Sawyer's cocker spaniel was bigger than Jessica's Rosie… Someone needs to warn her. No doubt she'll be grateful.

"Wait!" I call out. Jessica turns around, one perfectly shaped eyebrow cocked.

"Yeah?"

"Um, is Rosie okay?" I say. God forbid Rosie has already gone the way of Rich's dog.

"Why?" Jessica says sharply, eyes narrowing.

"Oh, I didn't mean to… she's usually with you, is all." My mouth floods with saliva and I gulp it down.

"Right," Jessica says, biting her lip. "She's… she's at the beauty shop."

"Oh, good," I say. "I wanted to tell you, in case you hadn't heard… you know Rich Sawyer? Lives over on Magnolia Road?"

"Sure, I know Rich," she says, her lips pursed.

"Well, his dog was killed by an alligator last week," I say, waiting for a gasp, or a 'Seriously?', or even something that could be taken for surprise on her Botoxed face.

She waits a beat, then says, "Yes, I heard about that. Awful. So… awful."

"Yeah," I say. "I figured, since Rosie is pretty small, you know, be careful."

"Sure," Jessica says. "I'll see you tonight, Sadie." Without another word or even a smile, she trots away, her toned legs flexing under the expensive fabric of her leggings.

"Sounds good!" I call after her, trying to do the mental calisthenics in my head. If I need to be at the party by seven, I'll have to shift Holly's night feeding to 6:30, which will mean I'll have to shift her afternoon naps and feedings a half-hour earlier, and I'll have to tell Cash how to put her down, and what to do if she wakes up, and and and…

And nothing! This is something normal, something doable. I get moving again, Tater Tot at my side. In the warm light of day, with Jessica's—and by extension, the entirety of the Yoga Moms—incipient approval, I wonder yet again if everything with the stupid fairy and the woods and the tree and the broken baby monitor and the knife in the picture and the pile of dead bugs in the corner was all a bad dream. Hormones can do crazy things, can make you question what is real, right? But here's something I know with certainty: the Yoga Moms are real. This party tonight is real.

Up ahead, there's a branch I've never noticed before hanging precariously over Sweetgum Street. A stiff wind would probably send it plummeting into the road. There's a name for branches like that—they're called widowmakers. A horrendous epithet, and somewhat misogynistic, too. Perhaps 'widower-maker' doesn't have the same ring to it?

I trot under the threatening branch, thick as Tater Tot around the middle, splintery twigs sticking off at all angles, dead leaves clinging to the rotten bark like leeches. How long would it take for someone to find me if that branch came hurtling down, crushing me? Would Cash be devastated by my death, or elated at Holly's survival? How many people get taken out by freak tree limb accidents per year?

Overhead, the widowmaker creaks, the sound like a door opening on rusted hinges. Instinct seizes control of my body and I surge forward, yelling for Tater Tot. My little parade is barely five feet beyond the tree when the widowmaker comes crashing down, screaming through the air like an arboreal banshee, hitting the road with a resounding thud that sends splinters and crisped leaves flying through the air.

"Jesus H. Christ!" a familiar voice booms, and I spin around wildly to find Ron's golf cart screeching to a stop beside me.

My body sags, spent adrenaline turning sour on my tongue.

Ron whistles. "If that had hit you, you'd be a goner."

I open my mouth, but nothing comes out. I look back at the destruction, and that's when I spot something strange. On the decapitated remains of the tree trunk, hack marks scar the wood, as though someone had tried to remove the branch but lost steam halfway through. Or… as though someone were orchestrating an accident.

"I keep running into you at the worst time, Sadie." Ron studies the branch, too, but I don't know if he sees what I'm seeing. He shifts his focus to me, my chest still heaving with panic. "Or is it the best time? Come on, I'll take y'all home."

We board Ron's golf cart the same as before, when he found me after the chainsaw incident. One accident can be ignored, but two?

And what about Rich Sawyer's dog? Was that really an accident?

God, was there any alligator involved at all?

Echoing my thoughts, Ron says, "Lots of strange things happening around here, eh?"

"Yeah," I choke out, clutching Holly's car seat.

"Rich Sawyer's dog, now that was sad," he says.

"Horrible."

"And then that boy going after that other pooch…"

"Huh?"

"Scuttlebutt is a kid around here tried to drown some fluffy little thing the other day. Tate McClain saw the kid and the dog in the fountain over on Lantana Ave. He yelled and the kid ran away."

My stomach roils. "Was it a Shih Tzu?"

Ron shrugs. "Could have been. Tate didn't say."

Why would Jessica lie to me? My head starts to pound in time with my aching guts.

"You keep a close eye on Mr. Tater Tot. Dogs around here are having a rough go of it lately."

I put one arm around Tater's neck. "Is it always like this?"

Ron chuckles. "Agua Roja's never dull, that's for sure."

CHAPTER TWENTY-FOUR

Girls' Night

"But what if Holly wakes up? What if she gets hungry?" Cash says, looking for any excuse to keep me home.

"She won't. Even if she did wake up, I wouldn't feed her right away—it would mess with the whole schedule."

"But if she does wake up… what do I do?"

I glare at him. "You're not an idiot, Cash. Comfort her, hold her a bit, check her diaper, then put her back down. It's not that hard."

Cash frowns, sulky. "What if she has a blowout?"

"What if she does? You have two hands, same as me. You can change it. You did a fine job this morning."

"But I don't know where the extra sheets are!"

"The drawer next to the bed."

"Or the onesies!"

"Also the drawer next to the bed." I finish changing Holly and snap her onesie back into place.

"How late are you going to be out? I have an early meeting tomorrow and I don't want to be tired."

I want to scream. I want to rip my hair out at the roots and shove it down his throat. "Not that late, Cash. Come on. I haven't done anything like this since before Holly was born, and even before then, I didn't go out much. Is it really that much to ask for you to be on duty for a couple of hours so I can feel like a human being again?" I pick Holly up and transfer her to the bassinet. Her little mouth puffs out in a pout, but tiredness overcomes her, and she lays down on the thin baby-safe mattress with nothing more than a tiny, adorable sigh.

He drops his gaze, shame contorting his perfect features. "Wow, Sadie," he says. I expect him to follow this up with some sort of understanding speech about how he had no idea how much I was hurting, and how sorry he is, and how he'll do better in the future so that I don't have to be a soulless, sucked-dry husk of a person. "I didn't realize being a mom was something you hated so much."

"Christ, Cash," I say. Cash trails behind me like a lost puppy as I walk out of the room. My fingers find their way into my hair, scratching my scalp, pulling at the tender roots. The postpartum hair loss that my doctor assures me is entirely normal has kicked in, and it's not difficult to pull clumps of ragged strands from my head. "I don't hate being a mom. I hate not being anything more than a mom."

"What do you mean? You're not just a mom." We're in the kitchen now, the quartz island an unfathomable gulf between us.

Cash doesn't get it. He truly doesn't understand, can't even recognize or comprehend the profound transformation I've undergone. His life has been changed, sure, but he hasn't. His essential personhood, his identity, his entire sense of himself as an independent actor in control of his life has remained the same. Meanwhile, I've metamorphosed into something different, more primal, more feral. Is it any wonder we have trouble communicating now?

Instead of responding, I shrug.

Instead of apologizing, or groveling, or anything else more appropriate, Cash says, "So, like, what? An hour?"

"An hour what?"

"You'll be gone like an hour, you think?"

I drop a clump of hair onto the floor. I hope he slips on it like a banana peel in an old slapstick comedy routine. "No. More like two, maybe two and a half if I'm having fun."

Cash's mouth twists. "I hope it's more like two."

"You don't want me to have fun?"

"Of course I want you to have fun," he says through gritted teeth, and now I know for sure I'm not the only one who tells lies in this marriage.

"Sure. Well, I'm going to get dressed, and then I'm leaving. I'm only going across the neighborhood."

"It feels so far away," Cash whines.

"Cash. You are a grown ass man. You are a father. You can handle two and a half hours with a sleeping baby."

He looks down at the floor. If he notices the dark blond clump of my hair, he doesn't acknowledge it. I wish he would; I'd love to explain to him how taking over my body, sucking me dry daily, interrupting my sleep, and aging me prematurely isn't enough. The baby is also making my hair fall out in greasy, tangled clumps, and there's not a damn thing I can do about it.

I leave Cash grumbling in the kitchen and head into my bathroom to freshen up my minimal makeup. It's 6:45, and it takes five minutes to get to Mandy's, so I've got ten minutes to pick out something that makes me look like I belong.

I change outfits four times, finally ending up in a black shift dress and sandals. The material pulls a bit at my bloated waist, but it's not horrible. With any luck, the moms are tipsy enough to ignore my lack of style. I may look like a wallflower, but at least I don't look like a pariah.

I hope.

* * *

There's already a line of cars—Escalades, Navigators, a Lexus here and there, a veritable showcase of snazzy mom cars—outside of Mandy's house. The dashboard clock on my Subaru reads 7:02. Sweat threatens to erupt in my armpits. Did Jessica purposely tell me to come later, or is everybody else extremely punctual?

"Stop," I tell myself, pulling to a halt behind a silver Lexus, a sticker on the back windshield proudly proclaiming, 'Mom of an Honor Roll Student at Macready Elementary.' That's great and all, but is this worth broadcasting? Isn't it enough to have perfect bodies, perfect homes, and perfect husbands—do they need to tell the world about their perfect kids, too?

"Stop," I repeat.

I take a deep breath and roll my shoulders back. I want to study the Yoga Moms in their natural habitat, not through filtered Instagram photos. I need to know: are they actually having fun, or are they pretending to have fun for the likes?

I fan my armpits with a takeout menu from the passenger seat. I send up a silent prayer—*Please, whoever's up there, let me look like I belong!*

It's 7:04 by the time I work up the courage to turn off the engine and get out of the car. Pink-orange lantana flowers tickle my ankles as I walk along the narrow stone path to Mandy's front door. I've passed by her house countless times on my walks, always intimidated by the double layer of front porches and the large, shuttered windows that look like scrutinizing eyes.

"Pull it together," I mutter, trying to channel the woman I was before I had Holly, before we moved here, before I met Cash, even. I used to be the kind of person who could walk into a room full of people I didn't know and strike up a conversation, join a group, make a few jokes, liven things up. I used to be completely unafraid of improvised social interaction with strangers.

Now, here I am, about to join a party I've been invited to with people I already know, and I'm perspiring like I'm in a sauna.

I run my index fingers under my eyes to wipe away any stray mascara crumbles or melted eyeliner. They need to see me at my best, to believe that I belong here, that my invitation wasn't a pity gesture or a mistake.

I pause at the front door. Am I supposed to knock? Do I ring the doorbell? The sound of tipsy laughter rolls out into the night. Should I just go in?

I settle for a knock.

There's a few seconds of delay, during which I seriously consider turning around, running back to my car, cowering in the front seat, then driving away once the door closes again. Instead, I hold my ground, like a competent, secure adult.

When the door opens, I'm greeted by Jessica's Chiclet smile. She's overlined her lips, giving her a slightly clownish appearance that instantly puts me at ease. She may act like this is her house, her party, but she looks more circus performer than Kim Kardashian. I examine her body—she's cloaked in a pink sundress, strappy and revealing. It looks like too much for a girls' night, but what do I know? At least I'm wearing a dress, too.

"Sadie!" she squeals, hitting me with a wave of alcohol breath. Jesus, when did they start drinking? Were they all pregaming together before this? Do moms in their thirties and forties even still pregame?

"Hey," I say, shifting from foot to foot like I have to pee. Behind Jessica, there's a circle of Yoga Moms draped over Mandy's white couches, slouched in her white armchairs, sprawled across her white rug. It's a bold choice to decorate your living room with only white when you have children. I can't even keep my wood floor looking clean, and wood will hide pretty much anything.

"I'm so glad you came!" Jessica says, wrapping me in a sloppy hug. She's not wearing a bra, and her hard-as-rocks breast implants press painfully into my sternum.

"Me, too," I eke out, pushing her mane of brown hair out of my face.

When she pulls back, bleary-eyed, she grabs my wrist. "Well, don't just stand there! Come on in!" She yanks me inside, and I nearly trip on the door frame.

Jessica wastes no time. She pulls me further into the house, to the circle of Yoga Moms reclining around the living room like they're part of some suburban bacchanal. They're all dressed similarly to Jessica, a rainbow of candy-colored sundresses.

"Ladies!" she commands, commanding everyone's attention. "I think you all know Sadie?"

From the floor, Mandy raises her glass of what looks like white wine. "Welcome!"

Tiffany, reclining on a plush couch, nods with approval. "Hey!"

A woman I've studied in every one of Jessica's party Instagram posts, who I'm fairly certain is Heather, pipes up from within the cozy cave of a deep armchair, "Sadie! It's so good to see you!" I wonder, with not a little bit of scorn, how often she sees her kid in juvie.

"It's about time, right, ladies?" Jessica asks, and I'm not sure if she's taking a dig at my tardiness or welcoming me into the fold.

Relief and unease battle in the pit of my stomach. The whole scene is off-putting. Besides the occasional waves and how-are-yous, I've never spoken to most of these women at any length, much less any depth. Why are they being so nice?

"Come, what can I get you?" Jessica says, tightening her grip on my wrist once again. "We have white wine, red wine, rosé… you name it!"

Ah. Now I get it.

All of this—the niceties, the enthusiasm, the friendliness—it's the alcohol. Every single one of them is gripping a glass of something white, red, or pink. From the thick, smudgy lipstick marks lining the rims, I'm guessing none of them are on their first glass, either.

Jessica is staring at me, eyes wide, waiting for an answer.

"Oh. Um. I can't drink, actually." Clocking Jessica's blank, uncomprehending look—or is that the Botox making her look like an expressionless mannequin?—I gesture to my inflated boobs. "Breastfeeding."

"Oh," Jessica says, her voice a few octaves lower. "Right. I forgot."

"You can always pump and dump!" Mandy shouts, taking another slug from her glass.

"Oh God, I did that all the time after Trayson," a woman I think is named Matilda slurs.

"Me, too, after the twins," a brunette with obvious eyelash extensions adds. She tips back her glass of red wine and downs the contents in one gulp.

"Oh," I say, trying to direct my voice at Jessica only. "I've never pumped. I just, you know, breastfeed."

Jessica lets go of my wrist. "Okay. No worries. Water, then?"

I nod, and Jessica runs off to the kitchen to get me a glass. The group is looking at me again, some of them frowning, as though they can't fathom a mom who doesn't drink, even though it's for a very legitimate reason.

The silence stretches on, growing more and more uncomfortable, until Jessica gets back from the kitchen and shoves a glass of water into my hands. Ice cubes clink, and the sound puts me even more on edge.

I'm so happy when Tiffany breaks the silence that I could hug her. "Did you guys see the huge tree that fell?"

Jessica tilts her head toward the pile of ladies, gesturing at me to make myself comfortable. She doesn't grip my arm again, and I'm not sure if I should be grateful or concerned. Has some magic spell been broken? Has my failure to accept a drink confirmed her suspicions that I'm not one of them? Oh God, I should have accepted a glass. I could have held it all night, pretended to sip. They're all so drunk, no one would even have noticed.

Jessica takes a central spot on the couch, between Matilda and a woman with a face the color of a ripe strawberry. She catches me staring, and mutters, "I had a chemical peel this morning."

I nod, gingerly taking a place on the white plush rug next to Mandy, trying to wrangle my legs into a ladylike position. My stomach bulges against the stiff fabric of my dress.

"Yeah, I saw it," Matilda says, taking another sip. "That was a huge branch, plunked right in the middle of the street."

"Where was it?" Heather asks.

"Over on Sweetgum," Tiffany says, and my heart rate accelerates.

"Oh, I saw that," I add, taking a nervous sip of my water. It's too cold, and it hurts my throat when I swallow.

"Maintenance has got to do something about that," Jessica says, and all the ladies nod like bobbleheads. "That could have hurt someone."

"Actually, it almost fell on me," I say, and the entire group turns to look at me in unison, as though they share a hive mind. It's eerie.

"Seriously?" Tiffany asks.

"Yeah," I say. "I was out walking, and I heard this creaking sound, and I had this sense that something bad was going to happen… so I ran ahead, and the tree came crashing down right behind me."

Next to me, Mandy looks stricken. "Oh my," she breathes, expelling a cloud of wine-scented breath. "That's terrifying."

"Yeah," I say, nodding solemnly. This semi-near-death experience might be the most interesting bit of conversation I have for this group. I've already slipped up by not drinking; maybe I can salvage the evening with a good story.

"That almost happened to me on that weird trail," Jessica says, and I splutter on my water. Could it be possible?

"What was that?" I ask, too sharply.

"Oh, nothing," Jessica says, waving her hand and taking a gulp of wine. "You're lucky you're okay."

"Yeah," I say, stretching the word out like it's taffy. "It could have crushed me. In fact, it almost looked like someone had tried to cut it—"

"You must have been so grateful," Matilda cuts me off, fingering the silver crucifix at her throat.

"Jesus works in mysterious ways," Jessica agrees, nodding.

"Praise the Lord," Mandy adds, but her state of drunkenness makes it sound more like 'Pays alert.'

I stay quiet, sipping my too-cold water. Is this the part where they all get to talking about their church fellowship groups and Bible study classes?

"Pastor Kenneth said something really pertinent in worship the other day," Heather says, and I cover my mouth to suppress a groan. Are girls' nights actually nothing more than getting drunk on cheap wine and talking about church and kids? Is this what I've been so distraught over missing?

"That's right, Heather, I remember," Jessica says, taking over. "He said 'The Lord may place trials and tribulations in our path, but he always shows us the right way to go.'"

All the women oooh and aahhh as though this is profound information worthy of pride of place right next to their other motto, 'Live Laugh Love.'

"Sadie, what church do you go to?" Tiffany asks.

"Um," I say. "We haven't found the right one yet." This isn't a complete lie, but it's not that close to the truth, either. Cash and I have zero interest in finding a church.

"You should join ours!" Heather squeals, and a headache blooms behind my sinuses. Clearly, her church didn't keep her child out of juvie, so…

"Yes, absolutely!" Jessica adds, her acrylics clicking against her glass as she raises it to her clownish lips.

The conversation continues in that vein for thirty minutes, then another thirty minutes is spent comparing the pros and cons of the daycare at the church versus secular preschool. My ice has completely melted by the time I tune back in. Mandy, now on the verge of blackout drunk, yells "Selfie time!"

All the women stumble and squish toward Jessica like dogs running toward a shaking treat bag. Luckily, most glasses are empty, otherwise Mandy would have one hell of a cleaning bill. I stand on stiff legs and walk to the back of the couch, squeezing between Heather and Matilda. Jessica grabs Mandy's phone and tilts it up at an angle. The screen wavers in her unsteady hand. "Say 'Girls' Night!'" she bellows, and everybody yells, "Girls' Night!" I plaster a soulless smile on my face and silently pray to the God I don't worship in church that this photo will not appear on social media. If Kendall sees this, she's never going to stop making fun of me.

This is what I've been so broken up about? This is the group I wanted so desperately to be a part of?

God, it's been nearly two hours, and my breasts are starting to ache. The water I sipped constantly throughout the inane conversation has collected in my bladder, which is full to bursting.

I slip through the kitchen and off to the bathroom, hungry for a bit of relief and privacy. There's a eucalyptus essential oil diffuser in the room, and it's so strong it almost makes me gag. I do my business as quickly as possible, washing my hands with Mandy's expensive hand soap and drying them on a ridiculously high thread count towel. I'm about to twist the handle and go back to the party when voices from the kitchen drift underneath the door, making me freeze.

"Has she done it yet?" someone whispers.

"I don't know," another whispers back. If they're trying to be discreet, they're too drunk to do a good job. I can hear every word.

"I thought you said she was looking better," the first one says. I think it's Tiffany.

"She is," the second one answers. Jessica?

"I'm not buying it," Tiffany says. "She'd be… different if she'd done it. You know that."

"Of course I know that," Jessica hisses.

"Did you see the baby?" Tiffany asks.

"Yes," Jessica says.

"And?"

"She looked fine," Jessica says.

"Did yours look fine after?" Tiffany says.

After what? I press my palm to my mouth to stifle my ragged breathing.

"I… I don't remember," Jessica says, and even though I can't see her, I can tell she's lying.

"They look different after, you know that," Tiffany says. "Kayden…" she trails off, sniffles, and then resumes. "Kayden was bigger. Even though he was only gone for a day. And… and his eyes were different."

"I know," Jessica says. "I know."

"Jared didn't even notice," Tiffany says. "He had no idea. He still has no idea. He thinks Kayden has some behavioral problems, normal stuff."

Jessica sighs. "It still could be normal stuff."

There's a beat of silence, and when Tiffany speaks, her voice is sharp enough to cut. "It's not normal stuff, and you know it. Just wait. Chesley is still little. You'll see."

I press my ear against the solid wood door. I know it's wrong to eavesdrop, but this is the most fascinating and horrifying conversation I've heard in ages. I silently suck in breath, praying they keep talking.

"Was it worth it?" Jessica finally asks, and there's a hitch in her voice.

"I don't know. But… but when I think about Janie, and what happened to her little boy…"

"Stop," Jessica says. "I don't want to talk about that anymore."

"You think I want to?" Tiffany says. "I should have warned her. I should have said there was only one choice."

"You didn't know," Jessica says.

"Of course I didn't know," Tiffany says. "But I guessed."

"Put your faith in Jesus," Jessica says. "You know He'll forgive you."

"I want to believe that," Tiffany says. "But I don't think I can ever forgive myself."

I can't hold my breath anymore, and it comes out in a whoosh. The voices on the other side of the door cease abruptly, and I want to slap myself. What have I done?

There's a click of heels as Jessica and Tiffany hustle out of the kitchen and back to the living room. I wait in the bathroom for another thirty seconds before I emerge, my face flushed.

"Sadie!" Mandy yells. "You sure took your time in there!"

My face grows hot, and I want to sink into the plush carpet. Do Jessica and Tiffany have any idea what I heard?

"Uh-huh," I say, smiling painfully. My breasts are throbbing, and now I'm embarrassed, and my mind is a maelstrom of thoughts. I need some peace and quiet to parse through everything. Who is Janie? And what happened to her son?

My bra grows damp as milk leaks from my full breasts. It's time for me to go… but I want to talk to Jessica first. She's drunk and loopy, and this might be my only chance to find out what's going on, to understand what I overheard.

While I was in the bathroom, the women coalesced into a booze-scented puddle on the couch. I take a step forward, trying to locate Jessica.

"Hey," I say, and, again, they look at me en masse, like one organism. "I have to head out—time to feed Holly, you know."

"No!" Jessica says. Her eyeliner has melted, giving her a raccoonish look. "You have to stay! We haven't even picked the movie yet!"

The thought of staying for an additional two hours as this harem of cartoonishly drunk women cavort and cry and have strange and disturbing conversations and otherwise act like buffoons makes me want to vomit.

"I'm so sorry," I say. "I've got to get back. Thank you so much for having me!"

"Bye, Sadie!" the ladies shout in various flavors of slur.

I try to catch Jessica's eye. "Hey, Jessica, I was hoping I could talk to you real quick—"

"Have a good night, Sadie!" Jessica shouts, drowning me out. She may be drunk, but her eyes spark with panic.

"Yeah, I will, I—"

"Bye!" Jessica says again, and this time there's a hard edge to her voice. Better not push my luck.

I let myself out. As I close the door, someone—Tiffany, maybe—leads the group in a version of the Lord's Prayer so sloppy it's barely intelligible.

Jesus Christ, indeed.

CHAPTER TWENTY-FIVE

Sparks Will Fly

My throat is raw from laughing. Several times on the drive home from Mandy's, I have to swerve to stay on the road, blinking away my hysterical tears. All those hours I spent on my couch, wallowing in misery and self-pity after stumbling across an Instagram post about yet another party I wasn't invited to that looked unforgettable and awesome, and now I can see those parties for what they really are: a colossal, embarrassing, completely boring waste of time. Hardly unforgettable, too—most of those women were so drunk, they'll be lucky if they remember their children's names.

I pull into the driveway feeling giddy, but that euphoria is extinguished by darker thoughts. Jessica and Tiffany's whispered conversation scratches at the back of my mind.

"Nope, nope, nope," I say as I open the car door. I don't want to think about any of that right now, about the unease curling around my guts. All around me, the night is alive with chirping frogs, buzzing insects, and the persistent hoot of an owl. My dress is plastered to my back, and I pull it free with a wet smack.

The nighttime chorus pales in comparison to the wails that assault me as soon as I enter the house.

In the living room Cash reclines on the couch, his dirty shoes propped up on a cushion, his arm draped over his face. Holly thrashes on the floor, crying so hard I'm afraid she'll swallow her own tongue.

"What the fuck, Cash?"

Cash doesn't even move his arm, before croaking, "She won't stop crying."

"Why didn't you put her down in her bassinet?" I say, fury kindling within me like a bonfire as I scoop Holly up. Bouncing her on my hip turns down the volume, but she's still upset.

"I did!" he insists. "But then she woke up and started crying and she won't stop!"

"Why didn't you try to hold her or something?"

"I did!" he says, finally removing his arm from his face. His eyes are bloodshot yet again. "I can't take this anymore. I have a pounding headache!"

My lips press into a thin, hard line. I want to yell back at him, 'Oh really? A pounding headache from less than two hours of caring for your daughter, while I've been spending twenty-four hours a day, seven days a week catering to her every whim, no matter how much it physically and mentally drains me?'

Instead, I say, "I don't understand. I was only gone for two hours!"

Cash sighs dramatically, rolling his eyes. "Okay, I get it. I suck as a parent. You know everything."

Without responding, I perch myself on the couch as far from him as I can manage, wrestle myself out of my dress, and get to feeding Holly. She's so hysterical she can barely latch, but she eventually gets it and suckles greedily. Milk stains my dress in the process, and this off-schedule feeding means she'll be up again in the night for sure.

"I tried my best, okay?" Cash says, dragging himself to a sitting position.

A sweet stink wafts into my nostrils, and I lift the edge of Holly's onesie to check her diaper. Sure enough, there's a full load.

"Did you legitimately not know she's got a full diaper, or did you ignore it on purpose so I'd have to deal with it?" My body is tense, poised for battle. Cash stays silent, bent over his knees, his fingers worrying at his temples. I switch Holly to the other breast, trying not to squeeze any poop out of the diaper in the process. This is not the way the evening is supposed to go, not the way this family is supposed to be. Here we are, each of us burrowed deep into our individual thoughts, trying to make our own respective hurts small enough to swallow without choking.

Cash stands up. "I'm going to go to bed."

"Fine," I say, my voice flat, keeping my gaze trained on the nubby carpet as Cash stomps off to his room.

When Holly finishes, she's heavy and sleepy. I hate to wake her up again by changing her diaper, but I can't let her sleep like this. She fusses again as I unsnap the onesie and bring cold wipe after cold wipe to her butt. My own head pounds, and when I finish everything and lay her down, she's still sniffling and snorting like an outraged bull.

Tater Tot comes padding into the room and jumps up on the bed. I'm too tired to do anything else but slip into the sheets myself, dress crumpled in a heap on the floor, makeup crusting on my face, seething.

CHAPTER TWENTY-SIX

If You Know What's Good for You

"Don't take my baby!" I bolt upright, the words thrown like daggers from my mouth. My chest heaves, my head snapping frantically around to find the thing, to...

It's my bedroom. My vision clears and there's Tater Tot, lifting his fuzzy head and blinking. He shakes, rattling his collar, before settling back down.

"Only a dream," I mutter, collapsing back against the damp pillows. Flashes of my nightmare pop and sparkle in the darkness—the tree, the bones, the door, the fairy, reaching not for me, but for Holly...

I can't go on like this.

My hands grab handfuls of sheet and twist, knotting them into horns. What was it Tiffany said? *When I think about Janie, and what happened to her little boy...*

I need to know I'm not alone. I need to know who Janie is and what happened to her little boy.

I unstick myself from my sweat-soaked sheets and slip out of the room. Tater follows me, nails clicking against the wood floor.

"We're going to figure it out, boy," I whisper, petting his back.

As the sun fills the bathroom with pink light, I rub tinted moisturizer into my skin, dust myself with blush, and slather my lashes with mascara until they're stiff as the starched collars on Cash's button downs, psyching myself up to confront Jessica. I contort myself into a pair of pre-baby leggings and the most stylish nursing-accessible tank top I own. Dress for the job you want, right?

Holly wakes with a gurgle as I finish double-knotting my tennis shoes.

I glance at my watch. Jessica is a creature of routine. I know she'll be doing the school drop-off around eight, then she'll spend an hour on her porch doing yoga. After that, she'll take Rosie the Shih Tzu for a walk.

And that's when I'll pounce. Easy as pie.

My stomach lurches.

After Holly's fed and changed, I load her into the stroller and head down the road. Tater whimpers at my side.

"It's okay, boy," I say.

His whimper turns into frenzied bouncing, and when I turn, there's Ron in his driveway, a pile of mail in the crook of one arm.

Tater takes off, lunging for Ron. I'm panting by the time I catch up to him, even though Ron's house is only a few dozen feet away from my front door.

"Morning, Sadie!" he says, grinning.

"Morning, Ron."

"What's on the agenda for today?"

I shrug, leaning on Holly's stroller to take some of the weight off of my overtaxed thighs. "Oh, you know. The usual."

"Good for you," Ron says. "I always love seeing you out and about, enjoying nature and getting your little girl some fresh air. You're keeping me young!"

"I don't know about that," I say. "I don't feel so young anymore."

Ron reaches down with a grunt to scratch under Tater's chin. "When you get to be my age, anybody under sixty is young."

I laugh and attempt to glance at my watch without Ron noticing. It's eight fifty. If I don't get a move on, I'll miss my shot at talking to Jessica.

"Sorry Ron, I need to get going."

Ron quirks an eyebrow. "Oh? So you do have an agenda today, after all?"

"I'm supposed to walk with Jessica this morning." The lie spurts out of my mouth like vomit.

"Jessica? You mean that girl who never picks up after her dog?"

"Huh?"

"She's got brown hair, about your height, always wearing clothes that are about four sizes too tight. But maybe that's the style now? What do I know?"

I can't help it—I grin. "Yeah, I think we're talking about the same woman."

"You should tell her to pick up after that dog of hers. The little fluffy thing."

"Sure," I say.

"Honestly, the way some of these younger people have overtaken the neighborhood, so entitled…"

"I call them the Yoga Moms," I blurt.

Ron guffaws. "They all certainly dress like they could drop into a downward dog at any moment!" Seeing my amused smile, Ron adds, "What? I do yoga too, you know. Keeps these aching joints limber."

"I'm impressed, Ron."

"Well, I won't keep you any longer. But remember what I said about that dog, and tell your friend. I'm not pleased at myself for thinking this, but those ladies—Yoga Moms, as you would say—are not a net positive to Agua Roja. And those kids of theirs… yeesh."

A heaviness I've been carrying for far too long begins to lighten. "Thanks, Ron."

"I don't know what I did, but if I made you smile, it was worth it!"

I have to drag Tater away from Ron by the collar, but eventually we're back on our way down the street, Ron waving us off. It's eight fifty-five, and all I can do is pray I haven't missed Jessica. I can't take another restless night.

We're halfway down Sweetgum when I spot her. A shiver runs through my body.

When we're close enough that I don't have to yell, I wave and say, "Hey, girlie!" I cringe as soon as the words are out of my mouth. 'Girlie?' Ugh.

Jessica stops a few feet from me, Rosie adhered to her ankles, avoiding Tater Tot's intrusive nose.

"Hey, mama," Jessica says. Her outfit today is electric turquoise, and the only physical evidence of her overindulgent evening is a few threads of red woven through the whites of her eyes.

I engage the brakes on the stroller and pick at my cuticles. "So, um, how's it going?"

Jessica laughs. "I'm pretty hungover, not gonna lie," she says.

"Oh," I say, trying to chuckle, but it sounds as disingenuous as it feels, I'm sure. "That sucks."

"You're the smart one for staying away from the wine," she says. Her smile looks like my laugh sounded: as fake as her half-inch-long nails.

"Right," I say. "About last night, actually."

I pause, unsure where to go next, how to get the answers I need.

"Yeah?" she says, but there's something in her eyes, something shifty and nervous behind those whorls of scarlet.

"I mean, well," I say. Where do I begin? Janie? The trail? The eavesdropping? Finally, I spit out, "Like, when we were talking about that tree branch, the big one that fell, I heard… well, I thought I heard…"

Jessica stares at me, her magenta lips pressed into a thin line.

When she doesn't say anything, I keep going, my voice shaking ever so slightly. "You said something about a weird trail?"

If her face wasn't so plastic, I'm sure she'd be scowling. "What weird trail?"

"Oh, you know, you said there was a weird trail, and something almost happened to you on it..."

"I don't remember that."

Ah, so that's how it's going to be. If I weren't so desperate, I'd give up at this point. If I still cared about her opinion of me as much as I used to, I'd back down. But I am desperate, and I don't care.

"I think you do," I say slowly, keeping my gaze locked on hers. "What weird trail did you find, Jessica?"

Her lips twitch, the pockets of filler dancing underneath her flesh like wriggling worms. "I didn't find anything," she whispers, but the lie is so bald, so obvious.

"Okay," I say. "Right."

The only sound in the humid air is the hum of insects. Yes, it's uncomfortable, but I'm willing to endure it.

Apparently, Jessica is, too. She stares at me, her eyelash extensions brushing her brow bones.

I'm the one to cave. If I've come this far, I might as well go all the way.

"I heard you and Tiffany talking about me," I say.

Jessica's face doesn't change.

"I heard everything."

Still nothing from Jessica. With all of her facial enhancements, she'd make a great poker player.

"Jessica," I say wearily. "Come on. Please. Will you..." I pause, take a deep breath. "Who is Janie? What happened to her?"

Jessica's hand shoots out to clamp onto my wrist with such speed and strength I cry out. Tater growls softly next to me. Jessica leans in so close I can smell the alcohol lingering on her breath, underneath the toothpaste and green tea. "We don't talk about her," she hisses. "Do you understand me, Sadie? What happened to Janie... to her son... it was an accident. Don't go digging, okay? I don't care that she used to live in your house. I mean it. And as far as the other stuff goes, I'm going to warn you one last time. We. Don't. Talk. About. It."

My vision goes blurry at the edges, all of my attention focused on those perfectly manicured fingers tight like a manacle around my wrist. She's cutting off the circulation to my hand. "She lived in my house—wait, what?" I whisper. There's a click deep in my brain. Ron had told me there was some unpleasantness with the former owners. The need to understand, to know the full story beats at me like an insect, fluttery and urgent.

She doesn't stop squeezing. "We've all seen it, Sadie. We've all gone down that trail, and we all know what's at the end, okay?"

"What?" I gasp, my heart pumping out a staccato rhythm.

"Me. Mandy. Tiffany. Matilda. Heather. All of us. We all had our turn with it, and now it's picked you."

"What's picked me?" I whimper.

"You know," she says. "And you know what else?" She finally releases me and leans back. Her hands gesture toward her body, her shimmering hair, her flat abs, her toned thighs, and everything in between. "You think all this is free, that it comes easy? Or do you think this is all because I worked hard and earned it?"

When I don't say anything, my eyes dry from staring, she goes on. "No, babe, I sacrificed. I gave it what it wanted, and it gave me this. Beauty. Security. Perfection. All for only a few hours with my baby. My Chesley. And I got her back, exactly like it said I would. Do you get it now? Do you understand, Sadie?"

"But what did it take from your baby? What did it want?"

"Only time. Time with my little girl." Jessica's eyes, gleaming with tears, refuse to meet mine.

"But Tiffany said—"

"Hush," Jessica says, pressing her long, pointed fingernail against my lips. Her finger smells of something acrid, like cigarette smoke. "Forget what Tiffany said. We don't talk about it. We don't say a single word,

Sadie. Or else all this goes away." She gestures at herself again. "And all that goes away." She points in the vague direction of her house, her family. "Don't forget it."

We stare at each other, the silence crackling with electricity.

"Is it worth it?" I say.

"What?" she growls.

I nod at her taut body, her youthful face. "Is all that worth the sacrifice?"

Her jaw tenses, and a single tear escapes her right eye, leaving a pale track through her blush. "Yes," she whispers, her voice reedy. She wipes the tear away. "Yes," she repeats, more firmly.

"And if I don't?" I ask.

"Don't what?" she says, her puffy lips quivering.

"If I don't sacrifice? What happens?"

"I think you can guess," she says. "I pray for you, Sadie. I pray you don't have to find out. All you need to remember is that I sacrificed. We all sacrificed. And if you know what's good for you, and for your family, you'll sacrifice, too. Or else you'll pay the price, just like Janie did."

An approaching car rumbles behind me, and as though she's whipped off a mask, Jessica's face reverts immediately to that earth-mother-naturally-beautiful expression she presents to the world as genuine. The car passes, we both wave—her vigorously, me halfheartedly—and then she turns to face me again.

"Don't be stupid, Sadie. You don't want to know what will happen to you if you don't listen to me," she says, and then she's off down Sweetgum, dragging Rosie behind her. Before she disappears around a curve in the road, Rosie squats on the shoulder. Jessica never stoops down to pick up the mess.

Tater Tot growls. If my throat weren't so clogged with shock and anguish, I'd growl, too.

CHAPTER TWENTY-SEVEN

No More Weirdness

By the time I get home, despite the long, thin bruises Jessica's steel grip has left on my arm, I've fully convinced myself I didn't understand her correctly.

As I feed Holly, I replay the conversation in my mind, over and over and over.

There's no way Jessica sacrificed her baby. There's no way she made a deal with an evil fairy living in the woods. There's simply no way we were talking about the same thing.

There can't be.

Before I know what I'm doing, I've got my phone in my hand and I'm calling Kendall, something I almost never do. She's a texter through and through.

The phone rings and rings, and I'm about to press End when Kendall answers.

"Sadie?" she says, a little breathless, her voice at a higher pitch than usual. "Everything okay?"

"Yeah," I say.

"Cool," she says, and her voice slips down into its normal register. "What's up?"

"I have to ask you something."

"Shoot," she says. There's rustling in the background. It's almost lunchtime, and my stomach growls. "What's up?" Her voice is muffled, like she's talking through a mouthful of something, and my stomach rumbles again. I've never been hungrier in my life than when I'm breastfeeding.

"This might sound weird…" I start, then falter.

"Spit it out," she says, then swallows loudly.

"Did you know the people who lived in our house before us?" I ask, nearly whispering. I feel naughty, like I'm a teenager sneaking out past curfew.

"Hmmm," Kendall says. "What were their names?"

"I don't know the last name," I say, "but it was a youngish couple. And they had a son."

"Hmmm," Kendall says again.

When Kendall stays quiet, I add, "Did something… happen to them?"

"Happen to them? What do you mean?"

"I heard this rumor… that they had an accident or something?"

Kendall is quiet for a full thirty seconds, and then she whistles through her teeth as she exhales, long and low. "Okay. I didn't want to tell you this before—there was no reason to freak you out, you're already dealing with so much."

"Please. Please, tell me."

"Ugh."

"What? What is it?" I'm terrified Kendall's going to clam up, or echo Jessica and tell me we don't talk about it.

"It's a sad story," she says.

"Kendall," I say, my voice tight. "Please. Tell me."

"Are you sure you want to know?"

"It doesn't matter what I want. I *need* to know, Kendall."

She huffs out a breath. "Fine. But only because you asked, alright?"

"Yeah, of course."

"Nobody around here likes to talk about it. I don't know that much about what happened, since we were new here back then. Basically, the wife—her name was Janie—woke up one day and decided to go nuts. I know that sounds crass, but I don't know how else to explain it. We met them once, and they seemed normal… anyway, Janie was running down the middle of the street one morning, butt-ass naked, covered in… in blood. Or that's what I heard, at least. She was screaming, and then an ambulance came and took her away. I never heard about what happened to her son, or to her husband. Nobody ever talked about it after that, and it didn't feel right to ask. I only know this much because Larry—you know, the security guard who always gives out dog treats—saw it all happen and told me. I think he was really shaken up and needed someone to talk to. Next thing everyone knew, there was a for sale sign in the front yard and that whole family was just… gone."

My breath comes out in a painful rush. I hadn't realized I'd been holding it. "Jesus Christ, Kendall. That seems like something you should have told me like… a long time ago. Especially since they lived in my freaking house."

Kendall sounds dazed. "I know, I know, I'm sorry. But honestly, it happened so long ago. And since nobody talks about it, the whole thing sort of… faded away. In fact, until you asked, I'd forgotten any of that ever happened."

"And you have no idea where they went?"

"None," Kendall says. "But if I had to guess—nowhere good."

Holly lets out a cry of frustration, and I switch her to the other boob.

"Thanks, Kendall," I say.

"Yeah," she says. "Why are you asking about that, anyway?"

How much to tell her? I mean, I don't seriously believe all that craziness Jessica was spouting, do I?

"I heard someone mention the name Janie the other day, and that something happened to her. And Ron told me a while ago that there was some unpleasantness with the people who used to own our house. I thought… I thought maybe it was all connected."

"Well, you were right, I guess."

"Yay," I say without any enthusiasm.

There's a heavy, uncomfortable pause. "Well," I say. "Again—thanks."

"See you later," she says, hanging up before I can say anything else.

I put my phone down, reeling. So Janie—the former owner of my house—was running down the street completely nude, bloody, and this is something that's been… what? Covered up? Ignored? Forgotten? In a neighborhood that loves its gossip almost as much as its luxury cars?

My heart is racing, and I try to take several deep breaths to slow it down. What Kendall described doesn't sound like some monstrous evil fairy; it sounds like a mentally ill woman having a psychotic break. She deserves my pity, my empathy.

But all I can muster up is terror.

Holly's tiny eyelids are fluttering, and a drop of milk escapes down her cheek. Seeing her this way, so sweet and vulnerable, I know there's nothing I wouldn't do to protect her.

Even if that means protecting her from me.

After laying her down for her morning nap, I unearth my prescription bottle from the back of the medicine cabinet.

I chug the pill with a full bottle of water.

I'm done with the hallucinations, the fear, the uncertainty. I'm done with the Yoga Moms and their lame parties and whatever crazy, awful shit they believe. I'm done with neglecting my own health and wellbeing. I have to be strong for my child, even if it makes me feel foggy in the process.

No one—and no thing, no illness, no cruel twist of fate—is taking my baby away from me.

I don't know Janie, but I do know one thing: even though I live in her house, I will never end up like her.

CHAPTER TWENTY-EIGHT

The Worst Thing

I don't know what wakes me. Lying on my side facing away from Holly, I think I can make out her normal baby snorts, barely audible over the white noise machine. The air smells of my night sweats, stale perfume, and urine-soaked diapers—nothing new there. Moonlight seeps through the thin curtains, illuminating the vast expanse of the king bed in front of me, and that's when I notice: Tater Tot is gone.

Did Cash come and take him after I fell asleep? Or did Tater get a sudden hankering for food or water in the middle of the night? Is he sick? Either way, it was probably his scrabbling jump off the bed that woke me…

I roll to my back, trying to get comfortable. Wherever Tater Tot is in the house, I'm sure he's fine. Even though there is that ever-present degree of mommy alertness, my brain is fuzzy, and all I want to do is go back to sleep.

If only I could find a good position.

I lift myself off the bed and twist to the other side, facing Holly, lids squeezed shut, praying for sleep. When I hear a low grunt, I open my eyes, squinting through the moon-tinged darkness at her sleeping form.

No.

There's something looming over Holly's bassinet. The moonlight shines on chunky, miniature fingers, stocky, stunted legs, feet adorned with long, split toenails perched on the bassinet's edge, digging into the soft mesh surrounding the tiny mattress.

As if sensing my gaze, the thing turns to face me. Locking its eyes with mine, it grins, exposing a mouthful of impossibly sharp teeth set into a skull the size of a doll's head.

I'm too stunned to move. Somewhere under the covers, my weak pelvic floor gives way, and my bladder releases a gush of warm urine all over the bed. My tongue is floppy and useless, like a dead fish in my mouth. I can't seem to take a proper breath, and sick moisture pops out in fat beads all over my body. My heart is beating so fast and so hard it seems to shake the bed.

The thing perches there on the bassinet, staring at me and grinning, while I lay paralyzed, praying to wake up, to move, to scream, anything. The purgatory of waiting for the danger to come, for the horror to descend and sweep me away in a tidal wave of agony, is excruciating, is worse than labor.

Then, the thing speaks.

"Will you let me take the baby?" Its voice is creaky, like a rusted door being pried open. "It won't be forever. You'll get her back. The babies always go back."

My brain jitters like a battery short-circuiting. What is it saying? I'll get her back? When? What will this thing do to her? What has this thing already done to the children in this neighborhood? Jesus Christ, Jessica was telling the truth…

"A few hours. A few hours the baby will be away from you, and then you'll be yourself again. You'll have what you always wanted, Sadie. Beauty. Harmony. Peace. Perfection." The words sound ugly and deformed coming from its horrible little mouth.

As if a switch has been flipped inside of me, my terror transforms into rage, a fury so hot and bright it threatens to scorch the sheets around me. Is that what this thing thinks it gave to all the Yoga Moms? Beauty? Harmony? Perfection? Their beauty is plastic and fleeting, and even I can see how thin the illusion of their perfection truly is. And what about the children? What about Tiffany's son Kayden, with his 'behavioral problems?' What will happen to Jessica's daughter Chesley? If I let this horrible little thing have Holly, even if only for a few hours, will the baby I get back still be my Holly? Or will she be something else, something that still looks like my daughter but who is twisted and transformed on the inside?

This is no real promise, no fair exchange. This is a dirty trick.

My body moves automatically. Without thinking, my fingers grab for the SOCP knife hidden under my pillow. I spring from the bed, my feet landing with a thud on the hardwood. Before I'm fully conscious of what's happening, the knife is slicing through the air.

It connects with flesh. There's a sticky sound as I pull the knife out. I rear back and bring the knife down again, and this time there's a yowl, a deep, inhuman wail that sounds far too loud to come from a creature so small. Something hot and wet sprays my face, and the smell of my urine is replaced by the iron scent of blood.

I pull the knife away and lift my fist high. But before I can bring the knife down again, there's a plop and a skitter, and the creature scrambles through the dark, leaving a trail of black ooze.

Is it gone? Have I killed it? What will this mean for Jessica and all the others?

Holly starts crying, but they don't sound like her normal sobs. They're deeper, more breathy.

I reach across the bassinet to flip on the light.

"What are you doing here?" I scream at Cash, who's slumped on the floor, blood gushing in a torrent from an ugly wound on his arm.

No. Please, no.

The knife slips from my slick grip and clatters to the hardwood floor.

Cash yelps, his breath coming in shallow gasps.

I look down at my body, at my pajamas plastered to my skin, at the blood splattering my clothes. I did this. Me.

Oh, God. Have I become Janie? Have I echoed everything that happened to her?

I think this is the worst thing that could have happened… until I look in the bassinet.

Holly is gone.

CHAPTER TWENTY-NINE

Big Girl Crib

"Where is she?"

Somebody is screaming, and it must be me, but I can't feel my mouth moving.

"Where is she?"

The voice is raw, angry. Sinister.

"Where the fuck is my baby?"

On the ground, Cash recoils, pressing one hand to his bleeding wound. I take a step forward, my toes squelching into the pool of warm blood. It's thicker and stickier than I imagined it would be.

"What did you do with my baby?"

This last question, like all the others, is directed at the evil fairy, the one who was just here, the one who peered in at my sleeping child and thought it could take her from me, who thought I would ever allow it to touch her.

There's a primal roar echoing throughout the room, bouncing off the tall tray ceilings, reverberating in waves in the charged atmosphere. Is that coming from me?

"Give me back my baby!"

Something tears in my throat, like a piece of fabric ripping. I am all animal. I have never been less human, more mother.

Before another roar can claw its way out of my ragged throat, Cash grabs my ankle with one blood-sticky hand. “I took her!”

My eyes lock onto his. I want to kick him. I want to stick my dirty fingers in his wound, to push until they break through to the other side. I want to punch his teeth down his throat.

“I took her!” he says again, sobbing. “I moved her to the crib upstairs while you were sleeping! I… I miss being in my own bed, and I wanted to see how Holly would do in her room by herself!”

A million thoughts run through my head, but I am still the animal-mother, and I can’t process any of them. “You… you took her.”

“I—I came down here to check on you and… Sadie, did you… did you stab me?”

I’m not sure if it’s how he says my name—reminding me that I have one, that I am not only Mama—or the raw emotion he pushes into the word ‘stab,’ but his question breaks me out of whatever mother-sick trance I’m in. The red curtain of rage falls away from my eyes like the removal of a veil.

“Oh, God,” I breathe, staring down at Cash.

“Where did you get a knife? Why do you have one in here?”

I don’t know how to begin to answer him.

His questions keep coming, fast and hot and furious, as he pushes himself upright. “Why would you keep a knife in the same room as Holly? Aren’t you taking antidepressants? Aren’t they helping? Goddammit, Sadie, what is wrong with you?”

There’s no point in lying anymore. “I stopped taking them,” I say, so quietly Cash has to ask me to repeat myself. “I stopped taking them,” I say again, louder. “But… but then I restarted, I swear!”

I’ve never seen him this angry. It’s as if he didn’t hear the last part, how I fixed it, how I made it right. If he weren’t bleeding on the floor, I’d be afraid he might hit me. “How could you do this, Sadie? You don’t take your antidepressants like you're supposed to, you keep a knife in the room, and now this? God, that hurts!" He winces, pressing a corner of his shirt to the wound, trying to staunch the bleeding.

"I thought… I thought I saw…"

"What? What did you think you saw, Sadie?"

"That… that fairy! It was here! It's been leaving dead things in the house, and it broke that picture of us, and it won't leave me alone! It wants my baby!"

Cash collapses back on the floor and puts a bloody hand over his face. "There is no fairy, Sadie. There is no fairy!"

"There is!" I scream. "I saw it in the woods! It eats all these bugs and animals and leaves their bones all around its tree! It broke the baby monitor! And I'm not the only one who saw it! Jessica did, too, and Mandy, and Tiffany, and all of them, and she told me I'd have to make a sacrifice, and that if I didn't, I'd end up like Janie—"

Cash laughs, drowning me out, and it's not a nice laugh. It's the kind of sound people make when they've accepted that their entire world has imploded into a ball of fire, and there's nothing they can do about it but howl.

"I can't do this, Sadie," he says, and all the fight has gone out of him. He presses his hand back against his wound with a squelch. "I can't do it anymore. Why can't you be normal? Other moms don't go crazy after having babies! Other moms don't stab people because they're not getting enough sleep!"

If I still had the knife in my hand, I'd be tempted to stab the bastard again. Did he not hear what I said about Jessica and all the others? And anyway, what does he know about other moms? What does any man know about what it's like to be a mother? How dare he tell me what my body and mind should or shouldn't do after a baby ripped me right up the middle in two?

From somewhere far on the other side of the house comes a wail.

"I have to get Holly," I say.

Cash grabs my ankle, squeezes. "No," he says. "Not anymore."

* * *

It's not until a few hours later, when I'm lying in the hospital bed at the mental health intensive care unit, that my rage twists into frustration and fear. If I'm not with her, how will Cash feed Holly? Will he switch her to formula? He'll have no other choice, right? What if her tummy can't handle it? After all, she's only ever had breastmilk, straight from the source. I don't even have a stash of pumped milk. How will Cash be able to figure out a transition to formula when he can't even find the baby wipes in the goddamned house?

Was this the punishment Jessica was talking about? Is this what happened to Janie after the ambulance carried her away?

As if in response to my anxiety, my breasts throb. They're aching and swollen, and I feel like a dairy cow that needs to be milked.

When I clench my teeth against the pain, there's a strange pressure between my molars, as though something's stuck back there.

I try to lift my arm so I can pick it out with my fingers, but there are restraints around my wrists, and I can't bring my hands anywhere near my mouth.

My tongue attacks the spot, worrying at the crack between my molars. I work it and work it and work it, letting the tip of my tongue grow raw and irritated. I'm about to give up when something thin and pointy finally comes free. I turn my head and spit it onto my pillow.

I crane my neck awkwardly to get a look at it.

No.

No, please. No.

It's a roach leg. Pointy, shiny, brown, the little hairs sticking out of it at odd angles.

That was in my mouth—it was in my *mouth*—

I turn my head again and vomit, the hot bile gushing from between my lips with very little warning, spilling over my cheek and onto my hair, my pillow, the bedsheets. Another wave of nausea rises, crests, and I close my eyes as a fresh heave wracks my body, propelling more vomit from my throat.

When it's over, I lay back on my pillow, exhausted and shaky. The drip-drop of my vomit falling from the bed to the linoleum fills the room. My eyes are still clamped shut, keeping the world out.

The click of the door cracks like a gunshot through the fetid air.

"Oh, my," a nurse says, rushing to my bedside. I pry my eyelids apart, and we both see it at the same time.

My vomit is a grayish-pink color. Swimming in the goop are pieces of insect bodies. Clumps of gray-brown fur dot the lunar landscape of my puke. A shard of tiny bone sticks up like a minuscule flagpole, a tuft of fur resting at the top like a gruesome flag.

"Mother Mary," the nurse says.

It's the last thing I hear before I start screaming.

Cash was right all along: there is no evil fairy living in the woods.

There's only me.

Right?

EPILOGUE

Jessica's Story

"Jessica!" Henry roared from the kitchen. Jessica flinched, curling protectively around the baby. "Jessica, get in here right now!"

On trembling legs, Jessica rose from the couch, Chesley clutched to her chest.

"What?" she said, her voice barely more than a whisper.

"Goddammit, Jessica, what the fuck is this?" Henry swept a hand in the direction of the sink. Piles of dirty dishes filled the basin, leaning precariously against one another. She could see dried cheese crusted on one plate, and grease from hamburgers congealing in a skillet.

"A sink?" she squeaked.

"Don't get smart with me, bitch," he said. "I know it's a fucking sink. What I want to know is why is it full of nasty-ass dishes?"

Jessica sputtered, "I'm sorry, Henry, really I am. I've been so busy with the baby, I haven't had a chance to… I know I've fallen behind on cleaning…"

"Fallen behind? Is that all? Jessica, the dishes at the bottom are starting to grow mold, for Christ's sake. I've been watching, expecting you to get off your ass any day now and deal with this. How much longer do I have to wait?"

Henry's eyes glittered with malice, and Jessica shrank further into herself, gripping Chesley like a life preserver, the only thing keeping her afloat in the raging sea of Henry's fury.

"I'll do it right now," she said. "I promise."

"It's about time."

"Could you hold Chesley for me?"

Henry snarled. "I don't have time to sit around holding a baby. It's a work day, Jessica, or did you forget that? I have to go to the office. That's my real job, the job that bought us this fucking house, the job that pays for your Lexus, the job that got you the gym membership you're clearly not using. You want to switch, huh? You want to go out there and try to find work with your substantial skills as… wait, that's right. You didn't go to college, I remember now."

Jessica choked down a sob. Henry zipped across the room and grabbed her arm, squeezing it. "You're hurting me," she whispered.

"I paid two hundred dollars for the best baby carrier I could find. Go use it." He shoved her away with a look of disgust.

Jessica waited until the door slammed behind Henry before she let the tears come. He hated seeing her cry; her tears were like a red cape to a bull—they only made him angrier, more violent.

In her arms, Chesley whimpered. Jessica missed her night nurse Irma fiercely, but Irma's contract ended when Chesley hit the eight-week mark.

"It's okay, baby, it's okay," Jessica said, kissing the top of her daughter's head.

* * *

Jessica never told Henry about the trail, or the clearing, or the freaky-looking tree. Definitely not about the door.

And definitely not about the thing that lived behind it.

Chesley was three months old when the baby monitor crackled

to life in the night, her tiny screams instantly jolting Jessica out of a nightmarish sleep. Henry rolled over to face her and gave her a shove. "Go take care of it," he hissed.

Jessica stumbled out of the room, her feet freezing on the hard floor, and ran to Chesley's room. The door stood ajar, and Jessica's heart seized.

With one fingertip, she pushed the door fully open.

In the glow of a nightlight, she saw the thing from the woods. It was perched at the top of Chesley's crib, one dirty finger rubbing the top of her baby's head. Chesley squirmed, her face scrunched almost beyond recognition.

Jessica didn't panic. She glided over to the baby monitor and ripped the plug from the wall.

"Why are you here?" she asked.

The thing looked up at her and grinned, its rodent-like teeth caked with something dark and slimy. "You never gave me an answer," it croaked.

Goosebumps rippled across Jessica's swollen breasts, the hand-shaped bruise on her right arm, down her bloated belly, past her C-section scar, to her unshaven thighs.

When she remained silent, the thing said, "I can make it all better. You know I can. You've seen the others."

Jessica grimaced.

"Give me the baby," it said. "For a little while, that's all. And in return, I'll take the pain away. You'll be beautiful. Isn't that what you've always wanted?"

Jessica didn't want to tell the thing that more than beauty, she wanted love. She let out a shuddering breath. Whether it was fair or not, she knew beauty could be the prerequisite for love.

"You won't hurt her?" she said, her lips quivering.

"No," the thing hissed. "Of course not."

* * *

The transformation was painful, as all real transformations are. Chesley had been back for three days, and now she was napping peacefully while Jessica showered.

It started with a tingle in her calves, almost like a muscle cramp. The tingle traveled up her thighs and into her belly, growing stronger with each inch it rose until it made her rattle and shake like she was having a seizure. She fell to the shower floor, slamming her face into the slick tiles. Her nose crunched, and she tasted blood. The water continued to pound down on her body, curled into the fetal position. Her stomach clenched, and then, without warning, she vomited, splattering the shower glass with chunks of half-digested Oreos.

"Oh God," she moaned. Please, she couldn't get food poisoning now. Who would take care of Chesley?

Her body heaved again, and this time, she expelled from the other end. The skin on her abdomen felt tight and itchy, and her nose throbbed. Her scalp was on fire. Jesus, what had she eaten?

Vomit poured from her mouth a second time, and, Christ, why was it red?

"Hospital," she panted. But who would take her? Henry was at work. Her phone was in the living room. If she died here on the floor, they'd find her curled up in a pool of her own vomit and excrement, naked and filthy.

She reached out one trembling hand to the shower bench and tried to pull herself up. She managed to sit halfway up before dizziness overtook her. A crack ricocheted around the room when her skull collided with the tile once more, and then everything went black.

* * *

The faint smell of feces roused Jessica. She lifted her head and spluttered, getting a mouthful of cold water.

I'm in the shower, she realized, blinking the fuzziness out of her eyes. Reddish-brown stains marred the pale grout between the tiles around her.

Awareness came back to her slowly, but when it finally arrived, she rose slowly off the tiles and twisted the shower faucet off. She stood there, shivering.

She was sick, that was all. Bad seafood, maybe, or expired milk? Or that week-old Chinese takeout?

But… why didn't she feel ill?

She'd puked and shit her brains out. She'd crushed the bridge of her nose against the stone tile. She'd lain there for who knew how long, getting pelted by high-pressure droplets.

And yet… she felt amazing.

She risked a glance down at her body.

"No fucking way," she breathed.

Instead of the yellowed, bare nails she'd had, her toes were now tipped with a vibrant shade of bubblegum pink. The dark hair that had covered her legs was gone, replaced with baby-smooth skin, moisturized to a shine. Her C-section scar had disappeared completely, and instead of a slack pouch, her stomach was a veritable washboard. And her breasts… God, the world's best plastic surgeon couldn't have done better…

She tugged a towel off of a hook and wrapped it around herself. The glass shower door opened with a squeal, and then she was in front of the mirror, staring into a face so flawless it almost hurt to look at. Expertly arched brows framed wide, clear eyes—undoubtedly hers, but the lashes were now long and thick. Her cheeks bloomed with a natural, healthy blush. The small bump on her nose, which she'd always despised, was gone, the bridge now a gentle ski slope. Her lips were two fluffed pillows, pink and utterly kissable.

"Thank you, God," she said, even though she knew God had nothing to do with it.

* * *

Chesley grew up fast—she walked early, talked early, potty trained early. Jessica bragged about her to whoever would listen. As Chesley got older, Jessica kept bragging, even when her daughter came home from school with another girl's lopped-off braid in her backpack, or when their cat came screeching through the house, the tip of its tail singed, Chesley running after it with a box of matches clenched in her tiny fist.

"She's just a kid," Henry said, and kissed Jessica too hard on the mouth. "Kids do stupid shit all the time. Hell, I definitely did. She'll grow out of it."

Jessica didn't tell her new friends in the neighborhood about Chesley's tendency to bite the legs off of frogs. The blood would stain her teeth red for days. Jessica didn't tell her new friends about how she'd often awake in the night with a start, only to find Chesley at her bedside, grinning, her eyes dark and alien, hands cupping her cheeks still chunky with baby fat.

When her friends asked—and they did ask, of course they did—she told them Chesley was fine, was still completely normal. They didn't need to know the truth. It was enough that they knew about the bargain, everyone sharing in that secret. And after all, Jessica looked great, didn't she? Henry hadn't given her a bruise since she'd transformed. Things had never been better between them. She told herself, more than once, that there was nothing to escape. Her life was perfect.

And then Janie came along, and she wouldn't play the game. She thought she was better than all of them, too principled to accept the bargain. Jessica tried to tell herself Janie had sealed her own fate.

You had to play the game. You had to, because it was all worth it.

Jessica really thought Sadie would give in. Sadie was so weak. The desperation had rolled off of her in waves.

And yet.

Jessica shook her head and finished cleaning the cut on her hand, telling herself Chesley didn't mean to throw the scissors.

Of course she didn't.

AUTHOR'S NOTE

In August of 2021, my identity changed forever. I went from Viggy Hampton, MPH (Master of Public Health), to Viggy Hampton, MPH (Mother of Petite Human). And it wasn't just my identity that changed—as if that weren't enough—everything else changed, too.

A night of uninterrupted sleep became a thing of the past. Spontaneity went out the window. I couldn't walk out the door with only a purse—I now needed a car seat, a diaper bag, an extra onesie, a nursing cover… the list went on.

I quickly came to realize that the scariest part of building a family wasn't giving birth (mine was both uncomplicated and medicated)—it was having a newborn.

After the birth of my daughter, the nurses wheeled me into a maternity room, handed me my baby all swaddled and snug, ran through a bunch of helpful but totally overwhelming information, and left.

My husband and I were alone with our hours-old baby, feeling totally inadequate.

Of course, we ended up surviving and learning how to take care of our little girl, but at the time, we were terrified. I'd read books and blogs and articles about pregnancy and babies, but nothing compared to the real living, breathing thing.

I'd never felt more like a child than when I had a child of my own.

Of course, caretaking grew easier with time, but I still struggled with the massive shift in my identity, which came with an entirely new schedule and list of priorities. Lack of sleep combined with the terror of being completely responsible for a tiny human at all times created a whirlpool of stress I couldn't escape.

I think most people realize new motherhood is stressful, but what's not often discussed is the repetitive monotony of early babyhood: Wake up, feed the baby, change the baby, put the baby to sleep, wake up, feed the baby, change the baby, put the baby to sleep, etc, etc...

The repetition of this never-ending cycle can become maddening, which is what I wanted to explore in *Ripped Up the Middle in Two*. My daughter is now five, and my son is three. Writing this book served as therapy for me as I navigated the years of early parenthood, but it also, at times, felt like my third child. I've often felt writing a book is like giving birth—the electric flashes of ideas at the beginning are the sharp, sweet pains of contractions, followed by the actual writing, which is a very long, exhausting, and at times excruciating labor.

But, of course, it is absolutely worth it.

A million thanks to my incredible support system: Mom, Dad, Ryan, Camille, Wyatt, Katherine, and all of the friends and family in my neighborhood and my larger community. My amazing editor Alison Hodyna also deserves an enormous thank you—her attention to detail and excellent comments made this a better book, undoubtedly.

Thank you to my Purgatory Media team and my writer friends, especially Haley Newlin, Dawn Kurtagich, and Sophia Louisa Lee for all of your encouragement.

Finally, thank you to everybody who provided support and cheerleading for this book, including Joey Powell (who also created the absolutely fantastic illustrations throughout this book), Emma E. Murray, and Jacquie Walters.

If you or someone you know is struggling with postpartum depression or maternal mental health, contact the 24/7 National Maternal Mental Health Hotline at 1-833-852-6262 for help.

VIGGY PARR HAMPTON

is an epidemiologist, host of the podcast "Horror Humor Hunger," and the author of *A Cold Night for Alligators*, *Much Too Vulgar*, *The Rotting Room*, and *A Veritable Household Pet.* She is a graduate of Georgetown University and Emory University's Rollins School of Public Health.

Connect with her at her website, www.viggyhampton.com
or on Instagram or TikTok @viggyparrhampton

www.ingramcontent.com/pod-product-compliance
Lightning Source LLC
LaVergne TN
LVHW010053170826
845678LV00012B/2127

* 9 7 9 8 9 9 3 5 9 8 0 3 1 *